RING
of Truth

DOROTHY STEWART

Zaccmedia

Published by Zaccmedia
www.zaccmedia.com
info@zaccmedia.com

Published November 2018

ISBN: 978-1-911211-85-3

British Library Cataloguing-in-Publication Data
A catalogue record for this book is available from the British Library.

This book is a work of fiction and, except in the case of historical fact, any
resemblance to actual persons, living or dead, is purely coincidental.

Cover photographs © J. McDonald

ACKNOWLEDGEMENTS

This book draws on memories and research, woven together into complete fiction. Special thanks are due to my sister, Anna Rogalski, for aiding, abetting and encouraging me; and to my readers who have kept up the pressure for me to get this book, the last of the trilogy, finished! Thank you also to:

Aberdeen Public Library Reference Department for a plethora of background material on the 1964 Aberdeen typhoid epidemic

Katy Kavanagh at Aberdeen City and Aberdeenshire Archives, and Hannah Downie, Institute of Chartered Accountants of Scotland, for information about conferences in Aberdeen in 1964

Reception staff at the Caledonian Hotel, Union Terrace, Aberdeen

Graham and Janet, Rachel and Daniel Gibbs and the Gibbs family for help with Robbie's character and behaviour. I have tried to depict what life was really like for someone with Down's syndrome in 1964. Thankfully times have changed for the better.

The team at NUCLEUS: The Nuclear & Caithness Archive, Wick, for two lovely days studying the 1964 editions of *The John O'Groat Journal* which provided examples of job ads, details of the Queen's visit, a ring found on Dunnet beach, and the visit of Roberts Brothers Circus (augmented by a wonderful film: https://player.bfi.org.uk/free/film/watch-robert-bros-travelling-circus-1953-online). I was a trainee reporter on the *Groat* in 1967 and have drawn from those memories for *The Caithness Sentinel*, placing that fictional newspaper in the *Groat* building as it was when I worked there. I have borrowed a couple of ads but rewritten the report of the Queen's visit.

Janet McDonald for sourcing the wonderful photographs for the cover and for permission to use them

Howard Geddes, Highland Railway Society, for help with train times to get Gina home from Aberdeen

George Fraser and Ken Peters, *The Northern Lights* (Hamish Hamilton, 1978), for background on newspaper takeovers

And last but not least Paul Stanier of Zaccmedia and Mollie Barker for all their work on the book. All errors are of course mine alone.

The Mizpah Ring Family Tree

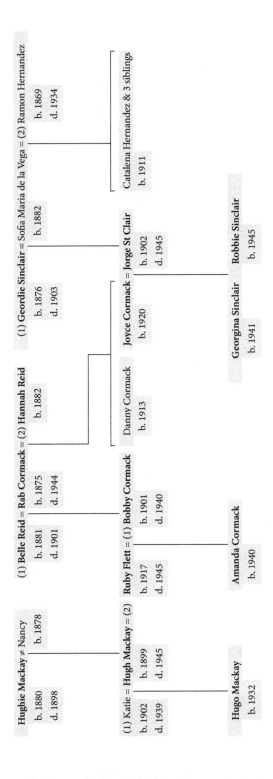

Hughie Mackay ≠ Nancy
b. 1880   b. 1878
d. 1898

(1) Belle Reid = Rab Cormack = (2) Hannah Reid
b. 1881   b. 1875   b. 1882
d. 1901   d. 1944

(1) Geordie Sinclair = Sofia Maria de la Vega = (2) Ramon Hernandez
b. 1876   b. 1882   b. 1869
d. 1903   d. 1934

Catalena Hernandez & 3 siblings
b. 1911

(1) Katie = Hugh Mackay = (2)
b. 1902   b. 1899
d. 1939   d. 1945

Ruby Flett = (1) Bobby Cormack
b. 1917   b. 1901
d. 1945   d. 1940

Danny Cormack
b. 1913

Joyce Cormack = Jorge St Clair
b. 1920   b. 1902
    d. 1945

Hugo Mackay
b. 1932

Amanda Cormack
b. 1940

Georgina Sinclair
b. 1941

Robbie Sinclair
b. 1945

CHAPTER 1

Wick, Caithness, Scotland, March 1964

The music of Billy J. Kramer and The Dakotas poured out of the Dansette portable record player, filling the comfortable attic bedroom with cheerful noise. The pretty dark-haired girl who had brought the record player, plugged it in and switched it on, despite her cousin's protests, laughed.

'Come on!' she said. 'Let's dance! I want to celebrate!' She waved a piece of paper. 'I'm free!'

The girl on the bed, so alike as to be her twin, gave her a worried smile.

'Are you sure, Mandy?' she asked. 'Aren't you even slightly sad?'

But Mandy just tossed her head and gyrated her body as she danced to the music.

'Plenty more fish in the sea!' she said.

'Yes, but…'

Mandy stopped dancing and planted her hands on her hips as she glared at her cousin. 'But nothing,' she told her. 'He turned out to be a no-hoper. I *wanted* to get divorced.' She waved the piece of paper at Gina again. 'And now I am. The final decree came through this morning. So now I'm footloose and fancy free again!' She began dancing again to the music. 'And I'm going to have fun!'

'Oh, Mandy,' Gina said, her face sad as she tucked her knees up under her chin and watched her cousin's apparent delight.

'What are you doing next weekend?' Mandy suddenly asked Gina.

'Me? Nothing,' Gina answered, surprised at the question. Mandy did not usually show any interest in the doings of anyone but herself.

'Good,' Mandy declared. 'I have a treat for you!'

'Oh yes?' Gina said. There had to be a sting in the tail somewhere.

Mandy stopped dancing and threw herself into the battered old armchair beside the dormer window with its panoramic view of the town and the bay.

'Now listen,' she commanded Gina. 'There's a conference in Aberdeen next Saturday – some kind of boring business briefing. My boss can't go. He's asked me to go instead, as an observer, and take notes. But...' Her eyes sparkled wickedly. 'But I have a better offer for that weekend,' she said, grinning at Gina. 'A certain someone who is showing great promise is taking me off somewhere nice and I don't want to miss that, do I?'

Gina blinked. Mandy's morals were clearly not what she herself was brought up to. She had always wondered but it seemed now there was no doubt...

'Oh, don't look like that!' Mandy said crossly. 'I'm a grown woman and now I'm free, I can do what I want!'

Fleetingly, Gina compared her own situation. She too was a grown woman and unmarried... but she was not free to do what she wanted. Truth be told, she wasn't sure she would want to. Or pay the price.

'Anyway,' Mandy said, crossing her legs and sitting back in the chair, the picture of confidence. 'I thought you could go to the conference in my place. That gets me off the hook. We look alike so if anybody notices you're there, it won't be a problem.' She gave Gina a disparaging glance. 'Not that anyone is likely to notice you.'

Gina flushed. It was true she didn't spend all her money on the latest clothes and shoes like her cousin did. She saw that Mandy's eyes had narrowed. She was clearly plotting.

'What is it?' Gina asked warily.

'Well, to pass without comment at the conference in Aberdeen you'll need to smarten up a bit. Why don't I lend you something to wear? We're the same size. And maybe you could wear some make-up for once?'

'You know I don't wear make-up,' Gina began, but Mandy batted away her words.

'If you're going to be me for a day, you're going to have to do it properly,' she said. '*If* we're going to get away with it.'

'I didn't say I would do it,' Gina protested.

'But you will,' Mandy said confidently. 'For me!'

CHAPTER 2

Aberdeen

It was not simply pouring with rain. There was sleet and, Gina Sinclair was almost sure, it was turning to snow. She pulled up her coat collar and ducked quickly off the street into the imposing entrance to the Caledonian Hotel. The metal canopy extending from the grey granite building kept the worst of the weather off the marble entrance, but Gina's wet feet made the ten steps up to the grand front door treacherous.

Glancing back worriedly, she saw the snow was getting heavier. Would she be able to get home tonight? She had taken a very early train down from Wick to Aberdeen that morning and had hoped to be able to get a train home. With the weather worsening, maybe she would have to find somewhere to stay overnight.

This was not at all what she had bargained for when she had finally caved in and agreed to stand in for Mandy. Somehow it was never possible to hold out against Mandy when she had her mind made up.

'But why would I want to go?' Gina had asked as a last-ditch attempt at wriggling out of it.

'Because you never go anywhere and it would be a day out,' Mandy had said. 'And anyway, because I've got better things to do and I'm asking you.'

Gina sighed. So now here she was. She had hurried up the steep road from the railway station, across Union Street and along Union Terrace to the Caledonian Hotel, got thoroughly wet from the sleet and snow, and was now hot and bothered with rushing so she would not be late.

Head down, she turned and pushed the door, and stumbled straight into the arms of a man coming in the other direction.

'I beg your pardon,' he said in a stiff voice, letting go and taking a swift step back from her.

'It was my fault,' Gina apologised automatically. 'I wasn't looking where I was going.'

Was that a Canadian accent, she wondered fleetingly as she looked up at the tall man before her. He had dark hair and shielded dark eyes, plus what would be a nice mouth if it smiled. Gina hesitated. There was something strangely familiar about him.

'Maybe you should come in,' he said abruptly and held the door for her.

Gina blushed. She hoped he had not thought she was staring, or interested, or anything. Because she was not. Definitely not.

He waited, unsmiling. Gina gathered up the remains of her composure and thanked him, before turning away as fast as she could to get away from him.

Gulp. He was rather gorgeous, she thought, then sternly repressed the thought. She focused her attention on the noticeboard in front of her, telling her where the conference she had come to attend was being held.

5

Following the direction notices, Gina hurried through the hotel to the reception table outside the conference room where a small queue of people were waiting to be registered.

As she waited, she removed her heavy, wet coat and folded it over her arm. Noticing what the other women were wearing, she realised Mandy had been right in insisting she borrow her little green suit. Wearing it did make Gina look the part she had come to play. But she wasn't used to dressing like this. The miniskirt felt almost indecently short and the zip-fronted jacket was tight. She tried to breathe deeply to calm her nerves. She knew her feet would be in agony by the end of the day, but Mandy's fashion sense had demanded she wear high heels. Looking around, it was clear that once again Mandy had been correct.

Gina sighed. She wasn't interested in fashion. She didn't want to dress to impress or to attract anybody. She preferred to be comfortable and able to move around quickly and freely. That's what she needed for her job as a reporter on the local weekly, *The Caithness Sentinel*. She thought of the younger lads at the works who found it entertaining to flick tiny sharp-edged pieces of lead from the letterpress forme as she went downstairs, trying to ladder her stockings. Female reporters were still quite rare and came in for a lot of teasing, but she had won her spurs over the years and was now a senior reporter.

'Name?' the girl at the desk asked, pen poised above a list of the attendees.

Gina jumped. She hadn't realised she had reached the front of the queue.

'Mandy Strachan,' Gina said. 'Mrs Mandy Strachan.'

She would have to pay attention if she was going to get away with this charade.

'You can do it,' Mandy had told her. 'We look alike, so if anyone remembers you being there, they'll think it was me. There's really no problem.'

And yes, they did look alike, but there the resemblance ended. Mandy, at only 24, was already at the end of one marriage and on the hunt for another man. While Gina, now 23, continued determinedly with her single life.

'You can't live like a nun for the rest of your life, Gina!' Mandy frequently lectured her. Gina did not see it that way. Being single was her choice. It suited her – and her family. It was really as much for them as for herself.

The girl at the conference reception desk was checking down through her list, pen poised. 'And your firm?'

Gina named the accountancy firm in Wick that Mandy was currently working for. After her marriage failed, Mandy had moved back to her grandmother's home in Lybster, a village a few miles south of Wick, and found herself a new job in town. She had airily announced that the move and the new job offered her much better prospects in the form of contact with 'a better class of man' as she had put it.

Gina had therefore been surprised that Mandy had not wanted to attend today's conference. There were plenty of young and middle-aged businessmen here who would surely have been of interest to her, but maybe Mandy's new 'someone special' was indeed more promising.

Perhaps if Gina had not been tempted by the conference itself, she might not have gone along with Mandy's request. But when she discovered it was on the subject of the latest business prospects in the north of Scotland and hosted by the Institute of Chartered Accountants, she knew it would provide up-to-date inside information that could not be got elsewhere. Her reporter's nose for a potential scoop warred with her deep-rooted horror of the dishonesty that would be involved. Somehow in the end, the reporter in her – and Mandy's determination – won.

Gina accepted a name badge and a thickly filled conference folder. As she turned away from the desk, trying to hold her heavy folded coat and the bulky conference folder, and pin the name badge on her lapel at the same time, the folder slipped from her grasp and the papers and booklets inside showered onto the ground at her feet.

Gina cringed. Now she was drawing attention to herself and for sure someone would notice her and see through her masquerade. It was obvious she didn't belong here. She couldn't even get herself registered and into the conference room without incident! She should never have been tempted to do this, she berated herself. There was no way she could carry it off.

Before she could move, a cool voice she had heard before said, 'Let me help.' And the Canadian man was there at her side, gathering up the documents from the floor and stuffing them back into the folder.

Gina stifled a heavy sigh. Now he'd know she was a total idiot! Not that it mattered, of course, but she knew she was blushing again. She closed her eyes.

Why did it have to happen when he was there to see? Why did it have to happen at all? And she knew the answer. It was perfectly simple and obvious. What she was doing was wrong. She was here under false pretences, at a conference she had no right to attend. At which, in fact, she was a spy.

And in her mind she heard the horrid, familiar voice that said, 'Bad girls must be punished.'

She realised the man was placing the folder back in her arms and taking the name badge from her nerveless fingers. He took hold of the lapel of her jacket and pinned the badge in place.

Gina opened her eyes and saw a stern yet somehow not unfriendly face. He stepped back.

'There, Mrs Mandy Strachan,' he said brusquely. 'Everything's sorted.' He waved to the door of the conference room. 'You'd better go in before the conference starts.' And he gave her a little push in the right direction.

The push woke her up. Dragging her emotions raggedly under control, she went.

CHAPTER 3

Hugo Mackay's eyes followed the girl as she stumbled away. Her reactions surprised him. He was used to high-maintenance, confident young women who hung about, trying to attach themselves to him despite his obvious lack of encouragement. It came with the territory.

Youngish, not bad-looking – though he said it himself – and rich. Funny how that last thing made all the difference, he thought cynically. But then women were always drawn to money…

This girl, though, was different. It was clear that she was just not interested. In fact, from the start she had almost run in her hurry to get away from him. She was like a young deer caught in the headlights of an oncoming truck. Surely he wasn't that fearsome?

That was a pity.

As was the *Mrs* on her name badge.

Hugo turned to the young woman at the registration desk and saw her eyes scanning him appraisingly. That was much more normal.

'Name?' she asked.

Hugo told her and waited for her reaction. Oh yes, she knew who he was. But then considering he was the guest keynote speaker and his name was plastered on the conference posters and brochures, she should. His eyes narrowed with dislike as hers widened with interest; then there was that tell-tale tongue lick over the fashionably pale lips, as she sat up a little straighter.

'Oh yes,' she said in a lowered confidential voice. 'Mr Mackay.' And there was the little intimate, knowing smile as she handed over the conference folder. Beginning to rise from her seat, and leaning closer, the name badge in her hand, she murmured, 'Shall I?'

But Hugo had had enough.

'Thank you, ma'am,' he said crisply. 'I can manage.'

He deftly removed the badge from her hand without touching her fingers and slipped it into his jacket pocket as he turned away.

Another one. Women attracted by his name and his reputation and the reports of his wealth. It was as if his success had drawn a big bullseye on his back for all the women in the world looking for husbands – or a wealthy provider – to aim at.

Hugo gathered his cynicism around him like a cloak and entered the big room set up for the day's conference proceedings. He always liked to arrive in good time and slip into an unnoticed place amongst the delegates so he could size up his prospective audience.

The back wall of the room was lightened by large windows looking onto a wide road busy with cars and other vehicles. The carved balustrades of Union Terrace Gardens flanked the pavement on the other side of the street, and in prime position halfway along, set back in a generous niche, was a statue of Robert Burns looking a little forlorn in the sleety downpour. On either side of the statue were entrances to the Gardens. Not weather for a stroll, Hugo thought regretfully.

He looked around the room for an empty seat unencumbered by more 'interested' females and noted that the girl he had encountered earlier had secreted herself away in the furthest corner. She had piled her coat and bag on the chair next to her like a barricade to stave off all comers.

For a moment, sudden mischief tempted him to invade her protective bastion. But that would be unnecessarily unkind. He noticed the girl's sudden heightened colour. She had spotted him looking at her.

He nodded brusquely and ambled in the other direction, seating himself where the event organisers could easily find him and call on him when it was his turn to speak. He set himself to read through the papers in the folder. After all, that was why he was here. He had thought it a half-decent trade-off: a short keynote talk in the graveyard slot after lunch, in exchange for an entrée to business in this area. He had heard it was an up-and-coming region, worth getting a foothold in. But first he wanted to find out what was going on, identify the people who might be useful to him, and stake out any prospects that might be of interest.

By the time a break for coffee was announced, he was ready to get up and stretch his long legs. He joined the queue for a cup of whatever infernal beverage they were serving and found himself almost homesick in his longing for decent coffee. And that brought back memories of his beloved grandmother and her faithful old coffee pot on the stove at her little house in Manitoba. His mind drifted. There had always been coffee…

Hugo caught a sharp breath as a sudden pain hit, hot and shocking him out of his reverie.

'Oh no!'

He found himself staring into the eyes of the dark-haired girl. And then he followed her appalled gaze to the coffee cup she was holding, the cup whose contents had tipped over onto his hand. Automatically he lifted his hand to his mouth to lick the spilled coffee.

'Oh no,' she said. 'Not you again.'

It was not the apology he was expecting.

'Yep,' he said, struggling manfully not to laugh at the disgruntled expression on her face. 'Me again.' He pulled a large white handkerchief out of his pocket and mopped the coffee from his hand.

She seemed to have frozen in the headlights again so he took the coffee cup out of her hand and set it down on a nearby table, reached for her elbow and determinedly guided her away from the queue.

'Wait a minute,' she protested, coming back to life. 'What are you doing?'

'I need coffee,' he explained. 'And I'd like my coffee now.' He waved in the direction of the queue. 'I don't reckon, from the sample I've had, that what they're serving is much good.'

She was still glaring at him.

Hugo continued. 'You're clearly too dangerous to be let out on your own so I'm taking you with me to the public coffee lounge where you can't do any more damage to me or anyone else. We'll have coffee there. You'll be perfectly safe and can run away any time you like. And if you decide not to run, we can simply sit and talk. Or not talk if you don't want to. All right?'

She glared at him again and he had to damp down the unexpected delight her reactions produced in him. In anyone else, that 'accident' would not have been so accidental but instead carefully created to get close to him. Somehow he was sure as sure could be that with this girl it had indeed been an accident, and one she bitterly regretted.

'Come on, Mrs Strachan. Let's get that coffee.'

And he led the way into the far lounge where a waiter hurried up to take Hugo's order.

'I suppose you're used to this kind of thing,' she grumped, perching on the edge of her chair.

Hugo bit his lip to stop the grin appearing. 'And you're not?'

Another glare.

He held up a placating hand. 'OK. No social chit-chat. We'll just drink coffee.'

The waiter arrived with china cups of coffee and a plate of shortbread.

'And eat shortbread,' Hugo added, reaching for the plate.

CHAPTER 4

Gina eyed him over the rim of her coffee cup. True to his word, he was simply sipping coffee and munching shortbread.

Silently she berated herself: how had she got herself into such a situation – having coffee with a man she'd never met before? And a man she kept embarrassing herself with! It was as if someone was pulling her strings and throwing her in this man's way. Well, it would not do.

Gina made herself sit very upright in the lounge chair. She would drink her coffee, say her thank-yous and get herself out of here as quickly as she could. She took a sip and had to stop herself from groaning out loud with despair. The coffee was very hot. She would be here for ages!

He looked across at her then, an eyebrow quirked enquiringly. She pretended to ignore it, but knew that the tell-tale blush was creeping up her cheeks again and giving away her horrible embarrassment. Swiftly she looked away.

But she had to admit he was rather nice to look at. If you liked a man with a golden tan, good skin, shiny dark hair that flopped over his forehead. Externals, she told herself. Superficial. But he had an intelligent face, quick sharp eyes. And a nice mouth…

She stopped that train of thought in its tracks. She was not interested in men however nice they looked. But, the thought came pushing into her mind, Mandy would be interested. Especially since he was probably successful and well off... exactly Mandy's type. She would be making the most of this opportunity.

If Mandy were here... Gina glanced up. He wasn't looking so she allowed herself an appraising inspection, allowing herself to think Mandy-style.

Yes, he was nice-looking. Tall and well turned out. Mandy would put this situation to her advantage. And if she was being Mandy for the day...

And then he caught her eye and she blushed for very shame, as if he could read her thoughts. She was not Mandy. She never would be, no matter how hard she tried. He was probably just taking pity on a stupid, clumsy, unattractive woman who was no threat and of no interest.

Even if she tried, she thought hopelessly, she'd never have a chance. She was not Mandy – even if for one day she was dressed up like Mandy, made up like Mandy, and pretending to be Mandy. Gina sighed.

Hugo watched with fascination as the thoughts and emotions played across Gina's face. For a moment, he had felt sudden disappointment when he saw a flicker of that acquisitive awareness so many young women showed in his company. The sign that it was time to get away from them, and fast. But then it was quickly replaced by... sadness? What was her story, he wondered.

'So tell me about yourself, Mrs Strachan,' he said.

Gina froze. What could she say? She dragged her thoughts together. What would Mandy say? It would be flirty, funny... Gina shook her head. She wasn't Mandy. She couldn't play the kind of game Mandy would play so there was no point trying.

'There's nothing really to tell.' She thought quickly, sifting the facts of Mandy's life. 'I work for an accountancy firm in the north. Nobody else could come to the conference so I was sent to take notes… I'm not an accountant or anything but I do shorthand.' Well, some of that was the truth, both about Mandy, and herself.

'Ah. And are you finding it interesting so far?'

Gina looked sharply at him. Was he making fun of her? The early talks had been tedious, offering nothing new or of interest and she had been wondering just how much use this conference was going to be either to Mandy's firm or to her own hopes of a scoop.

'Me neither,' Hugo said with a grin. 'Have another piece of shortbread. We may need it to get us through the next session!'

An hour and a half later, Gina was grateful. Her notepad was filled with hieroglyphics as she tried to keep up with the rattle of information from the last speaker. It had been genuinely interesting and she had an idea of how she could write it up for *The Sentinel*.

The room was busy with delegates getting up and making for the restaurant. Gina tidied her papers on the chair beside her and followed. She found a place at the end of a long table in the restaurant and concentrated on her lunch.

She was fending off questions from a very boring young man across the table when she became aware of a presence beside her, a hand on her chair.

'Mrs Strachan…'

The boring young man shut up.

Gina looked round, strangely unsurprised to find the Canadian at her side.

'I wondered…' Hugo waved to the window looking onto the street outside. 'The weather seems a little better. I'm going to take a walk to clear the cobwebs and get ready for the afternoon stint. I wondered if you'd care to join me?'

Mandy would, was Gina's instant reaction. Mandy would grab at the chance. But the question was: would Gina?

And it was as if a sudden madness seized her.

'Yes,' she found herself saying decisively, squashing down her usual reactions. 'Yes, I'd like that.'

And before she knew it she had been bundled into her coat and he was helping her down the slippery marble steps from the front door, then diagonally across the street to the Burns statue, and into Union Terrace Gardens.

'That's better!' Hugo said with relief. 'I don't like being cooped up indoors!' He smiled at her surprised expression. 'You think I'm a hothouse plant, spending my life in an office...'

Gina laughed, suddenly reckless with freedom. This wasn't her. She was someone else – just for a few moments stolen out of her usual careful, circumspect life – and she was determined to enjoy it.

'Yes, of course,' she replied, amazed that she was flirting, for the first time in her life. 'Jetting about every day in hothouse private jets...'

'Oh, is that what you think?' he teased her.

'Of course,' she said airily and discovered he had slipped her arm through his and they were walking along the wintry paths of the Gardens, comfortably together.

He pointed out a robin hopping cheekily among the pigeons. They laughed at the antics of a naughty puppy. Then as the snow started up again, a train came through on the railway lines sunk at the lowest level of the Gardens and Gina's face pulled into a little frown.

'What's the matter?' he asked.

'I'm thinking if the weather's going to get worse, I'd better catch an earlier train and get myself home. I don't want to be stuck in Aberdeen.' She tugged her arm away and consulted her watch. 'Mmm.' Gina looked up at him regretfully. 'I must go back to the hotel and pick up my stuff. I reckon if I get a push on I can get the 1.50 train.'

In another girl, it would be the beginning of the old ploy to spend the rest of the day, and the evening, and probably the night with him. But he didn't think this girl was playing that game. Playing any game, in fact. And now, surprising himself, he really didn't want her to go.

'Must you?' Hugo asked.

Gina gestured to the thickening snow tumbling down from a leaden sky. 'Yes, I think I must,' she said and turned to go.

Something made him reach for her arm and turn her back. Startled, she raised her face questioningly to his and a snowflake fell on her upturned nose. Unable to resist, Hugo dropped a kiss where it had landed. Flame rushed through her cheeks and Hugo bent and placed a soft kiss on her lips.

'Oh,' she said.

'Just so,' Hugo said, smiling inwardly. He took her arm and led her back through the swirling whiteness of the snow to the hotel, where he helped her gather up her conference folder and her notebook with her precious notes. Then he walked to the grand front door with her.

'Goodbye, Mrs Strachan,' he said. 'It was good to meet you.'

Gina blushed furiously, mumbling her goodbyes incoherently as she stumbled out of the door and down the steps to the street. She had reached the railway station and the 1.50 p.m. train to Inverness, found an empty carriage and collapsed onto the seat before she realised she didn't even know his name.

Hugo returned to the conference room.

19

'Ah, Mr Mackay.' The conference organiser was waiting for him. 'Everything's ready for your talk.' And she ushered him over to the lectern.

Hugo looked over his audience and considered it was probably just as well the snow had sent that delightful unaffected girl home early. She would never know who he was and so there was no danger that she would turn out to be like all the rest. Now he could believe that there was one more woman in the world, apart from his beloved grandmother, who was neither deceitful nor mercenary.

As he began his talk, he found himself thinking it was a pity she was married though.

CHAPTER 5

Wick, June 1964

'Typhoid?' Gina exclaimed. 'I didn't know it still existed!'

She pushed her chair back from her desk in the reporters' room and tried to ease the kinks out of her shoulders. She had been struggling to turn a very confused piece of copy from a correspondent with good ideas but not much of a grasp of spelling, grammar or punctuation into something *The Caithness Sentinel* could print without embarrassment. *The Sentinel* strove to encourage local writers and over the years Gina had learned the importance of tactful subediting. But this morning's offering had all but defeated her. She was glad of a break.

'Wasn't that what Prince Albert died from?' she added.

'That's right,' came the reply from *The Sentinel's* Editor, Danny Cormack.

Danny was Gina's uncle – her mother's brother. And his wife, Catalena – Auntie Cat – was her late father's half-sister. Each day before Danny went out to lunch with his wife, he would amble out of the Editor's sanctum and into the reporters' office for a catch-up on the morning's events. Today, however, it was Danny who brought news – and sensational news at that.

He waved the piece of paper in his hand. 'A wire has just come in. According to this, a typhoid outbreak has been confirmed in Aberdeen.'

Jimmy Macrae, the oldest of the team of three reporters, leaned back in his chair and puffed on his foul-smelling pipe.

'Well, Mr Cormack,' he said. 'And what can you expect from such a place? Cities are unhealthy places. All those people crammed in together!'

Gina grinned. Jimmy was a native Lewisman whose dream was to retire to a small croft there. He was, in fact, past retirement age but had not yet saved up enough money to fund the project. Henry, the trainee reporter and youngest on the team, had come in for heavy scolding when he had suggested that Jimmy should try the football pools to make up the deficit.

'Gambling!' Jimmy had roared, tapping his pipe out on the side of the office fireplace in time with his words. 'I would never stoop to that!'

So Jimmy remained a loyal and hard-working member of the staff, ably supported by Gina and Henry.

'We'll need to find out more about this,' Danny told them. 'There are Wick students at college and university in Aberdeen. Their families will be wanting to know what's going on.'

He looked at his watch. Auntie Cat was always prompt bringing the car up to the office door.

'I'd better go. Cat will be waiting for me.' He nodded to his team. 'Right. I'll leave it with you.'

The ensuing article was a triumph of moderation and reassurance – unlike the national papers which blared loudly about the 'Beleaguered City'.

'Says here,' Henry read out from one of the nationals, 'they've shut the place down – no one allowed to enter or leave the city.' He looked up. 'Do you think that's right?'

Day by day, bulletins were issued by Aberdeen's Medical Officer of Health, duly printed by the *Aberdeen Press and Journal*, but despite all attempts to calm misinformation, Aberdeen was shunned. Holidaymakers went elsewhere. And it was reported that the only local business that thrived was the one that sold ready-made will forms.

Word filtered out that the cause of the epidemic was tainted corned beef from Argentina. Catalena had been born and brought up in Argentina so it was unsurprising that she should find herself on the receiving end of questions. Visiting her mother-in-law one afternoon, she discovered that Hannah wanted to know how the outbreak of typhoid could have happened – and what the risks were of eating corned beef.

Cat answered her questions readily.

'It really shouldn't happen,' she said. 'My papa was in the meat-packing business and my brothers are continuing with it. There should not be a problem nowadays.'

'But clearly there is,' Hannah Cormack said.

'Yes,' Cat said sadly. 'When the cooked meat is put into the cans, they are cooled in tanks of water. In the old days, before people knew the dangers, they just used running water from a river – and who knew what was in the river! But the cans were sealed before they went into the water so there would have to be splits or holes to let polluted water in – and that's not very likely.'

Hannah raised an eyebrow.

'There were some problems a few years back,' Cat conceded. 'After that it was agreed that precautions would be taken. I know our factories back home in Argentina all have chlorination plants to treat the water before the cans go in for cooling.'

She sipped her tea, but Hannah could see the worry in her face.

'I think our plants are all right. I don't think any Hernandez products are involved,' she said.

'But you worry?' Hannah asked her daughter-in-law. She was very fond of the Argentinian girl who had come to Scotland to attend her half-brother George's funeral, caught Danny's eye and stayed to marry him and make him happy.

Cat nodded.

'But not about the corned beef,' she said. 'No, it's my mother. I haven't heard from her for a while. She usually writes regularly. Yes, I know she's an old lady now.' Catalena shrugged, a very continental gesture. 'She's 82 now and she's been ill for quite a while.' Her expressive mouth turned down at the corners. 'I worry about her, and I am so far away.'

CHAPTER 6

Aberdeen, June 1964

'With the way the epidemic is spreading, I really feel you would be best to get out of Aberdeen while you can, Mr Mackay.'

Hugo stared at his solicitor in dismay. He had selected this firm for its business reputation and acumen, never expecting to receive personal advice of this nature.

'I don't advise this lightly,' the solicitor said. 'I know how much the venture means to you, but surely your health is more important? I'd head to the hills myself if I could...' He spread his hands in helplessness. 'But I can't. You, however, can. And that's what I'd strongly advise. Get out while you can. The word is that there's going to be some kind of lock-down of the city to prevent the contagion spreading. Already all the schools are closed. Business is likely to grind to a halt so you'd be wasting your time staying.'

Hugo knew he was being given the best information and counsel the man could offer. But to leave Aberdeen when he had invested so much time and effort in preparing the ground for a take-over of a local firm that promised quick returns... He did not like giving up.

The typhoid epidemic seemed to have blown up out of nowhere and the daily newspapers were reporting increasing numbers of patients. The city was alive with rumour and fear.

'Seriously,' the solicitor said. 'I think it would be wise…'

Hugo returned unhappily to his hotel on the outskirts of Aberdeen and flung himself into a chair in his room. What was he going to do? People were saying it could take months before Aberdeen was open again for business. The fast turn-round he had been planning would certainly not happen now.

He had focused on Aberdeen as a likely up-and-coming place. He did not want to have to start all over again, easing himself into the business networks of another Scottish city before he could nose out the perfect opportunity for his capital and his reorganisation skills.

He could pack up and go home to Canada. Get back to the office and settle down to work there. But it felt like defeat. Surely there was still a prize to be had in this country, even if not in Aberdeen as planned?

The hotel notepaper on the table next to him jogged his conscience. He had not written to his grandmother for a while. Usually he sent regular postcards to keep her informed about where he was, but he had been based in Aberdeen for a couple of months now and had been so busy, there had been no time for jaunts and pretty postcards.

He picked up a pen and began to write, and as he wrote, he mulled over the problem. He had time on his hands – time to think, time to plan what to do next. Only not in Aberdeen.

Scotland was a country with a thriving tourist industry. He could have a holiday. But leisure was not a concept that had any place in his life. From the age of 13 he had set himself to work hard and climb the ladder of success, to ensure he had a solid business behind him and a big enough bank balance to fall back on should he ever need it.

But now, all that meant little. The Aberdeen typhoid epidemic had put paid to his plans and here he was, left kicking his heels.

'What do you think?' he wrote to his grandmother. 'A few weeks in the wilds?'

And then business as usual, he promised himself.

CHAPTER 7

Manitoba, Canada

'Mrs Paston?'

The sweet-faced old lady in the wheelchair smiled a welcome at the girl who hurried across the terrace towards her.

'I have a letter for you,' she said, waving it gaily.

'A letter!' Nancy Paston said. 'Thank you, Ella. I expect it will be from my darling Hugo.'

'You haven't heard from him for a little while,' Ella commented. 'I suppose he's busy. Now, have you got your glasses?'

Nancy fished down the side of the chair and pulled out a spectacles case. She brandished it with a triumphant smile. 'Yes, indeed.'

'Then I'll leave you in peace to read your letter.'

'Thank you,' Nancy said and bent her head to examine the envelope and the stamp. Scotland. Ah yes, so Hugo was still in Aberdeen. She opened the letter and began to read.

'You're thoughtful,' Ella commented when she came to wheel Nancy to the main building for lunch. 'There's no problem with that young man?'

'No, my dear,' Nancy said. 'I'm just wondering how to advise him. It's a little tricky...'

In the bright and cheerful dining room of the nursing home where she lived, Nancy tried to focus on the food and the friends around her, but her mind kept drifting to Hugo and what she would say to him. What would be best...

After lunch Nancy managed to attract Ella's attention.

'Yes, Mrs Paston?'

'My dear, would you mind taking me back to my room? I think I'd like a little nap after lunch.'

'That would be no problem,' the girl said and wheeled Nancy to her room.

'I'll just sit here for a moment,' Nancy said. 'Thank you for bringing me.'

'You're more than welcome,' and the girl took herself away.

Nancy heaved a small sigh as the door closed. Now she could really think – in the only way she could, talking it over with her Lord. And for that she needed privacy.

'So,' Nancy said, taking a deep breath and trying to marshal her thoughts. 'Hugo is in Scotland. His plans have all been wiped out by this typhoid epidemic... Do I detect Your hand in this, Lord? Oh, I'm not saying You're responsible for that – the epidemic, I mean! – of course not, but changing Hugo's plans?'

She paused, considering. 'Because now he can't simply do what he wanted to do in Aberdeen and then rush off back here, avoiding the north of Scotland and all it means to him. Oh, he'd say it means nothing – but actually it means everything, doesn't it? What happened up there.'

A little shakily, Nancy dragged her concentration back.

'I think he needs to go to Wick. I think he needs to go back as a grown man and face his demons there.'

She took a breath. 'You know I've always felt the way he lives – pouring himself into his work… OK, I admit, he plays hard as well, but it means nothing to him! A pretty girl on his arm is the same as another company in his portfolio – there for a while, then gone to make room for the next one.'

She caught herself up and refocused. 'I've always felt he's running from himself, from his feelings, from all that buried hurt.'

She gave a short mirthless laugh. 'The magazines all say he has no heart! Me, I think the problem is that he has a very big heart, and it got badly broken.'

Nancy firmly turned her mind back to the matter at hand.

'I think this is Hugo's chance to go back to Wick. Where things went really wrong, back in 1945. He can't avoid it for ever. And maybe – oh Lord, maybe You can use this opportunity for Hugo's good. Please!'

She sat for a little while longer, then reached for writing paper and a pen.

'*My darling Hugo…*'

CHAPTER 8

Somewhere in the far north of Scotland

Hugo consulted the map. Where was he? He looked up and scanned the countryside. Not a signpost or a house or a landmark. Just a winding road through a bleak upland moor. And sheep. Big woolly sheep, lying down on the edge of the road. And getting up without warning and walking slowly – insolently – across the road right in the path of the oncoming car. Almost as if they'd been waiting for a signal.

Hugo glared. He did not like sheep. In any shape or form. Alive, dead, or cooked. He never ate lamb if he could help it. The smell of the fat cooking made him want to retch. It was odd and something he just could not help. He wondered idly as he slowed for yet another sheep to make its way to the other side of the road whether there was anything in this idea of a race memory?

He knew from the stories he had been told as a child that his ancestors had been farmers in the county of Sutherland, growing crops and fattening cattle on fertile land leased for generations from the local landlords. In the early nineteenth century all this had come to a shocking end as the landlords – the Duchess of Sutherland

and her English husband – tore the land back from their tenants and drove them out, some in a terrible trek up to the rocky north coast. Others found shelter further up the east coast in Caithness. His family, the Mackays, belonged to this more fortunate group. They had settled in a small croft south of Thrumster from where his grandfather, Hughie Mackay, had set off to make his fortune in the Klondike gold rush back in 1897.

The landowners had put sheep on the now empty land. An old lady from church back in Manitoba had told him the ordinary folk of the time would never see mutton or lamb on their dinner tables. The only way you'd have sheep on your table, she explained, was if someone had stolen one or it had died of sickness. And you wouldn't want to eat that. Not unless you were desperate.

Hugo cast a wintry eye over the now barren landscape. The sheep experiment had not worked. The land had been much better managed and cared for under its crofting tenants. But at least in later years better provision had been made in Parliament for the protection of the crofters.

When he reached the village of Latheron, Hugo spotted a signpost at the road junction and on impulse turned his hired car off the main A9 road north, heading instead across the county. Thurso, that's where he'd go. Not Wick. He seized on the new destination with relief. He didn't want to go to Wick.

It was a small spurt of rebellion. He would wait a few days before sending his grandmother a postcard – and that would not be from Thurso but somewhere pretty and touristy and innocuous. She did not need to know he had not heeded her advice – or her wishes.

As he drove through the bleak moorland along the Causeymire road – so clearly a causeway across a 'mire' as the name attested – Hugo pushed down the momentary pang of guilt. He had never deliberately deceived his grandmother, and he felt he was deceiving her now.

'Since you're so close,' she had written, 'I wonder could I ask a favour? Would you go to your father's grave for me, and maybe put some flowers on? And I'd be so glad if you could find the time to visit Hannah and Joyce Cormack. They were so kind to me when I went across to Scotland for your father's funeral. We've kept in touch ever since. I don't think they've had it at all easy. They're good people and as much damaged by that George Sinclair as you and your father were.'

He had found that hard to read. He didn't want to go to Wick. He would go to Thurso, send Grandma a postcard, and then get out of there.

He could be back in Canada in a week.

CHAPTER 9

Wick

'No!'

It was a rainy Saturday afternoon and, unusually, Mandy didn't have a date, so the two girls were holed up in Gina's bedroom.

'No!' Gina repeated. She pulled her legs up under her in the big armchair and glared at her cousin.

Mandy was sitting on the bed, propped up on pillows piled against the wall. She was poring over the latest issue of *The Caithness Sentinel* spread out on her knees. She had managed to worm out of Gina the news that there was someone in Wick beginning to show an interest in her. But Gina wasn't interested in him.

Mandy arched a carefully plucked eyebrow.

'So you won't even give the boy a chance?'

'No,' Gina said crisply.

Mandy held up a hand. 'OK. I just thought it would be a giggle. Get you out on a date for once in your life...'

'Mandy!' Gina's tone was uncompromising.

'Oh well,' Mandy sighed. 'You can't say I don't do my best for you!'

Gina shifted uncomfortably.

'It wouldn't be fair,' she said. 'I don't fancy him in the slightest!'

'What's that got to do with anything?' Mandy asked. 'If he's willing to take you out, spend some money on you, give you a nice time... Where's the harm in it?'

'No,' Gina said. 'I'm not you, Mandy. I can't just use people for a bit of fun then toss them aside...'

The eyebrow was raised again, haughtily. 'I don't see why not. That's what men do to us.'

Mandy shook out the pages of the newspaper and resumed her perusal of the job advertisements.

Gina thought back to her encounter with the Canadian at the conference in Aberdeen. Was that all it had been for him? A moment's respite from the boredom of the sessions? She had liked him, though. And his gentle kiss. Her face softened at the memory. She had treasured it in the months that followed, despite her best intentions. It didn't matter. She would never see him again.

'Listen to this,' Mandy commanded. 'There's an ad: "*Young lady required by head of Scots firm in the South. Personal, Confidential, Private Assistant to take over running of residence. If interested, assist in business and entertainment. Pleasant personality, trustworthiness, adaptability essential. This is not a stereotype post; also offers some travel. State concise details and interests. Age group 21–30. Write to...*" It's a box number. No other information.'

She looked over at her cousin. 'What do you think? It sounds right up my street. Within a few weeks I'll have him wound round my little finger and married before he knows what's hit him!'

'Mandy!' Gina protested. 'He could be anyone...' And the dark-haired handsome Canadian flickered through her memory again. *Oh please, Lord Jesus, don't let it be him*, she prayed fervently. *And please, don't let Mandy go for that job and get it, if it's him. I couldn't bear it!*

'Shall I apply for it? I'm so bored where I am.' Mandy smiled, mocking. 'It would take my mind off trying to fix you up with someone!'

'I don't want fixed up with anyone…'

'I know. I know. That's what you always say, but you're not getting any younger and the decent men are getting fewer and farther between. One day, you'll be left with no choice and you'll wish you encouraged… what's his name?'

Automatically Gina answered, 'Alec Gunn.'

'Young Alec,' Mandy corrected her. 'Third in the line of Alec Gunns: Ould Alec, now passed away, Middle Alec – widowed, but he's too old for you, and Young Alec, first in line to inherit a fine farm and keep you in the manner…'

But Gina was standing up.

'Enough,' she said. 'I've told you. I'm not interested.'

CHAPTER 10

But when Gina's office door opened late the next Thursday afternoon to admit a blushing but determined Young Alec with the day's livestock market report, instead of crisply taking it from him and dismissing him without any encouragement to stay and chat, she found herself reaching for her coat and following him out to his car.

He had arrived later than usual. Jimmy and Henry had both left, and the compositors' room was silent and empty as she popped downstairs for her coat. Gina began packing her things up, putting the cover on her typewriter, and getting ready to go home. A glance at the window told her it was pouring with rain and she would be soaked by the time she got there. She hadn't brought an umbrella.

Which is when Young Alec appeared. She had grabbed the proffered piece of paper and was about to dismiss him as usual when he stumbled into speech.

'It's a terrible night out for the time of year, Miss Sinclair. I've got the car.' He had beamed then, so hopefully. 'I wondered, would you like a lift home? It would save you getting wet.'

And yes, considering the weather, she would like a lift, even from an embarrassingly besotted swain such as Young Alec. So she had accepted and followed him to the red Mini waiting outside.

He had opened the door for her, very politely, and waited till she climbed in before closing it and going round to the driver's side.

'Willowbank?' he asked.

'Yes,' she said, surprised that he knew where she lived. But he just grinned and started the engine.

The journey home was short and uneventful. Thankfully, Young Alec didn't try to make conversation and simply accepted Gina's thanks as she let herself out of the car.

But her mother had seen the flash of red from the kitchen window.

'That was good,' she said. 'A nice lift home so you didn't get wet.' She had come through to where Gina was taking off her coat. 'Who was that then?'

'Alec Gunn,' Gina said briefly. 'Young Alec.'

She hung her coat up on the peg in the little cloakroom under the stairs and went into the warm kitchen. Her grandmother, sitting on a chair by the fire, twinkled at her.

'Alec Gunn, did you say?' she asked. 'I remember an Alec Gunn. He came courting me a long time ago and I wouldn't have him!'

'I doubt it's the same Alec Gunn, Mum,' her daughter Joyce teased affectionately. 'If he's come courting Gina…'

'It was just a lift!' Gina protested, though she knew in her heart that poor Young Alec was doing his best to 'come courting' as her mother put it.

'Whatever,' her mother said peaceably. 'Anyway, he'll be a lot younger than your Alec Gunn, Mum.'

'He was never mine, though he wanted to be,' Hannah Cormack demurred. Her grey eyes gazed into the distance as she reminisced.

'That would be back the year my mother died. He was a good-looking man, Alec Gunn, and the farm even then was prosperous. I was fond of his parents. They were good people.'

She looked round at her daughter and granddaughter. 'But I was in love with your dad, your granddad, and there was no one else I wanted, so I waited for him.'

She paused thoughtfully and added with a smile, 'Alec waited for me too, though. During the war – that would be the first war – when we heard that Rab was missing, presumed dead, and I had the two boys to look after, he was willing to take us on, all three of us. But I still told him I would wait for Rab.'

She smiled, and the soft gentle smile lit into a deep glow.

'And that was the right thing to do. He came back to me, my Rab – and then we had you, my Joyce… and now there's you, Gina…'

Gina swallowed hard and tried to smile. To know that such love could exist made tears come to her eyes.

'And me!'

The interruption came from the young man sitting on the other side of the table. The words were loud and cheerful but spoken with difficulty, the lad's tongue too large for his mouth – one characteristic of the extra chromosome he'd been born with. His good-humoured face was broad and flat-planed, his build stocky. He grinned at the three women.

'Yes, of course, you too, Robbie my love,' Hannah said with a smile. 'My family. I am so grateful to God that I waited for Rab, and for you!'

39

CHAPTER 11

'*The Castle of Mey*,' Ella, the nursing assistant, read. '*Home of the Queen Mother*. Well,' she exclaimed, 'isn't that nice? I do admire the Queen Mum, don't you, Mrs Paston? She's such a nice lady.'

'She is indeed,' Nancy agreed. But what, she wondered, was Hugo doing up there on the north coast of Caithness, when she had asked him to go to Wick on the east coast?

He was killing time. And avoiding Wick. Hugo had taken himself off to John O'Groats and been duly impressed by the vistas of islands stretching out as far as the eye could see. In fact, he had been so impressed, he had managed to get a place on the *St Ola* ferry from Scrabster across to Kirkwall and spent a few pleasant days on Orkney, visiting the cathedral, the Italian Chapel, and a couple of the prehistoric sites – everything the guidebook told him to do.

And all the while, it itched at him that he was not doing what his grandmother had asked. But he could not do it. Not yet. So he decided to distract himself further with an attempt at what he was used to: business. A social/business gathering held in Thurso had welcomed the visitor from Canada. Hugo had been fascinated to discover that Thurso was a thriving, prosperous town, growing exponentially on the benefits of the nuclear power industry that was building a major site not too many miles away at Dounreay.

The same, unfortunately, could not be said for the county's other major town, Wick. In fact, one of the Thurso businessmen took pleasure in telling him so.

'No, Wick's not benefiting from the nuclear industry the way we in Thurso are. If you're thinking of investing, Thurso is the town for the future,' the man said.

Another chimed in. 'Even the Wick newspaper's in trouble. You wouldn't think it possible when it's got virtually a monopoly, all over the county, but that's the case.'

Hugo raised an enquiring eyebrow.

'It's not making the kind of money it used to,' the first man said.

'The building is old and inconvenient,' the second man elaborated. 'The machinery is old – and some of the staff are too! A bit set in their ways and not keeping up with modern times.'

'So?' Hugo prompted.

'It's owned by folk from the south. They've no interest in the north or in newspapers so they don't want to put any more money in.'

'So why own a paper up here?' Hugo asked, his curiosity piqued.

The second man shrugged. 'I think it was almost accidental. It was with some assets in the south that they were interested in a while back. At that time, it was ticking along nicely so they left it alone, but now...'

'Now it needs a cash injection,' the first man put in. 'And someone with a more hands-on approach to sort it out. Nobody up here has that kind of money, or interest...'

'It's got stuck in its ways!' the first man snorted.

'So this paper, what's it called?' Hugo asked.

'*The Caithness Sentinel*,' he was told.

41

'So *The Caithness Sentinel* was in their portfolio,' Hugo said thoughtfully, 'and while it was making enough money, they left it alone, but now they want to divest?'

'Aye, as speedily as possible.'

'I see.'

Hugo was intrigued. It sounded like the kind of deal he enjoyed and did well. He'd tackled a few small newspaper groups in the past so he thought it might be worthy of investigation. If it turned out to be his kind of opportunity, he could turn it round and sell it off at a profit, thereby rescuing his trip to Scotland from being a complete waste of time.

'Thank you,' he told the two men as he shook hands with them. 'That's very interesting.'

The fact it was in Wick need not be a problem. He could check it out from here in Thurso. His solicitor in Aberdeen would surely have contacts who could help.

He might have to nip across to Wick a couple of times to take a look at the newspaper building, see what the staff and machinery were actually like, and get started on whatever reorganisation or investment was needed. He could surely fit in a visit to his father's grave, and if he had time, a brief visit to the Cormacks to please his grandmother.

But he would stay in Thurso. His hotel was comfortable; the food was good. Yes, Hugo thought. That's what he would do. There was no need to actually spend time in Wick.

That was the last place on earth he wanted to go.

CHAPTER 12

'Next time, bring him in,' Joyce told her daughter. 'It's good of him to bring you home.'

'I don't want to encourage him!' Gina protested.

'I think once those Gunns get an idea in their heads, it's hard to stop them,' her grandmother offered with a smile.

'You are so right,' Gina agreed.

Somehow, her acceptance of a lift home on that one very rainy evening when the offer was welcome had turned into a regular pattern and now Young Alec brought her home in his car on the days he delivered the Mart report.

Even her Uncle Danny had noticed. The previous evening he had been leaving his office just when Young Alec was holding the door open for her as she found herself once again accepting his offer of a lift home.

'An admirer, Gina?' Danny had asked some time later.

Gina's attempt to brush off his enquiry had simply elicited the family twinkle and Auntie Cat had been round to Willowbank the next day to check out the story.

'There's nothing going on! In any case, he's too young for me,' Gina had protested when she heard. 'Why do people have to get all interested when there's nothing to tell?'

'It's because they care,' her mother told her. 'Anyway, Cat is family. You know she won't gossip. It won't go any further.'

But other folk had noticed and now each time Mandy dropped in, she took delight in teasing Gina about her rustic swain.

'You could do worse,' Mandy advised her.

The girls were having a coffee and a catch-up in Gina's room before Mandy had to catch the bus back to Lybster. Gina, ensconced on the bed, threw a pillow at her.

'And of course you might do better,' Mandy conceded, catching the pillow and cuddling it against her chest. 'But then you'd need to actually get out and meet some more suitable men.'

Gina shook her head. 'I'm not…'

'Interested. I know,' her cousin said. 'Poor you. How boring.' Mandy sat back in the armchair and examined her carefully manicured and varnished nails. She fluttered them at Gina. 'It's much more fun being interested and letting nice men be interested in you and take you out and pay for things so you have a nice time and…'

'No,' Gina said firmly, sitting back on the bed. 'I'm perfectly happy as I am. I've got my work and my family. I don't need anyone or anything else.'

'Boring,' Mandy repeated decisively. 'By the way, you remember that job ad I found in the paper the other week?'

Gina nodded, her heart catching suddenly.

'Well, I applied for it and I've got an interview down in Inverness tomorrow – all expenses paid. Do you want to come down for the day? We could make a day of it.'

'I can't,' Gina said. 'Mum and Granny are visiting Great-Uncle Jock at the Bignold Hospital this afternoon. You remember, Grandad's brother from out in the country. They're planning to go tomorrow too. He's not doing so well after that last stroke and Granny's worried about him. So I need to stay home with Robbie.'

Mandy pouted. 'I don't understand why you need to bother about Robbie. He should have been put in an institution when he was born; then you could all have got on with your lives.'

'Mandy!' Gina glared at her. 'Mum would never have allowed that! Just because Robbie's...'

'Mongol,' Mandy stated defiantly. 'Well, that's what he is, isn't he? Mental defective. Can't be allowed out on his own. Can't do very much for himself. Needs you all running around after him.'

'He can do plenty for himself...' Gina defended her brother.

'He can't even make himself understood. And dribbling all the time. Eugh! I don't know how you stand it!'

'So he dribbles,' Gina conceded. 'But so would you if your tongue was too big for your mouth! And he *can* make himself understood. If you take the trouble to listen to him, he makes perfectly good sense. Better than you sometimes! And at least he's nice!' Gina finished with a gasp.

'Well, I think he should have been put away from day one. That's my opinion,' Mandy declared defiantly. 'And I'm not the only one!'

'Sometimes I think you're just not a nice person, Mandy Strachan!' Gina told her.

Mandy flounced out of the door and down the stairs, only to meet Gina's mother and grandmother returning from their hospital visit.

'Must run!' Mandy said as she pushed past them. 'Bus to catch!'

Joyce hung up her coat and turned to see her daughter coming down the stairs in Mandy's wake.

'You'll never guess who we met at the hospital.'

She spoke with determined cheerfulness but Gina could see that it had not been a welcome surprise.

'Tell me,' Gina said, wondering who could have upset her usually equable mother.

'Auntie Joanie.'

'Ah,' Gina said. Auntie Joanie was married to Uncle Will, Granny's brother. Where Will was kind-hearted and easy-going, Joanie was mean-spirited and sharp-tongued. She was someone people preferred not to bump into.

Gina followed her mother and grandmother into the kitchen.

'And what did Aunt Joanie have to say for herself?'

'The usual,' her mother said, heading for the kettle to make tea. She glanced meaningfully towards Robbie who had come in to join them.

Gina nodded her understanding. She knew her Aunt Joanie's attitude towards Robbie was the same as Mandy's, if not held even more strongly.

'Was she laying down the law again?' Gina asked sympathetically.

Joyce's hunched back as she stood facing the kettle gave Gina her answer. She went over to her mother and gave her a hug.

'You mustn't let her upset you,' she told her. 'It's all talk. There's nothing she can do to hurt us.'

'Well, I don't know...' Joyce began unhappily. 'She was going on about this house again. You know she thinks we should move somewhere smaller...'

'So this can be sold,' her grandmother filled in. 'There's not a grain of human kindness in that woman. Oh dear. I really shouldn't have said that. It wasn't exactly kind of me either, but...'

'But only the truth,' Gina concluded. 'Still, she can't do anything about it while Uncle Will is alive.'

She saw her mother and grandmother exchange glances.

'Is there something I need to know?' Gina asked, looking from one to the other.

'The reason Joanie was at the hospital was because...' Hannah paused, then said in even tones, 'My brother Will had a turn this morning. She was visiting him.'

'Oh, dear,' Gina said.

'Quite so,' her grandmother said. 'So we'll all have to pray really hard that he recovers. We don't want to be left to Joanie's tender mercies!'

CHAPTER 13

Young Alec seemed even more bashful than usual as he stood in the doorway of Gina's office, waiting for her to put the cover on her typewriter and reach for her coat.

He held the door open for her and then as she moved past him, said breathlessly, 'I hope you don't mind but...'

Gina turned back, a question in her eyes.

Young Alec hurried to the outside door, face averted.

'Alec?' Gina asked. 'What is it?'

But he simply waved at the red Mini. There was a man sitting in the front seat.

'My dad had to come into town today, to the market. I couldn't just leave him to get the bus home...'

'No, of course not,' Gina said. 'I hope he doesn't mind a detour.'

'No, no!' Alec told her. 'He doesn't mind at all. He wanted to...' His voice dried up and his colour rose still further.

'Yes?' Gina prompted drily, though she dreaded the answer.

'He wanted to meet you,' Young Alec finished.

'I see,' Gina said.

So Middle Alec was aware of his son's pursuit of her. She straightened her shoulders and walked determinedly towards the car. Somehow she was going to have to make it clear to Young Alec that there was no hope for him in pursuing her or providing lifts.

The older man in the front seat opened the door as they approached, and climbed out of the car. Gina noted that he was smartly dressed in a tweed suit with a checked shirt and a heather-mix tie. Well-polished brogues completed the outfit – that of the well-to-do farmer on a day in town. His hair was thick and white, contrasting with the tanned skin of the outdoorsman, and he was smiling pleasantly, his hand outstretched.

'Miss Sinclair.'

'Mr Gunn,' she said politely, taking his hand.

'I've been looking forward to meeting you. Young Alec has told me all about you.'

The older man bent into the car and pushed forward the passenger seat. Before she could protest, he had nimbly climbed into the back of the car and pulled the seat back again.

'In you get,' he said.

'I'd have been quite happy to get in the back,' Gina began.

'Not at all,' he said. 'I'll be fine here.'

They managed some desultory chit-chat on the short journey to Willowbank, giving Gina time to order her thoughts.

'Won't you come in?' she asked them. 'My mother will want to say hello.'

The two men exchanged glances and Middle Alec spoke for them both. 'Thank you. We'd be delighted.'

Young Alec locked the car and they followed Gina down the narrow stone-walled entryway between the two tall houses. Middle Alec paused as they rounded the corner. A long garden spread

49

before them, and beyond it a fine view of the harbour and the sea beyond.

'This is very nice,' Middle Alec said, looking around appreciatively.

Gina's mother burst out of the front door.

'Robbie! Robbie! Where are you?' she called. She began hurrying down the garden path.

'Mum,' Gina said warningly.

Joyce stopped in surprise and stared at the small group.

'Mum, Alec brought me home and his father was with him so I thought I'd bring them in...'

'Yes, of course, love.' Joyce turned to her unexpected visitors. 'Mr Gunn, Alec, it's nice to see you. Gina, will you take them into the house while I locate your brother...'

'Maybe we can help, Mrs Sinclair,' Middle Alec offered, but Joyce shook her head.

'No, no, that will not be necessary. He's just playing hide and seek. I'll find him in a minute. You go inside with Gina. And Gina, put the kettle on.'

Gina could see that Middle Alec was perplexed but she knew her mother was fiercely protective of Robbie, and the Gunns, father and son, were strangers. She would never accept their help, nor risk their reactions if they suddenly encountered Robbie in boisterous mood. It was more than likely that they would react like Aunt Joanie...

'Boo!'

Gina jumped as Robbie appeared from behind the big front door. He clapped his hands with delight.

'Got you!' he told her in glee, his mouth stretched in a wide smile.

'Yes, you did!' Gina said. She turned and called down the garden, 'Mum, Robbie's here.' She waited till she saw her mother hurry up the garden, then she addressed Robbie.

'We've got visitors, love,' she told him. 'And they're staying for tea…'

She felt a hand on her shoulder. It was Middle Alec. He spoke quietly. 'I think we won't disturb you. We need to be getting home.'

All she could read in his face was kindness and a plea for understanding. Young Alec, however, was staring at Robbie as if he had seen a ghost. Middle Alec touched his arm and he seemed to pull himself together.

'We'll be going then,' Middle Alec said. He smiled at Gina's mother as she reached them. 'Nice to meet you, Mrs Sinclair.'

Joyce managed a polite nod, but her face was sad as she watched the Gunns make their escape.

'I'm so sorry, darling,' she told Gina. 'I expect that's the last we'll see of them.'

'I don't mind,' Gina said. 'In fact, I'm glad. I couldn't think how to get rid of Young Alec without hurting his feelings. He was so persistent!' She kissed Robbie on the cheek. 'Thanks, Robbie. You're an answer to my prayers!'

'*Me?* Why?' Robbie said, puzzled at Gina's words.

'Don't worry about it,' Gina said, taking his arm. 'Let's go in and have our tea!'

CHAPTER 14

'I told you Robbie ought to be put away!' Mandy told her sharply when Gina relayed the story to her cousin next time she came calling. 'He's spoiling things for you!'

'Not at all!' Gina defended him robustly. 'He's done me a good turn. I didn't want to encourage Young Alec and I didn't want to hurt his feelings by telling him to get lost! This way is best.'

'I don't know about that,' Mandy responded. 'Just when someone was interested and you'd half a chance of having some fun! I can't think of anyone else in town who would do for you. You'll have to cast your net wider…'

'I'm not interested,' Gina said. 'I've told you before. And anyway, I don't do nets!'

'More fool you!' Mandy lobbed back. 'Every girl needs a net in her handbag along with her lipstick and other essentials.'

'So did you take your net to that job interview?' Gina enquired. 'How did you get on?'

She was surprised to see Mandy looking unsure of herself.

'What happened?' Gina probed. 'Who was the man who was looking for a "Personal, Confidential, Private Assistant" and probably lots of other things besides? What was he like?'

Mandy hesitated. 'I really don't know. I didn't meet him. He sent some fearsome female that I'd have to report to. I didn't like her one bit either. Turned her nose up at me from the start. Well, I'd dressed to appeal to the boss man...'

Gina sighed. She could imagine. Short tight skirt, stilettos, skimpy blouse with the buttons popping...

'So what are you going to do now?' she asked.

'Well, I haven't heard either way,' Mandy said. 'It's most odd. In any case, it was just a first interview. The next one – if I get that far – is in Edinburgh. That's where the firm is based.'

She was quiet for a moment, then she looked up and the old glitter was back.

'Tell you what, if I get a second interview I'll come round and borrow some of your boring work clothes! Maybe that will do the trick!'

'And if not?'

Mandy's mouth turned down. 'I suppose I'll have to find something else.'

'Maybe there will be something in this week's paper,' Gina suggested. 'Why don't you come round Thursday evening after work and have a preview?' On Thursday night, Danny always made sure everyone went home with a copy of the next day's paper.

But Mandy demurred. 'Can't. I've got a date,' she said.

Gina was neither surprised nor disappointed when Thursday afternoon came that it was a different young man who shyly handed over the Mart report. She had not wanted to encourage

Young Alec and had found it hard to discourage him. Robbie indeed had done the job for her – but she could not help but think less of Alec for his reaction to her brother. He clearly could not cope with Robbie and that put him beyond the pale for Gina, if for no other reason.

By five o'clock when the last-minute rush had turned into the satisfying turning of the presses in the huge print-room downstairs, there was an odd tension in the building. Instead of Danny wandering around as usual, chatting with the staff and making sure everyone had an early copy of the week's edition to take home, he was closeted in his office. And unusually, he had decreed that there should be no interruptions.

'He's with a man from the south,' Cathy, one of the advertising staff, told her when Gina went to fetch her coat from the female staff cloakroom.

'Do you know what it's about?' Gina asked curiously.

Mrs Swanson, the office manager, reached for her scarf and jacket. 'No,' she said. 'But I'm worried. I think he's one of those finance people from the parent company and I know our revenues have not been good for a while.'

Gina slipped her arms into her coat. 'Well, no doubt we'll find out soon enough if it's anything we need to know.'

She smiled reassuringly at the two women and was glad to see them return her smile. It would not do for the staff to start worrying.

As she walked home, she considered maybe she should have a word with her uncle, see if there was anything she could do. Deep in her thoughts, it was only as she neared the entryway round to the house that she spotted the red Mini with the familiar number-plates outside. Surely that was Young Alec's?

But Young Alec had not brought the Mart report that afternoon. Another lad had come in his place. So what was the car doing there? Had Alec just been late and the other lad simply come instead? Gina sighed. She had been sure he had been put off by Robbie. She didn't want to have to deal with his hopes all over again.

Filled with trepidation, she let herself quietly into the house. The sitting-room door was closed and though she could hear a soft murmur of voices – one of them a male voice, she thought – she could not make out what was being said. She went to hang her coat up, listening intently and wondering what to do.

Dithering at the foot of the stairs, she heard a soft call from the first-floor landing.

'Gina!'

She looked up to see her grandmother beckoning to her and then holding a finger to her lips.

Intrigued, Gina went upstairs. Her grandmother seized her arm and pulled her gently into her bedroom at the back of the house.

To her surprise, Robbie was there too, comfortably ensconced in the big armchair by the fire.

'Me hide and seek,' he told her with a grin.

Gina's eyebrows rose.

Her grandmother nodded. 'Your mother has a visitor and we don't want to disturb them, do we, Robbie?'

Robbie shook his head, beaming with delight.

'Hang on a minute...' Gina began.

'Shh!' her grandmother chided her.

Gina automatically lowered her voice. 'I don't understand. Who's the visitor? That's Young Alec's car outside... So what's Mum doing closeted with Young Alec? You all know I don't fancy him...'

But her grandmother was smiling mysteriously.

'The visitor is not Young Alec,' was all she said.

'But that's his car...' Gina protested.

'I rather think they share it.'

'They?' Gina queried, then, as light dawned, 'Oh.'

Her grandmother smiled encouragingly.

'Middle Alec?' Gina ventured, her voice rising in surprise.

Again her grandmother shushed her. And smiled.

'Middle Alec?' Gina repeated softly. 'Come calling on Mum?'

Her grandmother smiled and nodded.

Gina sat down on the bed beside her grandmother.

'Well!' she said.

'Yes,' her grandmother agreed. 'So let's keep out of the way and give them a chance...'

CHAPTER 15

After a while they heard the sitting-room door open. Then voices – Joyce's and Middle Alec's – and the sound of the front door opening and closing.

Gina rose from the bed.

'Wait!' her grandmother counselled softly.

Gina willed herself to patience. After a few moments, they heard Joyce's voice calling.

'Where are you?'

At her words, Robbie burst from the room and rushed downstairs.

'Me here. Hiding!' he announced delightedly.

'Oh, my darling, you don't have to hide!' Joyce said, her voice breaking a little as she enfolded him in a warm hug.

Gina hurried downstairs, her grandmother in her wake. Joyce looked over Robbie's shoulder at them.

'You didn't have to hide,' she said fiercely. 'None of you! If he can't cope with my family...'

The 'he' clearly referred to her visitor.

'We weren't hiding. We were simply giving you your privacy,' Gina's grandmother said firmly. She added, 'You should be able to entertain your visitors privately. You would do the same for us, wouldn't you?'

Joyce looked from her mother to her daughter, seeing the same strength and encouragement in their faces. Slowly she nodded.

'Yes, all right,' she said. 'But…'

'But what?' Hannah said. 'Why shouldn't a pleasant man – a widower – call on you, a respectable widow? I don't see any problem. Do you, Gina?'

Her grandmother's sharp grey eyes fixed on Gina. She found herself looking at her mother with new eyes. She was only in her forties, and still lovely. Why shouldn't someone come calling? And Young Alec's father at that! Maybe some good had come out of that embarrassing situation! And suddenly she found herself grinning.

'Well done, you,' she told her mother. 'No, Granny, I don't see anything wrong in that.'

'Now, perhaps we can finish off the shortbread you put out for that man. If there's any left. What do you think, Robbie?' her grandmother asked.

'Shortbread? Oh yes!' Robbie headed into the sitting room.

The three women followed more slowly.

'Are you going to see him again?' Gina asked.

Joyce glanced nervously at her daughter but all she could see in her face was curiosity.

'I said I'd think about it.'

'Oh, Mum!' Gina said. 'You should have said yes! What was the invitation? Something nice?'

Joyce darted a glance at her mother. 'He wondered would I like to go to the circus. It's coming to town in the next few weeks.'

'Circus!' Robbie repeated, through a mouthful of shortbread. 'What's a circus?'

'It's a show in a big tent. A big top, it's called.'

'Big top,' Robbie said thoughtfully. 'Why?'

'Because it's big and they have animals…'

'Animals? I like animals.'

'Elephants, and horses, and oh, I don't know…'

'Elephants?' Robbie's eyes were huge and round. 'Elephants? Can I see the elephants?'

Gina exchanged a glance with her mother and grandmother. Because of the negative reactions many people had towards Robbie's condition, he spent most of his time at home. But it was no longer so easy to keep a 19-year-old at home and entertained as it was with a younger child.

'We'll see,' her mother said diplomatically. 'Are you going to finish up that shortbread?'

Robbie was willing to be distracted, but Gina began to think. It would be such a treat for Robbie to see the elephants. Surely there had to be some way to achieve it?

CHAPTER 16

Back at work next day, Gina was surprised to find that the usual Friday morning meeting – when the reporters reviewed that week's edition of *The Sentinel* with the Editor and checked over the galleys for what stories had not been used but might be usable next week – had been postponed. Instead her uncle had called a meeting of all the staff in the largest of the advertising offices downstairs.

'What's it about?' one of the compositors asked her.

Everyone assumed that as the Editor's niece she would know what was going on, but this time, she had to admit she had no idea. She followed the compositors, typesetters and reporters down the narrow stairs to the big room fronting the street, and perched on a table from where she could see and hear her uncle.

Gina noted that her Uncle Danny looked uncomfortable as he faced the staff: compositors in their aprons, hands already inky, office staff neat as pins, and the two male reporters shuffling, eyes alert for whatever was to come.

'You'll know I had a visitor yesterday,' Danny began. 'I was not expecting the visit, nor what resulted from it.' He frowned at the assembled group. 'You know we've been going through tough times recently. I've wanted for a long while to modernise the offices and the technology – but our parent company would not permit me to even start. And now I know why.'

He paused, his mouth set grimly. 'This newspaper has been sold to a foreign buyer. As far as I know, as a going concern...'

He held up his hand to still the anxious murmur that followed his words.

'As I say, as far as I know we'll continue as *The Caithness Sentinel*.'

His eyes scanned the group in front of him.

'I am assured that at the moment all our jobs are safe, but there will probably be some restructuring. There may be some opportunities for those of you who want a change or feel it's time to retire – if the package on offer is right, of course. And it appears that it is likely we'll get that modernising that I wanted to do.'

He took a deep breath. 'So let's get on with today as normal. I'm afraid I have no other details for you except...' He paused. 'Our new owner will be here on Monday, so please be here at nine o'clock sharp to meet him and hear what he has to say.'

Danny turned abruptly and left the room – to an uproar of questions and exclamations.

'Well, that could be interesting,' Jimmy Macrae asked Gina. 'Did you know any of this?'

'Not a thing,' she assured him.

'He's kept it close to his chest,' someone else said.

'Aye. Probably thought he was protecting us...'

Gina listened to the conversations around her. Her uncle had said that as far as he knew, all their jobs were safe – and that surely was the thing that mattered to most of them. But restructuring? That usually meant job cuts. Where could such cuts be made? Voluntary redundancies? Jimmy would be a likely candidate. Maybe now he could get the croft that was his heart's desire.

But what about modernising, new equipment? She looked at some of the older men from the print room. Would they be willing to learn new ways with new technology? Would there be difficult changes there?

It was worrying for them all, and her uncle had looked sick and ill as he told them the startling news.

She bumped into him as she left the reporters' office at lunchtime. He was, as usual, going out to meet Aunt Cat and have lunch with her at the Rosebank Hotel.

He caught her arm. 'Gina!' he said, searching her face. 'You mustn't worry. I'm sure your job will be safe. You're good at what you do. I'll do my best…'

Gina patted his hand. 'I know, Uncle Danny. I know you will, but what about the others? I don't suppose you can protect everybody.'

'I'll do my best,' Danny told her. 'You can be sure I'll do my best.'

CHAPTER 17

Manitoba, Canada

'*Dear Gran,*' Nancy read. '*As you can see from the postmark, I'm still here in Scotland. There is an interesting business opportunity someone here in Thurso has put me on to.*'

Nancy pursed her lips thoughtfully. So he was in Thurso, rather than Wick. That was a pity. Determinedly, she read on.

'*So I've been rather busy with meetings.*'

Knowing Hugo, that was probably an understatement, she thought with a wry smile.

'*There's a small local newspaper that should be doing better. All it needs is an injection of a modest amount of capital, a little shaking-up of old ways and out-of-date equipment and staff, and it should be running fine in a short while. Then I'll sell it off and be on a plane back home as soon as I can.*

In the meantime, I've been across to Wick as you asked – the newspaper is in Wick, by the way – and been to Dad's grave. I put some flowers on from us, not that he was ever into flowers!'

The rest of the short letter enquired after her health and ended with affection.

Nancy scanned the letter but could find no further clues. He sounded as dutiful as ever, though she noticed he had not yet been to visit Hannah and Joyce. His casual comments about what was likely to be a huge upheaval for a whole bunch of people betrayed a sadly ruthless side to Hugo.

The old pain clawed again in her chest.

'Mrs Paston? Mrs Paston?'

Nancy gritted her teeth against the pain and willed her eyes open. Ella was leaning over her.

'Can I get you something for the pain?' she asked and Nancy managed to nod. Everyone was so kind here. It took only a moment for Ella to pop the pill into her mouth to hold underneath her tongue.

'Better?' the girl asked.

Nancy nodded and the girl, reassured, left. 'Better' was a relative term, but she didn't want to worry them. And she especially did not want them calling Hugo and fetching him back to Canada. She felt deep in her bones that he was meant to be in Scotland, meant to be in Wick – not Thurso!

The pain jabbed again and she forced herself to slow her breathing and calm herself.

'Lord Jesus!' It was a prayer, a trustful call for help.

And as the pain eased, she focused on remembering the delightful child Hugo had been – before his dear mother Katie died. What a tragedy that the cancer had taken her away so young.

They had been a happy family – Hugh and Katie and young Hugo. Nancy shook her head sadly. It was impossible to understand why God would have allowed such a thing to happen, but happen it did. And then Hugh embarked on the series of... just mistakes, Nancy told herself. There was no malice in Hugh, no wickedness. If anything, he was one of the world's innocents. Like his father, Hughie, before him.

The ruthlessness that Hugo demonstrated in business – and with his girlfriends – that didn't belong to Hugo either. It was his reaction to all the hurt that had been too much for a young lad to bear.

Which was why, Nancy was convinced, Hugo had to go back to Wick to face his demons, and dismantle the walls he had built between himself and the rest of the world.

'Oh, let it be so,' she prayed. 'Lord Jesus, lead Hugo through this and out to Your green pastures. And oh, let there be love and joy for him, to make up for all that he lost.'

And a text from her beloved Bible came to mind: Joel, chapter 2, verse 25. 'And I will restore to you the years that the locust hath eaten.'

'Yes, Lord Jesus,' she whispered. 'For Hugo... Please restore the happy years!'

CHAPTER 18

Wick, Monday morning

The one morning it was super-important to get to work in good time – and Gina was late. There had been an upset with Robbie at breakfast. He was getting impatient with being treated like a child, and his occasional clumsy attempts at independence were putting a strain on his loving family. It was usually Gina who could smooth things over. But today she did not have time and as a result spoke more sharply than usual and one thing led to another and…

So she was late. For this very important meeting with their new owner that had so worried her uncle. Gina hung her coat up in the female staff cloakroom downstairs and very quietly eased open the door to the large advertising office. A tall man in a dark suit had his back to her, but as she tried to slide unnoticed into the room he turned round.

She stopped in her tracks, shock on her face. It was the Canadian she had met at the Aberdeen conference. The man who had stalked her dreams all the months in between, and here he was in the flesh. The blush flamed over Gina's cheeks as their eyes met. She could not help but admit that he was in reality as handsome as he had been in her memory and imagination.

His face betrayed his surprise at seeing her. The beautiful mouth quirked, his smile one of pleasure. His eyebrows rose in friendly enquiry.

'Mrs Strachan, I didn't know you worked here now?' he said in an easy tone. 'Have you changed jobs? I'm sure a newspaper office is much more interesting than an accountancy firm!'

He was inviting her to smile with him, but Gina froze. She had gone to the conference as Mandy. Using Mandy's name… She would have to explain.

But before she could begin, Uncle Danny intervened.

'No,' he said with a puzzled look. 'This is my niece, Gina. She's one of our reporters. In fact one of our best reporters. You're mistaking her for… someone else.'

The Canadian's smile vanished and the dark eyes that were fixed on her face narrowed.

'Gina?' he queried icily.

She nodded. Swallowed hard.

'Not Mandy?' He said the name quietly, remorselessly.

Gina shook her head.

'And probably not Strachan either. Would that be right?' he asked. 'Not Mrs Strachan?' There was a tiny emphasis on the *Mrs*.

Gina closed her eyes. She could not bear to see the anger in the face of this man.

'I can explain…' she stammered. She forced her eyes open and said pleadingly to her uncle, 'I was helping out Mandy…'

And she saw the sudden understanding in her uncle's face. But the man was still there, listening, and he had caught what she said.

'So there is a Mandy?' the man probed. 'A Mrs Mandy Strachan?'

'Yes.' Gina seized the opening. 'She's my cousin. She couldn't go to the conference so she asked me to go in her place...'

'And as a journalist, you thought it would be... useful?' The question was quiet and cruel. 'You wouldn't have been able to get in there otherwise.'

Gina's face flamed again. Yes, she had. She had thought it would be useful, and it had been. She had got a good article out of it. But better than anything else, she had met him. And then, fool that she was, she had let her emotional barriers down, let herself dream. And now she was found out and it was a disaster. She had deceived their new boss!

'So won't you introduce yourself,' he commanded, his face set like flint. 'Properly this time.'

But before she could get any more words out, her uncle stepped in again.

'Mr Mackay, as I said, this is my niece Gina – Georgina Sinclair.'

And she saw the flash of sudden fury and then outright disgust tear across his face.

'Georgina Sinclair!'

He flung her name at her, the stress on the first syllable of her Christian name *George*-ina. And he pronounced Sinclair as St Clair.

'I might have known.' His lip curled. 'One more St Clair cheat and liar! And I'll bet you only got your job here because of your precious uncle!'

He turned on Danny. 'I will want a full account of this from you, and you may consider your own position with great care!'

He whirled back to Gina. 'And as for you, Georgina Sinclair, you can get yourself out of my sight!'

CHAPTER 19

Gina willed herself not to faint. She wanted to scream at him, to denounce the injustice of his treatment of her. What she had done was not that bad! But she could see the worry in her uncle's face. His job was in danger now, because of her. She couldn't let that happen.

The man was moving away.

'One moment.' She spoke with careful control.

'I have nothing further to say to you, Miss Sinclair,' he flung over his shoulder.

'But I have something to say to you and I will say it before I go.'

He turned, surprised at her defiance.

She stood straight and faced him.

'I recognise that you have the right to fire me if that is what you wish to do, but you might find the grounds you have chosen won't wash legally.'

There was a gasp from the assembled staff.

'It would certainly be wrong to fire my uncle because of something *I've* done that you choose to disapprove of. He knew nothing of my trip to Aberdeen. He had nothing to do with it.' Gina swallowed hard and made herself continue. 'It would be wrong. He has worked hard for this firm and *The Caithness Sentinel* is what it is because of him. You'd be cutting off your nose to spite your face if you got rid of him. I hope you're not quite that stupid.'

The brown eyes bored into hers and she stared back, refusing to be cowed.

'Gina!' her uncle protested.

She looked at him. 'I'm sorry. It had to be said. This man clearly hasn't even bothered to do a bit of background research on the paper or he'd know that, not to mention who we are!' The colour that flared in her cheeks now was anger.

'Oh, I know who you are,' the man said with savage emphasis. 'You're George St Clair's daughter.'

Gina flinched.

'And quite clearly a chip off the old block. As I said, one more St Clair cheat and liar.'

'And how would *you* know?' Gina fought back. 'What do you know about me – apart from my name and a chance meeting at a conference?'

That seemed to anger him further.

'Don't you recognise me?' he said, coming closer, like a panther stalking prey. He stopped full square in front of her. 'Allow me to introduce myself – or rather re-introduce myself.'

Gina stared at him defiantly. 'I have no idea who you are.'

'Oh yes, you do. I'm Hugh Mackay's son.' His eyes bored into hers. 'Do you remember my father? And what your father did to him?'

But Gina was staring at him in horror.

'Hugo? You can't be Hugo...'

Her voice trailed off as whirling blackness overtook her and she crumpled to the floor.

CHAPTER 20

When Gina came to, she discovered with shock that she was lying on the floor of the female staff cloakroom. A wet cloth was on her forehead and she was being fanned enthusiastically by one of the younger girls.

'What happened?' Gina asked.

'You fainted,' said Mrs Swanson, bending down to talk to her.

'I never faint!' Gina protested, but Mrs Swanson merely tut-tutted.

'You were amazing,' the girl whispered. 'Speaking up to him like that!'

'I'm a fool,' Gina groaned. 'I've probably lost us all our jobs.'

She tried to sit up and remember just what had happened, but all she could think was… that man was Hugo. Hugo whom she had loved from the first moment she had seen him. He would have been 12 or 13 back then and she was maybe 4. He had come over from Canada to live with his father and his new wife…

She had followed Hugo around like a little shadow and he had been patient and kind to her. And she had loved him. Adored him. No wonder he had seemed familiar when they met in Aberdeen! No wonder she had felt it was entirely natural for him to kiss her... Hugo had been her special friend. Until everything went wrong.

And now she remembered the last time she had seen Hugo – before that day at the conference in Aberdeen.

Her father had persuaded Hugo's father to invest all his money in the family garage business as his partner. Then on the day that Robbie was born, her father had stolen all the money and tried to get away with it – and with Hugh's new wife, Ruby. They had been killed in a terrible accident, crashing over Berriedale Brae in their car.

When Hugo's father had found out, he'd tried desperately to rescue the business, their homes, their livelihood – but he couldn't. The terrible double betrayal had broken his heart. He'd had a massive heart attack and died.

Hugo was supposed to be at school in Edinburgh but he had come back to support his father. And he was there, in the office at the garage that day, at that moment – when his father died.

On the day of the funeral, Gina had seen Hugo go walking by and had run out to him. She had tried to take his hand and comfort him, but he had uncharacteristically pushed her away. And he had shouted at her.

'It's all your dad's fault! Everything's his fault! He killed my dad! Your dad is the worst person in the whole world. George St Clair! George Sinclair! I hate him, I hate him, I hate him! I never want to hear that name again. George Sinclair! I'll hate that name till the day I die!' And he had stormed off and left her there.

They called her Georgie in those days, her full name Georgina, named after her father. She had turned Hugo's words over and over in her mind as she made her way back to the house where all the relatives had gathered after the funerals.

'Georgie,' her mother and her grandmother had greeted her. But she couldn't bear the name now, not now that her beloved Hugo

72

hated it and said he'd hate it till the day he died. She needed to have a different name so he wouldn't hate her.

So she'd chosen her middle name, Belle. And that turned out to be worse. Her grandmother could not abide it. It reminded Hannah of her wicked younger sister who had set in train all the mess that had entangled the Cormacks and the Reids and the Mackays and the Sinclairs, and caused so many people so much harm.

So she let herself be persuaded that Gina was an acceptable compromise. She had been Gina for close on twenty years now, and she had thought, between them, they had put to rest the dreadful results of her father's wickedness.

He was never mentioned. Her mother and grandmother had gathered together the shattered fragments of their lives and managed, on the rock-solid foundation of their Christian faith, to make a decent life for her and her brother Robbie – a happy life, resolutely turning their backs on George St Clair and the past and all the shame. Granny's oldest brother, Uncle Will, had let them have the house in Willowbank to live in. Gina got the job at *The Sentinel*, so there was some money coming in. They were managing. They were doing all right.

But now it seemed, the past had come back to hurt them once again. And this time she had to admit it was her own fault. She had done something wrong, something bad, and now the old familiar voice echoed in her head: 'Bad girls must be punished.'

Well, she was certainly being punished.

CHAPTER 21

Gina went home. Where else could she go? Hugo had told her to get out of his sight, so there was no point going up to the reporters' office where he could easily find her and physically throw her out. No, she wouldn't risk another confrontation. She needed to go home. To the people who loved her.

She gathered up her bag and coat and slowly walked home.

Her mother met her at the door.

'What's the matter, love? Are you ill?'

Gina shook her head, struggling to think what to tell her mother. She didn't want to worry her with the news that she might be out of a job. Not yet. Even so, surely if she needed to, she could find another job quickly so her mother would barely need to know, let alone worry? The solution came instantly: she would ask Mandy. *She* would know for sure what jobs were around. Mandy had been job-hunting for ages.

'I wasn't feeling very well,' she told her mother. 'So I came home.'

'But what about your important meeting?' her mother asked. 'With the new owner. Did you have to miss that?'

Gina shook her head.

'So, what happened?' her mother asked worriedly. 'He's not closing down the paper and firing you all?'

'No,' Gina said.

She hung up her coat and went into the kitchen. To buy thinking time, she slowly filled the kettle and put it on to boil. But what could she say? She didn't want to lie to her mother.

'It's a bit of a disaster, really,' she said, deciding honesty as always was the best policy. She turned back to the table and sat down. 'And it's all my own fault.'

Her grandmother had come into the kitchen behind them and now sat down at the table across from her.

'Tell us all about it.'

Her mother nodded agreement.

'Well,' Gina began unwillingly. 'Do you remember that Saturday when I went to Aberdeen for Mandy – to the conference?'

They nodded.

'I met someone there. A man. A nice man, I thought. We had coffee... talked a bit.' She went pink as she carefully edited out the kiss. 'I liked him and I think he liked me, but...'

The kettle was boiling so she got up to make the tea, busying herself with warming the pot, spooning the tea-leaves out of the caddy, pouring on the hot water.

'But?' her grandmother prompted.

Gina set the teapot on its stand on the table and sat down heavily.

'That man turns out to be the new owner of *The Sentinel*,' Gina said. 'And when I walked into the meeting this morning, he recognised me.'

'So what's the problem? If he liked you, surely...' her mother began, a hopeful light in her eyes.

But Gina's grandmother held up a hand. 'Wait a bit. There's more to this, isn't there?'

'I was at the conference as *Mandy*,' Gina reminded them, the ache of regret in her voice. 'Wearing a name badge that said Mrs Mandy Strachan. Wearing Mandy's clothes. Being Mandy for the day.'

'Oh.'

Her mother and grandmother exchanged glances as they realised the implication of what Gina was saying.

'And of course, this morning,' Gina continued doggedly, 'Uncle Danny introduced me. As Gina Sinclair.'

'Yes, well, that would be awkward,' her grandmother said. 'But I'm sure you explained?'

'I tried,' Gina said. 'But that wasn't the only problem – or the real problem. The real problem is who *I* am. And there's nothing I can do about that.'

She took a deep breath and spoke words that had not been heard amongst them for nearly twenty years.

'It's all about my father. He…' Gina faltered. 'He said because I'd been pretending to be Mandy, it was obvious that I'm the same kind of person as my father. A cheat and a liar! And then it got worse. He said that I'd probably only got my job at *The Sentinel* because of Uncle Danny. More cheating and lying. And then he threw me out. Told me to get out of his sight.'

There was a shocked silence; then her grandmother asked, 'But how does he know anything about your father?'

'And what does it have to do with him – or the newspaper?' her mother put in.

'Who is this man, Gina?'

Gina turned tragic eyes on her grandmother.

'It's Hugo, Granny! You remember Hugo? Hugo Mackay! He's the new owner of the paper, and he's the man I met in Aberdeen when I was being Mandy, to help Mandy out. I didn't know it was him, but maybe that's why it seemed so easy and natural to be with him…'

She turned to her mother. 'Oh Mum, it's Hugo and he still hates me!' And she burst into helpless tears.

As she wept, head burrowed into her arms, her mother and grandmother came round and enfolded her in their arms, their eyes filled with concern.

When the storm was nearly over and Gina was hiccupping the last sobs, her grandmother withdrew her arms and poured the tea, adding milk and extra sugar. She dropped a kiss on Gina's bent head.

'Gina, my dear.'

Gina looked up and saw the proffered cup of tea. She managed a watery grin.

'Tea! The remedy for all ills!'

But she accepted the cup with a soft thank-you and took a sip, wrinkling her nose as the sweetness and strength of the tea hit her palate.

'Go on. You need it.'

'Yes,' Gina agreed with a sigh. 'I think I probably do.'

The three women sat quietly while Gina drank down her tea. At last she set the cup neatly on its saucer.

'I fainted!' Gina told them. 'Would you believe it? Me! I never faint! But I... I just passed out. When I realised it was Hugo and what he was saying and...' She took a breath and added on a calmer note, 'Next thing I knew, I was lying on the floor in the cloakroom having my face fanned by one of the girls and a cold cloth on my forehead! It's so embarrassing. I'll never be able to show my face...'

And then she remembered: Hugo had said to get herself out of his sight. Would she ever be allowed to return to the office while he was in charge? She went cold. She needed her job. She was the breadwinner for the family.

She stared at her mother and grandmother in growing horror.

'Gina, love, what is it?' her mother asked.

'Nothing,' Gina said quickly. 'Nothing to worry about.' She stumbled up from the chair. 'I just remembered something I have to do. I'll be back soon.'

And she grabbed her coat and dashed out, one thought uppermost in her mind: Mandy. She had to see Mandy. Mandy would know what to do.

CHAPTER 22

'You've got to help me,' Gina told her cousin fiercely. 'I need a new job and I need it fast.'

'But why?' Mandy's eyes sparkled with curiosity. 'I thought you loved your job?'

The girls were tucked away at a little table in a corner of the Central Café on the High Street. When Gina had hurtled into Mandy's office 'as if the world was on fire' as her cousin put it, Mandy had managed a quick excuse to her boss and followed her outside.

'Let's go somewhere quiet and you can tell me all about it.'

The girls had ordered a hot orange squash each and selected the quietest table, furthest away from the jukebox. Once they had got settled, Mandy stared at her cousin with avid interest.

'So what is the matter? What's going on?'

'Oh, Mandy!' Gina wailed and the story came pouring out. The new owner of the paper was the man she had met that Saturday at the conference when she had been pretending to be Mandy and he had virtually fired her on the spot.

'He can't do that!' Mandy blazed. 'You didn't do anything wrong! If anything, it's me who should be fired if my boss ever found out.' She paused. 'He won't tell, will he?'

Gina shook her head. 'I don't think he's really bothered about that. It's me he's got it in for.'

'Why? What did you do?'

'Nothing.' Gina shook her head, the tears beginning again. 'It's nothing I can do anything about either...'

'What are you talking about? You're not making sense!'

'Oh, Mandy,' Gina sighed. 'It's about who I am...'

'You mean that you're Danny's niece? He thinks you've got your job just because your uncle is Editor?' Mandy considered. 'Well, it would be pretty easy to show him you got the job on merit. You've got all those awards and prizes and things... Anyone can see you're properly qualified...'

Gina held up her hand to stop the flow. 'No. No, it's not that – though that's bad enough and Uncle Danny's job is under threat too because of me. No.' Gina sighed again, heavily. 'It's because I'm a Sinclair...'

'What? And he's a Gunn keeping up the old feud! Oh, don't make me laugh!' Mandy erupted. 'In this day and age. That's primeval! Feudal!'

'No!' Gina protested. She dropped her voice. 'Will you just listen! It's because I'm...' She faltered, visibly steadied herself, and continued. 'It's because I'm Georgina Sinclair, daughter of George Sinclair... and the deception at the conference proves I'm just as much a cheat and a liar as my father was.'

Mandy sat back with a thump, staring at her cousin with growing horror.

'Good grief!' she said. 'That's ancient history, and anyway, it's not as though you can do anything about who your father was...'

The two girls sat in silence, sipping their drinks. Then Mandy leaned forward.

'Wait a minute,' she said. 'This man. Your new boss. How does he know anything about who your father was? And what's it got to do with him anyway?'

Gina flushed.

'Gina!' Mandy said slowly. 'There's something you're not telling me. This rich entrepreneur who bought your newspaper. He isn't some stranger, is he? If he knows who you are... Who is he?'

Gina gulped and looked away. She really didn't want to tell Mandy.

'Gina!' Mandy prodded.

Gina swallowed hard. 'It's Hugo,' she admitted. 'Hugo Mackay. Remember him, when we were young?' She tried to say it nonchalantly, as if it didn't matter.

Interest blazed in Mandy's eyes.

'Hugo,' she said. 'Well, well.'

'And he blames everything that happened to *his* father on *my* father,' Gina added.

'Well, he's right there,' Mandy said slowly. 'It was all your father's fault. Still, I don't see it's anything to do with you. And I don't see why you should lose your job because of it. Still...'

'What is it?' Gina asked. Mandy was looking at her thoughtfully.

'So Hugo's come back rich enough to buy up things like your newspaper,' Mandy said. 'And he's about to fire you.'

Gina nodded miserably.

'Well, we'd better find you a new job, hadn't we?' her cousin said, with a satisfied grin. 'You don't want to bump into him again, do we?'

CHAPTER 23

'*Clerkess wanted for Garage Office in Wick,*' Mandy read aloud. 'Well, your family used to be in the car business till your father wrecked it. You might have a chance at that one.'

Mandy had popped out of the cafeteria and bought some newspapers. She was now trawling down the Situations Vacant columns. Gina had replenished their drinks and returned to the table to find her cousin determinedly at work. She sighed and obediently noted down the box number.

'Oh, this might be better,' Mandy exclaimed. She read out the next advertisement that had caught her eye: '*Shorthand-typist, with experience, for law firm. Good salary and conditions. 5-day week.*'

'But I know nothing about what law firms do,' Gina protested. 'I don't have that kind of experience!'

'You can do shorthand and typing,' Mandy said firmly. 'And a law firm would be a nice place to work.' She glanced disapprovingly at Gina. 'If we weren't doing this for you, I might have a go at it myself. I still haven't heard whether I've got a second interview for that job I went for.'

'Oh, Mandy!' Gina said. 'I really don't want another job but I can't see what else I can do. Hugo said to get out of his sight, and he warned Uncle Danny that because of me, his job wasn't secure.'

She sighed heavily. 'Hugo has bought the paper. There's no going back on that now. And, quite honestly, it needed a new owner willing to put in money for new equipment and drag it into the twentieth century. If Hugo and Uncle Danny get on together, it will be the best thing that could happen.'

She set down her drink on the table.

'I care about *The Sentinel* and the people who work there. And it seems to me that staying there is just going to mess things up for everyone. Every time Hugo sees me he'll be reminded of the past and that will annoy him and he'll lash out and who knows who else might get hurt?'

She fixed her cousin with miserable eyes. 'I don't want another job. I certainly don't want another kind of job! I love working on *The Sentinel*! From the moment I started there, I knew it was the only thing I ever wanted to do!'

Sharp eyes met hers. 'Well, if that's the case, you'll have to look further afield.' Mandy folded up the local paper and reached for the *Aberdeen Press and Journal*. 'Let's see.'

After a moment, she gave a low whistle. 'Well, your luck's in. Listen to this: "*Reporter – Confident young man...*" Well, with your experience I'm sure they'd be willing to make an exception.' She read on. "'*Confident young man with reporting experience for daily newspaper work. Higher Leaving Certificate standard of education. He should be a good mixer and able to drive...*" Oh.' Mandy's excited voice went flat. 'That's a pity. You can't drive.'

'No,' Gina said. 'I can't.'

'Wait a minute,' Mandy said with a glint in her eye. 'That Alec Gunn – the young one. He has a car, right?'

'Yes, a red Mini,' Gina said. 'But I rather think I've seen the last of him.'

'That needn't be a problem,' Mandy told her firmly. 'You just have to find a way to cosy up to him, and then when you're friends again, you get him to teach you to drive. Easy!'

'I couldn't,' Gina said.

'You want the job?' Mandy countered.

Gina frowned. Mandy's solutions always looked easy – and probably were for her. She always got her way.

'Where was the job?' Gina asked in an attempt to side-track Mandy. 'Out of interest.'

'Dundee,' Mandy said.

'Oh,' Gina said. 'Well, I couldn't have done it in any case. Not in Dundee. Not leaving Mum and Granny and Robbie. They need me here.'

Mandy raised arched eyebrows. 'I thought they needed the money you bring in?'

'Ouch,' Gina acknowledged the hit. 'I know.' She sighed deeply. 'Oh, Mandy, what am I to do?'

In answer, her cousin thrust the newspapers at her. The Dundee job was circled in red.

'Beggars can't be choosers, my dear. You may have to make some hard choices.' She glugged back the rest of her drink. 'I must get back – or I'll be out of a job too, and that would never do!'

And with a jaunty wave, Mandy was on her way.

Gina pulled the newspapers towards her and smoothed down the pages folded back to the Situations Vacant columns. Her eyes scanned down. There were hotel jobs, nursing vacancies and traineeships, positions for policemen in forces all over the country, jobs at the new nuclear test establishment at Dounreay where Mandy

84

had met her ex-husband, farm jobs and building work. And that one vacancy for a reporter. In Dundee.

Tears came to Gina's eyes as she realised that if Hugo was adamant in his opposition to her very presence, then before long the paper would carry an advertisement of another vacancy for a reporter – her own job at *The Caithness Sentinel*.

How was she going to bear it?

Worse, what if Hugo fired Uncle Danny and the next job ad in the *Press and Journal* was for an Editor?

CHAPTER 24

Carefully, Gina tore the advertisement out of the *Press and Journal* and slipped it into her purse. Mandy was right. She was in no position to be choosy. Admittedly she couldn't drive, but surely she was capable of learning? Perhaps she had been a little short-sighted not to encourage Young Alec Gunn. As Mandy had pointed out, he had a car and if they were friends again, perhaps she could ask him to teach her. But she would ask straight out, not play Mandy games.

Thoughtfully she made her way home, only to find that same red Mini parked outside the house. She was sure it wouldn't be Young Alec, so it had to be Middle Alec visiting her mother again. She hoped so and smiled to herself. And she hoped this time he wouldn't take no as the answer to his invitation to go out. Her mother deserved treats and outings.

The sitting-room door was standing open as she went past.

'Gina,' her mother called to her from inside so she went into the room.

'Mr Gunn just popped in...'

'Good morning, Miss Sinclair,' Middle Alec said and held out his hand.

Gina shook it.

'Gina, please,' she said.

'Gina,' he acknowledged. 'I just popped in to ask your mother if she would like to go out for a little drive. I thought maybe we could have a bite of lunch,' he said.

Gina smiled. 'What a lovely idea.'

'But your mother said she couldn't come,' Middle Alec continued. 'She needs to stay at home and be with your brother and grandmother.'

Gina cottoned on at once. 'But now I'm here, that doesn't apply,' she said with another smile. 'So you can go, can't you, Mum?'

Her mother hesitated.

'You would like to?' Middle Alec asked gently.

Joyce nodded. 'It's very kind of you. I can't think when I last…'

'Go and get your coat on, Mum,' Gina coaxed her. 'And powder your nose! I'll hold the fort while you're out.'

'I'm not sure…'

'I am,' Gina said and gave her mother a gentle push towards the door.

'Thank you, Gina,' Middle Alec said. 'You're sure you don't mind?'

'Of course I don't. It will be lovely for Mum to have an outing.'

'I'll take good care of her,' Middle Alec said and within moments he was ushering Joyce out of the house and into the car. The family came out to wave them goodbye and then Gina led her brother and grandmother back into the house.

'Well, that's good,' her grandmother declared with satisfaction. 'See how everything turns out well? If you hadn't come home, your mother could not have gone out.'

'Yes, but me coming home was because of something rather bad.' Gina sighed. 'And I can't see how that will turn out well.'

Her grandmother patted her hand. 'It says in the Bible that "all things work together for good to them that love God".[1] She smiled mistily. 'Someone said that to me a long time ago. I wasn't too sure I believed him but it turned out to be true.' She looked at her granddaughter. 'Your mother loves God and trusts Him. I'm sure He has good plans for her – and for you too.'

Gina looked at her beloved grandmother, her faith shining so steadily in her frail elderly body.

'I wish I had your faith, Granny,' she said huskily. She thought of the folded newspaper advertisement in her bag. 'I could do with a solid lump of it right now!'

---

1   Letter to the Romans, chapter 8, verse 28

CHAPTER 25

Hannah looked at the clock in the kitchen.

'We'd probably better get some lunch for ourselves.'

'What was Mum planning for us to eat today?' Gina asked.

'I think there's some stew and I know she'd peeled tatties to go with it.'

'Tatties!' Robbie echoed with a wide grin.

'Yes, my love,' his grandmother said. 'There will be plenty of tatties for you!'

Robbie clapped his hands. Then a loud knocking on the front door had him jumping from his chair to see who it was.

'Wait for me.' Gina hurried to catch up with him.

'Oh,' she said when she opened the door to find Uncle Danny standing there. Tears filled her eyes as she thought back to the embarrassing scene in the office. 'Uncle Danny, I'm so sorry! I can't tell you...'

'Can I come in, Gina?' Danny asked gently.

'Yes, of course,' she said, wiping the tears with the back of her hand. 'Uncle Danny, I didn't *know* it was Hugo. I didn't mean any harm...'

'Let's have none of this nonsense. I know *you*. I know you didn't mean any harm. Hello, Robbie,' Danny said and accepted Robbie's hug with a smile. 'Where is everybody?'

'It's just Granny and us,' Gina said. 'Mum's gone out. Come through to the kitchen.'

Robbie took Danny's hand and led the way.

'Uncle Danny!' he told his grandmother with a beaming smile.

Danny gave his mother a kiss.

'Any chance of a bite to eat?' he asked.

'Why?' Hannah asked in alarm. 'Where's Cat? Is she ill? What's the matter?'

'Cat's fine,' he reassured her.

Gina waved Danny to a place at the table and he sat as bidden.

'You know Cat hadn't heard from her mother for a while?'

Hannah nodded. 'Yes, she was saying just the other day.'

'Well, she got a telegram from her sister that the old lady is on her last legs and to get home to Buenos Aires as fast as she can.'

'So of course...'

'I put her on the plane to Glasgow early this morning,' Danny said. 'She made the connecting flight to Argentina from Prestwick and she'll be in Buenos Aires later tonight.'

Danny looked over apologetically at Gina. 'What with one thing and another, I wasn't able to tell you this morning.'

Gina shrugged wryly. 'Yes, well. One thing or another.' She gestured to her grandmother. 'I've told Gran and Mum what happened.' She walked over to the stove. 'If there's four of us for lunch I'd better get on with it.'

'Gina,' Danny began.

She turned and he could see the shine of tears in her eyes. She spoke, forestalling him.

'Uncle Danny, *The Sentinel* needs Hugo and his money and his new ideas. With him on your side, you can make all those improvements you've been wanting. You can expand, make the paper the way you've always wanted...' She took a deep breath. 'I'd only be in the way.'

She reached for her handbag and took out the folded advertisement. She unfolded it and handed it to him.

'You mustn't worry. I can get another job.'

She turned back to the stove and busied herself among the pans.

Danny unfolded the piece of newsprint and read the advertisement. He looked across at Gina.

'Not if I can help it,' he told her. 'We need you here. Whatever Hugo thinks, you earned your job by your own talents and hard work. Your place is at *The Sentinel*, doing what you do best – reporting and writing.' He waved the piece of paper. 'Please don't apply for this – not yet. Give me a few days to talk to Hugo. I'm sure if he's the businessman he's cracked up to be, he'll see sense. You are one of the most valuable assets of the business and he needs to realise that.'

Gina looked at her uncle. 'I doubt he'll come begging me to return,' she said with a wry smile.

'Maybe not. A man has his pride,' Danny said. 'But just give me a few days. Please.'

CHAPTER 26

'We went down to Latheronwheel harbour,' Joyce said.

Gina thought she had rarely seen her mother look lovelier – and certainly not for a long while. There was a new glow in her face, a sparkle in her eyes.

'I love the little Caithness harbours,' Joyce continued. 'We sat in the car and talked for a while, then we went for a little walk.' She looked at her assembled family, eager for her report. 'He's a nice man,' she told them.

'Where did you go for lunch?' Gina asked.

'The Portland Arms Hotel.'

'Oh, nice!' was the family response.

'Yes, indeed. And maybe a bit expensive...' Joyce flushed. 'I tried to choose something modest, but he insisted I have whatever I liked! He said... He said I was worth it.'

Gina's grandmother beamed. 'And so you are, my love, and it's time someone noticed. I'm glad this Alec is a good man.'

'I think he is,' Joyce said.

'So what was wrong with the first Alec Gunn?' Gina asked curiously. 'Ould Alec? He came courting you, didn't he, Granny?'

'Yes, he did,' her grandmother replied, with a small chuckle. 'Give him his due, I'm not sure there ever was anything wrong with him. But I was in love with your granddad and basically no matter how nice any other man was, they couldn't hold a candle to him!'

'So you sent Ould Alec packing?' Gina asked.

'I did that. Twice!' Hannah twinkled at her granddaughter.

'Oh, Granny! So he didn't give up easily. I wonder will Middle Alec be like that?' Gina considered.

Her mother frowned. 'I don't know, but I'm not sure I should give him any encouragement.' She glanced across at Robbie who was chewing his lip as he concentrated on the picture he was colouring. 'It wouldn't be fair… to any of us.'

Gina caught the glance. 'Mum,' she said slowly. 'You've been thinking only of us for a very long time. Don't you think maybe you deserve some happiness for yourself, when you have the chance? Has he suggested you go out again?'

Joyce nodded.

'And what did you say?'

'I said I'd think about it!'

'Oh, Mum!' Gina groaned. 'Not again! The poor man!'

'I don't know, my dear,' her mother said. 'Yes, he's a nice man, a good man, but we're fine as we are…'

'Would it hurt to just go out a few times, for the company?'

'I've got plenty of company.' Joyce indicated her mother, son, and daughter.

'You know what I mean,' Gina said.

'Yes but… we're not exactly like other families,' Joyce said quietly. 'I have to think of Robbie and I can't expect Alec to have the same viewpoint as I do. As we do… And you saw how Young Alec reacted to him. I'm afraid that could be a real impediment to any friendship between us.'

Gina recalled the look on Young Alec's face – horror or shock? – when he first saw Robbie. Yes, that could be a problem. She knew a lot of folk – Auntie Joanie and her cousin Mandy to name a few – who thought Robbie should have been put into an institution at birth. Would Alec Gunn be of the same opinion?

If that was the case, he would certainly go down in her mother's estimation. And hers too, Gina thought. They loved Robbie, loved him for who he was. Anyone who wanted to be part of their family would need to love him too and accept him as he was.

But maybe that was too much to ask of any man?

CHAPTER 27

'*Dear Gran,*

Please forgive the long gap between letters. Quite a lot has happened.'

And that was the understatement of the year, Hugo thought. Instead of making a brief appearance at *The Caithness Sentinel* offices to check out his purchase and get the restructuring and investment in place, he had lost his cool. His reaction to Mrs Mandy Strachan *alias* Georgina Sinclair had set the whole staff against him. As one they had sided with her and were making his task virtually impossible.

He knew he had overreacted. What was it about this girl? Twice only in his whole life had he given way to his feelings – and both times had been with this girl. The first time had been long ago. He excused himself for that because he had been young, alone, and in shock after his father's death. Of course he should not have shouted at Georgie (as she was then), but he was hurting.

And then on Monday morning. How could he have let himself down so badly? But he knew. His memory provided him with a mental video of a lovely trusting face upturned, snowflakes falling softly, and two gentle kisses. She had somehow got through his defences. He had thought she was innocent of all dishonesty and deceit.

When he saw her on Monday morning and for a moment felt again that tenderness towards her – and even a leap of hope – the last thing he could have dreamed of was to discover that he had in fact been deceived. Thoroughly deceived. And worse was to come. He had been deceived by George St Clair's daughter.

'*Basically, I let myself down,*' he wrote to his grandmother, hoping she would sympathise. '*I blew it! I'd met this girl at a conference in Aberdeen. Her name badge said she was Mrs Mandy Strachan. I liked her. She seemed to like me but not in that horrible chasing-after-the-rich-boy way so many girls have. We had coffee, talked, went for a walk...*'

Hugo edited out the kiss. Her comment 'a chance meeting at a conference' still stung. But perhaps that was all it had been to her. He himself had been captivated.

'*But it turned out it was all pretence. She was only pretending to be Mandy Strachan. She shouldn't have been anywhere near that conference. It was an exclusive business briefing. And when I arrived to meet the staff at my new acquisition on Monday, there she was, as bold as brass.*'

Hugo stopped again. That wasn't quite fair. She had slid in late. Like a windswept mouse. Her delectable nose red.

He snorted. What was he thinking? He had to get this letter written. His grandmother would be worried that she hadn't heard from him for a while. Canada must feel a very long way away from Scotland when you were old and alone. She deserved a decent letter. Continue!

'*It turned out she wasn't who she said at all, but*' – his hand hesitated over the page – '*someone else,*' he concluded. '*And I blew up in her face. I told her to get out of my sight and she went. And now the staff won't cooperate with me. They think I'm being unreasonable. Every obstacle possible is being put in my way – but not so you can put your finger on it and deal with it straight out. The Editor is her uncle and he will not agree that it was sheer corruption and nepotism for her to have that job. (She's a senior reporter on the paper by the way.) He says they need her. That she's really good at her job...*

But how can I back down? I'm about ready to admit defeat – simply close them down and get out of here!'

Hugo looked at what he had written. Was it really that bad?

Yes, it was. And part of it was his fault. He should never have blown up at her. But if she hadn't been so dishonest...

But how could she be anything else? She was George Sinclair's daughter.

CHAPTER 28

Manitoba, Canada

It was a fine Sunday morning and Ella was wheeling Nancy back to the nursing home from church in town. An old friend was walking slowly alongside so they could chat as they went.

'So how's Hugo?' Nancy's friend asked. 'It seems a while since we've seen him.'

His grandmother smiled. 'I think he's doing fine,' she told her. 'He's in Scotland at the moment. Business,' she added.

Her friend nodded. 'Yes, of course. He's a busy young man.'

Nancy agreed, but her curiosity had been piqued by Hugo's letter. In her opinion, and reading a little between the lines, there was more going on than the usual business matters. That young woman he had fired up at in a fit of anger? That was totally out of character for Hugo. He was always so controlled. There was only one time in the past that she had known Hugo to lose that control and that was a long time ago when he was still in shock after his father's death. Poor little Georgie St Clair had taken the brunt of it and it had quite broken her heart.

Plenty of young women had set their caps at Hugo over the years but he had sent each one packing. Not one had seemed to get under his skin – let alone anywhere near his heart. And now, out of the blue, an unnamed young woman in Scotland had somehow got under Hugo's skin. The evidence was in the way Hugo had reacted! How Nancy longed to know more! The names Hugo had mentioned meant nothing to her. She would need to do a little digging...

She parted from her friend at the gate to the nursing home. As Ella wheeled her up the path to the main door, she said, 'I think I'll just answer that latest letter from Hugo before lunch.'

But when Ella had taken her back to her room and left her, Nancy settled with paper and pen and her address book from her bureau, and instead began to write:

'*My dear Hannah,*

It's quite a few months since we exchanged Christmas cards. I hope that you are well and that Joyce, Gina and Robbie are thriving.

I've just received news that my grandson is in your neck of the woods and I wonder has he come calling? He's a high-powered businessman nowadays and may be too busy for social calls! I hope you'll understand, even though he was in and out of your house as if it were his own home when he was thirteen! You always made him so welcome.

Anyways, his letter tells me he's got involved in a business venture at the local newspaper, The Caithness Sentinel. I was trying to remember was that the paper your son Danny worked on before the war?

Do you remember how he unexpectedly appeared that day in your house when we were all sitting round, drinking tea and catching up on our complicated and multiply-entwined and entangled family stories? That gathering of good-hearted women made all the difference to me at such a hard time. It was a difficult time for us all – so many funerals!

I was delighted that he and Catalena made a match of it. I thought she was a lovely girl and I rated her highly for making the effort to come all the way from Argentina to her half-brother's funeral. She had a loving heart.

Speaking of loving hearts, my Hugo does have a heart (despite all his attempts to appear to the contrary!). It would seem from his most recent letter that he has at last met someone who has had an impact on him. I'm reading slightly between the lines here. You know what men are like for not sharing their innermost secrets, not even with those who love them!

So I'm wondering if you've seen Hugo and if you have any news of what he's been up to. I'd be grateful for any snippets!

Scotland is a long way from Canada and he's still my beloved grandson, even though he's grown up now! Maybe you could keep a gentle eye on him for me.

Fondest regards,

Nancy.'

She folded the letter and tucked it in an envelope, carefully addressing it to Mrs Hannah Cormack. Then she took another sheet of paper:

'*Dear Hugo,*

You do seem to have got yourself in a bit of a pickle but I trust you have the wisdom not to do anything rash. I'm sure you know my advice is always to take it to the Lord.

If you need a little break from business, do see if you can find time to visit my old friend, Hannah Cormack. I believe she was kind to you when you were a youngster, and she was certainly kind to me when I went to Wick for your father's funeral.

I'd be grateful if you could find the time, and then write to let me know how she is. We're none of us getting any younger.

Your loving grandmother.'

Well, Nancy thought, that and my prayers are probably all I can do. Now we wait and see.

CHAPTER 29

Wick

Hugo was in a bad mood.

Everything that could go wrong seemed to be going wrong and now his hire car had died on him. There was no representative closer than Inverness and a replacement was going to take at least a week. Meanwhile, his luggage was in his hotel in Thurso and the only way to get there was on the bus. And if he was going to get to work next morning, he would need to take an early bus back to Wick.

He groaned. It had been a very long time since he had been on a bus! He did not need this.

Danny, just about to leave for lunch, paused and looked back at him.

'Anything I can help with?' he asked.

Hugo stared. Danny Cormack had been unfailingly courteous to him and as helpful as he could be, right from the start. The only thing they disagreed about was his niece and her job. And even despite that stumbling block, Danny had gone out of his way to cooperate with him and all the changes he wanted to make. And here was Danny, offering help again.

Hugo felt churlish. He had turned up in these people's lives out of a clear blue sky and turned everything upside down. Turned what had been one happy family – admittedly losing money – into a hostile, tight-knit guerrilla movement fighting him every inch of the way, risking their own jobs and livelihoods over one deceitful girl. And her uncle, while unyielding in his support of his niece, was now offering him – the invader – yet more help.

He found himself saying 'Thank you. But I don't know how you can...'

Danny came back into the Editor's sanctum and sat down. He had given up his desk and chair to Hugo on day one without a murmur, and now he sat on the other side of what had been his place of authority.

'So tell me and let's see what we can do,' he invited.

Hugo was touched by the undeserved kindness. Deciding he had nothing to lose, he told Danny what the problem was.

'So I'm stuck,' he finished.

Danny steepled his fingers, his forehead furrowed in thought. Then he said, 'I have an idea. I don't know what you'd think but...'

And he laid his suggestion in front of Hugo. His wife Catalena was visiting her mother in Argentina and would be away for the foreseeable future. Danny was alone in their house. There was a spare room. Hugo would be welcome to come and stay. They could pop over to Thurso this evening in Danny's car and pick up Hugo's things. Hugo could pay his bill at the Thurso hotel and get settled in at Danny's tonight. He would find Danny's house conveniently within walking distance of the office.

And no, he wouldn't be any trouble. They'd get their own breakfast but have their main meal at Danny's mother's. And no, she wouldn't mind. There was always plenty. Just let him make a phone call – then Hugo could phone the hotel in Thurso.

Hugo was taken aback. He had heard of Highland hospitality, and he had been taught as a child at Sunday school about the Christian duty of taking in strangers. But to see it in action... More, to be the recipient...

He gathered his thoughts together.

'If you're really willing to take me in, I'd be most grateful,' he said. 'It shouldn't be for too long... I wasn't meaning to stay more than a week or two...'

'Aye, well,' Danny said, rising to lead the way out to his car. 'We'll see.'

CHAPTER 30

'I see,' Hannah said thoughtfully.

She looked up and noticed that Mrs Henderson had removed herself from earshot. It was a blessing that their next-door neighbour was willing to let them use her telephone, but she could be a little... interested... at times.

Now free to speak openly, Hannah continued, 'And you'd like to bring Hugo over for lunch tomorrow? Well, my dear, I'm sure you know what you're doing.' She listened carefully. 'Make sure Gina isn't there? Yes, I can see that would be best but it might take a bit of doing. This is her home, but I'll do what I can.'

She returned thoughtfully to their own house and wandered into the sitting room. Her eye caught the unfamiliar sight of Nancy's letter sticking out of her Bible on the table. It was no coincidence, she was sure, that it had arrived that morning. Dear Nancy. She had last seen her nineteen years ago, as she waved her off at the railway station on the first stage of her journey back to Canada, taking a shocked and silent Hugo with her.

There had been three deaths – George's and Ruby's and Hugh's – then three funerals. Afterwards three bereaved women had drawn close to one another in their time of sorrow. And God had brought good out of that terrible time. She and Joyce had made a peaceful home for Gina and Robbie. But now their peace was threatened. Somehow that old destructive entangling of the three families was happening again in the next generation, and this time it appeared that Gina stood in the line of fire.

Hannah settled into her chair with the Bible on her lap. Quietly, she rededicated her family to God's loving care.

'You are our Refuge, our Shield and our Defender,' she prayed. 'We depend on You to sort this all out and protect us from harm.'

But that evening, it appeared that it was not going to be easy. Hannah had shared the news and Nancy's letter with Joyce.

'I think we should give the boy a chance,' Hannah said. 'Let Hugo come and see who we really are – where Gina really comes from. *Our* family. It might help...'

And though Joyce was reluctantly willing, the one person who was not in on the secret appeared intransigently unwilling to cooperate. Gina was determined to stay at home next day and help with Robbie.

'I'm not going in to work tomorrow so I need something to do! Shall we go for a walk?' she asked Robbie. 'Tomorrow afternoon after lunch if the weather's nice.'

'Yes!' Robbie said with delight and clapped his hands. 'Walk! With Gina!'

'Where do you think you might go?' Joyce asked.

'I don't know,' she said. 'I've some letters to write tomorrow morning and then I'll need to post them. Mandy found me a couple of jobs I could apply for...'

'Anything that appeals?'

Gina shook her head. 'Not really. But there's one newspaper job… They really want a man, and a man who can drive,' Gina added disconsolately. 'So I wouldn't have a chance.'

'You hold down a man's job now,' Joyce said. 'And if the problem is not being able to drive…' She blushed delicately. 'I could ask Alec if he'd be willing to teach you.'

'If I'd been nicer to Young Alec,' Gina said, 'I'm sure he'd have been willing to let me have a go.' She remembered Alec's reaction to Robbie. 'But I don't think he'd want to now.'

'There might be a way,' Joyce said. She rose and left the room. When she returned, she was a little flushed but looking pleased.

'Young Alec can take you out for a trial run tomorrow,' she told Gina. 'But he can only manage it during his lunch hour, so if you could get down to the Mart for ten to one, he'll be happy to set out from there.'

Gina stared at her mother. 'You've fixed it?'

'Yes,' Joyce smiled. 'I popped next door and phoned Alec. When I told him what the problem was, he had a quick word with Young Alec… And now it's not a problem.'

And neither would lunch tomorrow with Hugo coming to the house, Hannah thought. She smiled at Joyce. Between them, and God, all would be well.

CHAPTER 31

'I'm not sure this is a good idea,' Hugo said, suddenly balking as he and Danny walked along Willowbank.

Danny looked at him in surprise. Was this the same super-confident Canadian tycoon who had appeared just a few days ago in the newspaper office and turned their lives upside down with a few hasty words?

'Are you sure I'll be welcome?' Hugo worried. 'They're *her* family, after all.'

'Highland hospitality,' Danny said laconically. 'If I bring you, you will be treated courteously and fed well. The rest is up to you.'

Danny watched Hugo's visible discomfort. Good. The lad had some inkling of the mess he had created.

He took pity on him. 'I believe it will just be my mother and sister, and of course Robbie,' he said. 'Gina had to go out.' He had rung and checked. There was no need just yet for any meeting between the two warring parties.

'Right,' Hugo said, visibly relieved. 'By the way, who's Robbie?'

'Gina's younger brother,' Danny said. 'He was born…' He paused. 'He was born the day his father was killed.'

'Oh?'

Hugo clearly was going to ask more questions, but Danny simply ushered him into the entryway between the two houses and as they turned the corner, waved at the fine view over the bay. The harbour was busy with fishing boats and lorries, the sea sparkled, and the grass on the north and south headlands was green and bright in the sunshine.

'Great, isn't it? I could almost envy them this house for that view,' Danny said.

Hugo found himself being led into a big old grey-stone house. The front door itself was big and heavy, the brasses gleaming. There was a small vestibule with an acid-etched glass-panelled door into a hallway. And then he was standing in a warm dining-kitchen, the focus of three pairs of eyes.

'Hugo Mackay,' said a warm female voice.

He looked at the elderly lady in front of him. Of course Granny Cormack had aged but he would have recognised her anywhere. Her now completely white hair was still pulled back in a small bun at the back of her head and those grey eyes… Hugo saw with a pang of sorrow that they were looking at him quite sharply, assessing him – and maybe finding him wanting? When he had known these people in his youth, there had always been a warm and accepting welcome for him.

He hesitated. Was he now unwelcome?

'Granny Cormack?'

'Hugo.' Another voice.

He turned. A second woman had turned from her work at the stove to greet him. This must be Joyce, Hannah's daughter. She would have been quite young – younger than he was now – when he had last seen her. And the memory came back of a washed-out, nervy girl. Back then he had not understood. Now he did. He saw that the traces of prettiness that he had been aware of back then had matured and there was a glow that lifted her face into a gentle loveliness.

'Mrs St Clair,' Hugo acknowledged her, but Joyce laughed and shook her head.

'Oh no, Hugo. We dropped all that nonsense as fast as we could,' she told him cheerfully. 'The name's Sinclair, as it always really was. And maybe we can drop the Mrs now you're grown up!' She smiled at him. 'That means I'm Joyce,' she said, and held out her hand. 'Welcome.'

Hugo heard himself say something appropriate as he took her hand, but his mind was struggling to absorb the impressions that were flooding his brain. Joyce had clearly moved on from the disaster of her marriage to George St Clair. She had put it all behind her. And there seemed to be no trace of bitterness, no jagged edges. She was serene and radiant, a woman at peace – and happy.

'And this is my son, Robbie,' she was saying. 'Robbie, say hello to Hugo.'

'Hello.' The word was slurred and accompanied by a sudden bear hug that took Hugo by complete surprise. 'Hu... Hu-go!'

The name came out triumphantly and the large young man who had embraced Hugo stood back and beamed at him, clapping his hands in delight.

'Hu-go! Hu-go!' he said.

And Hugo realised that Danny, Joyce and Hannah were watching him, waiting to see how he would react.

CHAPTER 32

He had passed all the exams he had ever taken, Hugo thought wryly, but for once in his life, he felt out of his depth, with potential failure staring him in the face.

What should he do? It was not at all the thing for one unknown young man to bear-hug another. And this particular young man was… Hugo hesitated. What would his grandmother advise? And he knew the answer. Pray! Hugo snorted inwardly. Prayer was her answer to everything! But he had not prayed since his prayers that his father would not die had been resoundingly ignored.

But yes, Grandma would pray. Wryly, he wondered, would a quick 'Help!' suffice? It only took a moment. What next? And he knew she would say 'Just be yourself.' Yes, but… which self? The hard-shelled businessman who most certainly was not used to spontaneous hugs from strange young men? Or the very uncomfortable visitor who was not at all sure of his welcome?

And then he remembered the oasis that Hannah Cormack's kitchen had been for him back in 1945. He recalled the welcome that the unhappy 13-year-old, not wanted elsewhere, had found there. A place in a family. With two surrogate little sisters: a bossy little madam who threw tantrums to ensure she always got her own way and a sweet adorable one who followed him around like Mary's little lamb.

Yes, there had been a welcome here for him. And kindness. And food. Always food. Before it all went pear-shaped.

He looked at Joyce and Robbie. Suddenly he realised that what George St Clair had done to this family had more than turned their lives pear-shaped. But somehow they had come through. He could sense that this was a happy family, contented with their lives.

And they were waiting for his reaction. It mattered because it would tell them who he had become in the intervening years. Was he still the lad they had known who fitted in and had patience – and love, he admitted it – for two little girls who pestered him and comforted his lonely heart? Or was he indeed the heartless tycoon he had made of himself as he worked to ensure he never made the mistakes his father had?

Someone shifted and Hugo realised he had to say something. He looked round at the waiting faces. He remembered only kindness here. Let there be kindness then, starting with him.

'Hi, Robbie,' he said. 'It's good to meet you.'

Robbie grinned. 'Hu-go. Dinner!'

'Yes, please,' Hugo replied with a grin. 'I'm starving.' And the words that fell from his lips were the words of that 13-year-old boy. He caught Hannah's swift glance and knew that she recognised it.

She smiled. 'Then we'd better all sit down or we won't get any!'

The meal was simple and delicious, the conversation wide-ranging. It was clear that Hannah and Joyce both knew what was going on at *The Sentinel* and the difficulties he was having. Tactfully, no one mentioned Gina.

Robbie's contributions were treated with respect, and where necessary translated for Hugo's benefit. He seemed delighted that Hugo was with them. At least with Robbie, there was none of that sense of being measured...

'How's Cat?' Joyce's question jolted Hugo back to the ongoing conversation.

'She won't be home for a bit,' Danny said. 'I got a letter this morning telling me that her mother has died so she's staying on to help clear up the house and sort things out. I meant to tell you. You'll surely get your own letter soon.'

He turned to Hugo. 'Cat didn't get home to Buenos Aires as often as she might have liked, but she has a sister and two brothers over there who looked after their mother.'

'I thought it was lovely that she came to George's funeral,' Joyce said. She caught Hugo's questioning glance. 'That's how we got Cat!' And both Joyce and Danny laughed. She explained. 'Catalena was George's half-sister. After his father died...'

Hannah made a disapproving cluck.

'All right, Mum,' Joyce said with a grin. 'Hugo knows the St Clairs were a bad lot! I'll tell it like it really was!' She turned to Hugo and explained. 'George's father, Geordie, married a rich Argentinian girl and then got himself shot for cheating at a poker game. Sofia Maria remarried – a good man named Ramon Hernandez – and had a second family. Catalena is the youngest of that family. She's a lovely girl with a soft heart and for some reason kept in touch with her half-brother even after he'd been thrown out of the family. So when he was killed, she came to the funeral.'

'And that's when we met,' Danny put in.

'And lived happily-ever-after,' Joyce teased, receiving a dour glower from Danny. 'Well, you have!' she protested.

'Yes,' Danny agreed peaceably. 'We have.'

'But she's not the only good thing that came out of that man's intrusion in our lives,' Joyce continued steadily. 'I have been blessed. I have a beautiful and talented daughter, and a loving gorgeous son. You could say George was an irritant in our lives – but that irritant produced two pearls of great price: Gina and Robbie.'

Hugo searched her face. Joyce meant what she was saying. She really meant it.

'Do you know your Bible, Hugo?' Hannah put in.

Hugo thought of his grandmother sitting with her old Bible on her knee, sharing stories and teaching him. It had been a long time since he'd looked in that old book. He'd given it up when he gave up praying.

'We have a favourite text in this family.' She and Joyce exchanged affectionate glances. 'Romans 8:28: "And we know that all things work together for good to them that love God, to them who are the called according to his purpose." We have found those words simply true. What looked like disaster has turned out for good.'

Hugo swallowed hard. Like his grandmother, clearly this family found strength and help from that old book that enabled them to make sense of their lives.

But Joyce, with a smile at her mother, was speaking.

'I've got another text that means a lot to me,' she said. 'I think it applies even better in my case. It's from Genesis, chapter 50. Do you remember the story of Joseph?' she queried. 'How his brothers sold him into slavery and he had a hard time of it, what with prison and everything. But then it all turned out good and he got a high position and was able to help his family.'

Hugo nodded. It was a story he remembered hearing at Sunday school and from his grandmother.

Joyce continued. 'Joseph said to his brothers: "But as for you, ye thought evil against me; but God meant it unto good..."[2] George St Clair certainly meant evil against our family, and against me. But he did not succeed. God looked after us.'

She looked into Hugo's eyes.

'God keeps on looking after us, so what might be meant for evil doesn't turn out that way.'

And it was more than a lesson from the past, Hugo realised. It was a warning for the future.

2 Genesis, chapter 50, verse 20

CHAPTER 33

Gina was pleased that Young Alec had apparently taken on board that she could never be interested in him romantically. It seemed he was an easy-going young man and friendship instead of romance was quite acceptable to him.

'Especially now,' he had said with a meaningful grin.

Gina pondered that. Did he know more about the progress of his father's courtship of her mother? If so, it sounded promising.

They had met at the Mart as arranged. Gina recognised this was to save Young Alec from encountering Robbie again and she had to bite her tongue not to challenge him about it. She loved her brother and she did not like people who looked down on him. On the other hand, she did not want to offend Young Alec – or his father. And this driving lesson was too good an opportunity to miss.

Young Alec drove the red Mini through the town, then up Newton Hill and out into the countryside beyond.

'The roads are quieter out here,' he said, as he climbed out of the car at the spot he had chosen and they swapped places. Gina settled into the driver's seat. Patiently Young Alec explained the various foot pedals and levers to her and then it was her turn to have a go.

Hesitantly and very slowly at first, Gina managed to ease the car over into the road. Young Alec seemed very relaxed, and after a little, Gina began to feel more confident.

'That's right,' he said after several minutes of driving very slowly but surely along a straight stretch of road. 'Now give it a bit more juice.'

So Gina pressed the accelerator pedal and the little red car shot forward. After a few moments of enjoying the new speed, Gina saw, to her horror, that they were approaching a T-junction. The car seemed to be going too fast and she could not remember which pedal to press to slow it down. She tried one at random but it made the car go even faster.

Horrified, she held on to the steering wheel helplessly as the car shot across the T-junction. There was an open gate immediately ahead into the field beyond. The car sped through and then kept going. It seemed only moments before they were approaching the top of the field and the solidly built dry-stone wall that marked the boundary. Terrified in case she wrecked the car on the stones, Gina wrenched the steering wheel to the left and the car dutifully made a sharp left turn and proceeded along the top of the field.

Oh well, Gina thought, in for a penny, in for a pound, so as the next corner approached, she turned the wheel again to the left and steered the car along the furthest edge of the field. Another turn, and she managed to manoeuvre the car along the bottom edge of the field, then out through the open gate and back onto the road.

At which point the car stalled and came to a stop.

Appalled, she turned to look at Alec only to discover that he was red-faced with laughter. When he saw her horror-stricken face, his laughter got louder, and suddenly she was laughing too.

'That's one of the best first attempts at driving I've ever seen!' he managed to get out. 'You really should see your face! Shall I take over now?'

And Gina was happy to relinquish the driving seat for the journey back into town.

CHAPTER 34

As he finished his meal, Hugo considered the veiled warning. But *he* was not intending any evil to anyone in this family! It was Gina who had caused all the problems. She had proven herself capable of deceit and he was not convinced she had come by her job at *The Sentinel* through merit.

Now he had seen the close-knit Cormack family, he could understand Danny giving Gina the job to help them. As Editor of *The Sentinel*, he could cover for her, prop her up. But that wouldn't wash now. There was no way *he* was willing to carry passengers.

Quoting Bible texts at him as though he was the villain of the piece, Hugo thought sourly. Maybe it was time for God to work it out for good for *him*.

Go on, then, he told God silently. *Let's see You sort this out for good.*

Then it was time to go. He thanked Hannah and Joyce politely for their hospitality and was prepared for the hug from Robbie who came to the door to see him and Danny on their way.

'My friend Hu-go!' Robbie said beaming.

They walked back into the centre of town in silence, Hugo wrestling with the problem. Hannah and Joyce and Danny were clearly good people. Robbie was a much-loved member of the family. He didn't want to hurt them but how could he resolve the problem with Gina without damaging the business or compromising his own integrity?

As they approached the bridge, Hugo said suddenly, 'What if we put Gina on a trial basis…' He glanced at Danny. 'You know I have reservations about her competence, and I only have so much time to turn the paper round and make it pay again. I'm sorry. I know she's your niece and the family have had a hard time, but I can't carry passengers.'

He could see that Danny was not pleased. As he paused, trying to put his thoughts in order, Hugo saw a small red Mini draw up on the street ahead. Gina and a young man got out. They were laughing and clearly enjoying each other's company.

Hugo felt a sudden blaze of fury. How dare she be so light-hearted when she had created such problems for him? But that was who she was – like her father. Careless of the harm she did to other people.

'You can tell her she's on three months' trial,' he snapped. 'If I'm not satisfied she is up to the job in that time, then she's out.' He glared at Danny. 'Understood?'

Danny's eyes flicked from Hugo to Gina and Young Alec laughing together and back to Hugo's angry face.

'Understood,' he said blandly, and continued to walk back to the office.

'Uncle Danny!'

A bright female voice brought Danny's head round. His eyes narrowed.

'Mandy,' Danny acknowledged her.

The fashionably dressed young woman hurried across the street towards them.

Hugo's head turned sharply, his eyes unfriendly.

'May I introduce my other niece, Mandy,' Danny said, when she reached them.

'Mandy?' Hugo's voice was icy as his eyes raked the girl's face. 'Would that be Mandy Strachan? Mrs Mandy Strachan?' There was a slight emphasis on the *Mrs*.

Mandy stuck out her hand. 'That's me,' she said cheerfully. 'Or used to be – the Mrs bit. I'm divorced.'

'Indeed?' said Hugo. He shook the proffered hand.

'And you are?' Mandy asked, her face a picture of innocence.

Danny watched as Hugo made a slight bow.

'Hugo Mackay, at your service.'

It was as discouraging as it could be without giving offence.

Mandy's eyes widened and she licked her lips. 'Hugo Mackay?' Her voice rose. 'Not Hugo! Hugo, you remember me! Amanda Cormack! *I* remember *you!*'

And before Hugo could move, Mandy had flung her arms around him and pressed her body against his, in the second unexpected hug of the day.

'Hugo! How wonderful!' she carolled. 'You've come back!'

CHAPTER 35

Mandy was well-pleased with herself. Yes, Hugo would do very nicely as Husband No. 2 – especially now he was rich and apparently available. And if he wasn't, she would soon see to that.

She had found out that he was staying in Wick, at Danny Cormack's. All she had to do was bump into Hugo, pretend she recognised him...

But would she recognise him after all this time? The only person who could help her would be Gina and there was no way she was letting Gina in on what she was planning. Gina had always adored Hugo. Hopefully helping her get the newspaper job in Dundee would take her far enough away to be no threat.

Mandy carefully applied hairspray to her bouffant dark hair, holding the mirror up to check. The back-combing had done the trick and Mandy felt she was looking her best.

Hugo had apparently taken completely against Gina – because of her father. Funny that. Everybody knew that Goody-Two-Shoes Gina took after the *other* side of the family. She was as noble and self-sacrificing as her boring mother. Still, if that's what Hugo wanted to believe, it could only help.

Mandy had given some thought to how she would play this. The magazines she'd read had painted him as cold-hearted and, though pursued by glamorous women (gold-diggers, Mandy thought), always managing to keep out of reach. Mmm. So he would need careful handling.

She slipped her bag over her shoulder and set off down the stairs from her bedroom.

'Bye, Gran!' she called. 'Don't know when I'll be back...'

'You never do,' the old woman grumbled. 'See if I care.'

Mandy stuck her tongue out and slammed the door behind her.

'See if I care!' she repeated; then she laughed. 'The sooner I get out of here, the better. And Hugo Mackay is going to be my one-way ticket to a better life! Canada, here I come!'

Mandy waited impatiently for the bus into town to arrive, stepping into it daintily in her high-heeled shoes. She brushed the seat before she sat down, making sure to sit with her knees neatly together and her legs at an angle as she had seen in the magazines. She may not have been born a lady but she was sure she was going to be one, one day, so she might as well get in some practice.

She now regretted not going to the conference in Aberdeen. That had been a mistake, letting Gina go in her place. What a waste of an opportunity! If she had known Hugo was going to be there... But of course she had not, and she had wasted the day instead on one of a long line of no-hopers. That had come quickly to an end. Like all the others. But now Mandy had her eyes set on bigger game. She had spent some time in the library researching Hugo's story. It appeared he had done very well for himself.

Well, now was his chance to do well for her. All she had to do was find him. Bump into him. She couldn't exactly hang around the office or Danny's house. Either would be far too obvious.

Was there any other place he was likely to go?

'Are you getting off, or is this a round-trip?' the bus driver called down the bus, jolting Mandy out of her thoughts.

'Hold your horses!' she shouted crossly. 'I'm going!'

She hurried down the gangway and out of the door. There she stood for a moment at the bus stop, considering what would be her best chance of encountering Hugo.

She had taken the day off – a calculated risk as she had already taken rather more days off than her boss liked. But it was an investment. Land Hugo and she could wave goodbye to the job – any job, including the intriguing one in Edinburgh.

She patted her hair, grateful for the holding power of the hairspray keeping it in place in the ever-present wind. It was a fine day and the trees alongside the road provided welcome shelter from the sun. The war memorial stood impressively on its plinth at the junction of five streets.

Mandy hesitated. Which one to choose?

As she scanned the streets around her, her sharp eyes spotted two men walking across the bridge. One was Danny Cormack. The other was a stranger: a tall, dark-haired man, well-dressed in a grey suit, and probably in his thirties. Mandy felt sudden excitement race through her as she realised the second man could be Hugo.

With another pat of her hair, she set off in pursuit of her quarry.

CHAPTER 36

Mandy batted carefully mascaraed eyelashes at Hugo.

'Were you in a hurry?' she asked in a soft voice. 'I suppose you've got to get back to work?'

'Sorry?' Hugo said. His mind was still on the unwelcome sight of Gina and her boyfriend.

Mandy produced a pleasant smile.

'I suppose it's a bit of a shock,' she said. 'Bumping into one another after all this time?'

Hugo dragged his thoughts together and made himself focus on the girl in front of him.

'Yes,' he said.

'And we've both grown up.'

She took a step away so he could appreciate the now grown-up Mandy.

As he looked at her, he recalled the two little girls – Georgina and Amanda. One was difficult, throwing tantrums to get her own way, and the other was sweet, quiet and adorable. Clearly Gina was the difficult one. That meant Mandy was the sweet one who had followed him around like Mary's little lamb.

Hugo's relief broke into a smile. Perhaps in the grown-up Mandy he had found a friend in this place.

'So tell me, Mrs Mandy Strachan,' he said lightly. 'What have you been up to since I last saw you?'

'Well, that might take a little bit of time to tell,' she said. 'And you have to get back to work.'

'I'm the boss,' Hugo said, 'and we've only just met up again. I reckon I'm allowed a little bit longer... for an old friend.' He smiled. 'Where would you suggest we go to catch up?'

CHAPTER 37

Gina stared at her uncle, open-mouthed with shock and outrage.

'Gina, we need you at *The Sentinel*. But we also need Hugo's money and new ideas. He's our only chance of survival. Please. Just think about it,' Danny said.

He had returned to his office but then gone back to the house in Willowbank where he had broken the news of Hugo's ultimatum to Gina. Now he picked up his jacket unhappily, nodded his thanks to his mother and sister, and left.

'How could he?' Gina demanded. 'I've worked there long enough to win my spurs and now *he* comes and starts throwing his weight around and suddenly, just to please *him*, I have to start proving myself all over again! And I've three months to do it in!'

'In that case it should be perfectly simple and straightforward.' Her grandmother spoke calmly.

Gina's face flushed. 'Not if his mind is made up and it's only an excuse to stay pally with Uncle Danny till he has an excuse to get rid of me!'

'Then you have to make sure he has no excuse.' There was steel in the steady grey eyes. 'If you want to keep your job.'

'Yes, of course I want to keep my job! I love my job!' Gina protested.

'Then, it's in your hands. He's given you an opportunity. I think you should take it.'

'You'd never forgive yourself, love, if you backed down now,' Joyce said. 'After all you've worked for...'

'Yes, but...'

'And you do have some extra good opportunities coming up,' Joyce reminded her. 'Danny said he's got notification that the Queen's coming to Caithness. You would always be the one to cover that.'

'Yes,' Gina agreed slowly.

'So...'

Gina looked at the two beloved, concerned faces. She knew they were as angry with Hugo as she was, angry at the injustice and his prejudice. But they were taking a more positive approach.

Easy enough for them, sitting here at home, she thought hopelessly. If she went back to work she would have to see Hugo every day and read his contempt for her every time she encountered him. Could she bear it? How crazy she was. To love someone who not only didn't want her but couldn't bear the sight of her.

The Queen's visit would give her an excellent excuse for being out of the office, she considered. They were well used to the Queen Mother's frequent visits to Caithness. Her cheerful relaxed approach to her life in the county, turning up at local shops in a headscarf and mac, had universally won hearts, and her privacy was now as protected by local people as her almost-ordinariness was approved.

To have a royal visit from the Queen and Prince Philip would instead be a grand affair, with many set pieces to cover, with lots of photographs. Gina barely realised she was already planning...

'So you'll go back to *The Sentinel*?' her grandmother murmured with a smile.

Gina started almost guiltily. The truth was, now she let herself think about it, she was itching to get back to work.

She grinned. 'Yes, Granny. I'll be back at my desk tomorrow!'

CHAPTER 38

But it wasn't easy. Next morning, Gina found herself fretting about what to wear for virtually the first time in her life. It was only work, she tried reminding herself. But today, she wanted to look smart.

She caught sight of herself in the full-length mirror and grimaced. She looked like a parody: Gina Sinclair, Girl Reporter. No, it wouldn't do. She tore off the clothes she had so carefully chosen and grabbed for the kind of things she always wore to work. Her favourite pale-green kilt and a white sweater. Whatever Hugo might think of her, she would not change who she was. And if he didn't like it… Her thoughts slowed. She did not want to think about that.

As always, she entered the building by the ground-floor door into the administrative and advertising offices. Unseen, she hung her coat up in the female staff cloakroom, took a surreptitious look at her face and hair, and stepped out into the corridor.

'Gina!' Mrs Swanson, coming through from the outer office, had spotted her. 'Oh my dear, it is so good to see you.' She took in Gina's strained face. 'We heard,' she continued in a lower tone. 'And we're all on your side. You can do it, my girl. Yes, it's unfair and the man is an idiot who can't see the nose in front of his face, but if this is the only way for you to be fully reinstated then we'll all be doing whatever we can to help.'

'That's lovely, and thank you,' Gina said. 'But I think the point of this trial period is that I have to show that I'm capable and competent all on my own.'

'Humph!' came the reply. 'As if there could be any doubt. Well, you'd better get on up to your office. Come down when you're ready for your coffee and more moral support!'

And Gina was ushered swiftly through the warren of the ground floor to the narrow stairs up to the compositors' room and the corridor to the reporters' room. As her head appeared up the stairs into the room where the comps were working, there was a loud chorus of greetings and cheeky comments.

'Had a nice holiday?'

'All right for some.'

'Wasn't any news for you to report anyway!'

Gina acknowledged the underlying friendliness with a wave and a grin. She headed for the reporters' room only to slam on the brakes as she realised Hugo had come out of the Editor's office and was watching and listening to all that was going on. He had a sardonic curl to his mouth.

Gina nodded and bolted into the office, closing the door behind her with relief.

'What's the matter with you? Ghoulies and ghosties chasing you?' Jimmy Macrae was filling his pipe. Now as he puffed on it to get it started, he looked across at Gina from behind bushy eyebrows and clouds of smoke.

Gina shook her head warningly and slipped behind her desk, automatically reaching to take the cover off her typewriter.

'Not a lot happening,' young Henry commented mournfully. 'No murders, no robberies. The usual drunk-and-disorderlies...'

'And the Queen is coming to town,' Jimmy said.

'Yes, I heard,' Gina said.

'Next Wednesday and Thursday,' Jimmy added.

'So we'll be able to cover Wednesday's visit for Friday's *Sentinel* and then carry over the Thursday events for the following week,' Gina said. 'Have we got a programme yet? And what about photographers?'

'Sorted,' Jimmy said.

'Has Danny said anything...' she began slowly. If she were indeed only at work on sufferance and being treated like a hopeless probationer, there was no way he would be allowed to let her cover the Queen's visit. She would be reduced to the least demanding tasks. With a pang, Gina realised how much it mattered to her.

'He said you would do it, as usual,' Jimmy said kindly. 'Don't worry, Gina. You're the only one of us who's any good at that kind of reporting! It has to be you.'

'But what about...' Gina began.

'As far as we know, Danny is still Editor here, and editorial decisions are still his to take,' Jimmy said. 'That man Mackay seems to be more concerned with the money, and his new ideas,' he added darkly. 'He's not troubling us – and we won't let him trouble you.'

Gina searched the kindly faces of her two colleagues. With humble gratitude she realised that everyone here was on her side. They wanted her to succeed and be properly reinstated.

'In that case,' she said, 'where's the programme? I'll need to get started.'

And, she thought, make sure she didn't let them down.

CHAPTER 39

'You've got your name in the paper!' Joyce pointed to the bold-type byline above the double-page article on the Queen's visit to Caithness. 'Well, we knew you wrote it...'

'It's strange,' Gina said. 'I had nothing to do with that and I didn't see it when I read the galleys, but when I got my copy before I left work tonight, there it was.'

Her mother and grandmother exchanged glances.

'They're making sure you get the credit,' Hannah said. 'Danny maybe?'

'The comps wouldn't do it off their own bat,' Gina said thoughtfully.

'Well, he can't help but notice,' Joyce said and it was clear to them all that 'he' referred to Hugo. 'And it's staring him in the face that you're a first-rate reporter! You got all the details that folk are interested in.' She picked up the paper and read aloud: '*A large crowd, including many schoolchildren given time off school, broke into loud cheers as Her Majesty the Queen descended from the bright red Heron aircraft onto the tarmac runway at Wick airport. She paused briefly to wave to them before...*'

'I know!' Gina laughed. 'I wrote it. But the pics are great.'

'But they're black-and-white photographs,' her mother said. 'You only get the full picture when you read that the Queen was wearing a deep turquoise coat and dress, and she and Prince Philip went off in a wine-coloured Rolls Royce. It's those details that bring it all to life. It means that those of us who weren't there can imagine it.'

Gina shrugged. 'Well, that's what it's all about. Painting pictures with words.'

'And you do it well,' her grandmother said.

'Yes indeed.'

Danny had arrived quietly in their midst. He smiled at Gina.

'You've done a good job. We'll run another double-page spread next week, and put in any of the pics we hadn't room for today. Stand by for any extra copy we'll need.'

Gina nodded her agreement. 'I've got loads of notes.'

'Good. Now,' Danny said, 'I have a suggestion for you. And yes, I know I've suggested this before and you've always said no.' He looked at his mother and sister and explained. 'There's an annual prize for young journalists – a national one – and I am sure Gina would have a good chance of winning it, if she would just enter for it. All she has to do is send in three examples of her best work over the past year. She's always said she's too young, too junior, not good enough…'

'Nonsense!' her mother and grandmother said robustly.

'If Gina would enter and win,' Danny continued, 'then it would be announced nationally. Her name would be in the big national papers. Of course, the announcements would say she works at *The Sentinel* and that would be good publicity for the paper.' Danny waited as they followed his thinking.

'Mmm?' his mother said. 'Two birds with one stone? National recognition that Gina is a first-rate journalist…'

'Winning the prize demonstrates that,' Danny agreed.

'So Hugo could no longer deny her ability and would have to fully reinstate her. How could he not?' Joyce added.

'And he could not help but be pleased at the publicity,' Hannah said slowly, 'which hopefully would soothe any annoyance at having to eat humble pie!'

Three pairs of eyes fixed on Gina.

'I reckon today's double-page spread on the Queen's visit is one of your very best,' Danny said, gesturing to the newspaper. 'I'd recommend that would be one of your three. We can take a look through the back numbers and see what else there is.' He smiled. 'The problem will be choosing – not finding – two that will do!'

Gina blushed.

'You will enter this competition?' her mother urged. 'There's no harm in doing that.'

'And I'm happy to sign off your application,' her uncle said. 'Think about it, Gina. Whatever happens, it will stand you in good stead.'

And as the pictures jostled in Gina's head – of Hugo having to apologise or going off the deep end again so she had to take the new job in Dundee – she realised Danny was right. Whatever happened, it would stand her in good stead.

'Yes,' she said. 'I'll try it.'

CHAPTER 40

The *Caithness Sentinel* building, Gina realised as she arrived at work the next day, was no longer the happy place it used to be. The staff walked around on tiptoe as if Hugo were an ogre they were afraid to provoke – as if they thought they would lose their jobs if they got things wrong.

Yes, he had lashed out at her but that was… personal. Surely the businessman that Hugo had become wasn't that bad? Out of curiosity for what he had been doing in the intervening years, Gina had read up on his background. It was clear that he had successfully turned round many businesses before – and none of the write-ups in the business press suggested that he was anything but good at what he did.

She raised her concerns with her uncle.

'Yes,' Danny agreed. 'The staff are nervous. But we did need a shake-up. Lots of things that needed done just couldn't be done in the past through lack of funding. I had ideas and took them to the bosses often enough – but they were always turned down. I think we'd all given up to some extent. Just plodding on, trying to keep going against the odds. And that goes for some of the staff too, hanging on to their jobs when maybe we'd have done better with new blood. Jimmy Macrae is a case in point. He's been wanting to retire for a long time.'

'I can see that with Hugo's money, there will be more up-to-date equipment,' she conceded. 'Hopefully there will be decent redundancy arrangements for those like Jimmy who are willing to take it. But the rest of the folk here need to feel secure and appreciated to give their best. And Hugo just seems to have alienated everyone.'

'Ah well, that was because of you,' Danny said with a wry smile. 'When he threw you out, they closed ranks against him. They just haven't eased off yet.'

'Oh, I see,' Gina said thoughtfully. 'Maybe I can do something about that.'

And when she went down to the advertising office for coffee at eleven as usual, she spent some time reminiscing about her childhood.

'Poor Hugo,' she told her fascinated audience. 'We plagued him – me and Mandy. He was thirteen and probably would have much preferred boys of his own age to kick a football around with, but he had endless patience with us.' She looked over the rim of her coffee mug. 'What happened with his dad was terrible and it's no wonder if that still hurts. I perfectly understand. But he's fine with us now. He had dinner at the house with us just the other day and of course he's staying with Uncle Danny while Auntie Cat's away.'

She managed to slip that nugget of information into another conversation, this time with the head compositor and Father of Chapel, Andy Chalmers.

He raised his bushy eyebrows. 'Is that so?'

'He was always in and out of our house,' Gina continued blithely. 'He even called my grandmother Granny Cormack, and that's what she was to him.' Gina smiled. 'Still is, I reckon! But I don't mind sharing.'

Gradually, the gentle but consistent strategy began to work and Gina could see a more relaxed attitude among the staff towards Hugo. The tense atmosphere eased and there was laughter and joking again.

The first time a slip of lead caught her stockings as she headed down the narrow stairs for her morning coffee, Gina turned in delighted surprise instead of the annoyance she used to feel. If the lads felt comfortable enough to revert to their old teasing, things must have got back pretty much to normal. She managed a pretend scowl, but they just laughed and she headed on downstairs with a lighter heart.

The only person who remained awkward was Hugo himself. He clearly remained unconvinced of her competence and insisted on being icily formal whenever they encountered one another. And when he had to actually speak to her it was even worse.

'Miss Sinclair, I wonder could I trouble you...' was how he began any sentence.

Gina longed to scream at him. Throw something. Anything to break through his icy façade and reach the Hugo she knew was in there somewhere.

Wasn't he?

CHAPTER 41

'I thought you wanted to come to the concert?' Hugo asked.

Mandy had been keen to accept his invitation. An event like that would be an excellent opportunity to demonstrate that they were going out together. She had dressed carefully, selecting one of her quieter outfits. Hugo, she was discovering, was a bit old-fashioned. But one of the benefits of going out with him was that he was tall. She could wear her favourite stiletto heels. It was so boring going out with short men. You either had to wear clumpy flats or look down on them all the time, which wasn't exactly conducive to romance.

She had carefully taken Hugo's arm as they entered the Assembly Rooms in Wick, and engaged him in low-voiced conversation, so he had to lean close. As expected, the other people going in to the concert noticed. She preened inwardly, and surreptitiously scanned the auditorium. She had made sure they would arrive almost on time so everyone would see them.

But there was no sign of Gina, or anyone she knew who would be likely to take the useful gossip of Mandy's obviously established relationship with Hugo back to her.

'There's nobody here,' Mandy muttered crossly.

Hugo looked startled. He gazed round at the audience.

'They seem to have got quite a good crowd,' he said.

Realising her *faux pas*, Mandy quickly tried to cover her mistake.

'Not as many as usual,' she tried, and offered a beaming smile of thanks to distract Hugo as he led her to their numbered seats.

She settled in for a boring evening. Why couldn't Hugo like modern music? If this was the kind of music he liked, there was no point trying to persuade him to take her to the dance next month when The Hollies would be playing. She had really wanted to go to that, but it was too much of a risk to accept someone else's invitation just to hear a pop group – and there was no way she would ever pay for a ticket for herself. That's what men were for.

As the accordion and fiddles started playing, Mandy closed her eyes and dreamed. When she and Hugo were married... What was Canada like? She would have to go to the library and have a look at some books. And not let Hugo know she was looking.

Toronto – that was in Canada, wasn't it? Montreal... Vancouver... The names played across Mandy's mind. Yes, a penthouse apartment in one of these wonderful modern cities would do very nicely. She began planning furniture and décor.

'Would you like an ice cream?' Hugo enquired.

Mandy realised with a jolt that the dreadful old-fashioned music had stopped and the audience were getting out of their seats and heading for the refreshments.

She considered. She didn't really like ice cream but it would be another opportunity to be seen with Hugo.

She managed a smile. 'Yes, please,' she said and carefully took his arm again as they left the hall.

There was of course a queue.

'Why don't you go back to your seat?' Hugo offered. 'I'll get the ices and bring them back to you.'

No, that would not do. The whole purpose of being here was to be seen with Hugo, and clearly seen as an item. Mandy was determined she would not leave his side, but what could she do when he was being so gentlemanly?

'Mandy! How nice to see you!'

Mandy turned to the speaker in surprise. She had not noticed Auntie Joyce in the audience. Her eyes narrowed. Perfect!

'And Hugo!' Joyce said, smiling. 'Alec, let me introduce the new owner of *The Sentinel*, Hugo Mackay.'

The older man with Joyce shook Hugo's hand and gave him a cautious smile.

'Mackay,' he said. 'Yes, I've heard about you.'

'And you'll know Mandy,' Joyce continued. 'Hugo's father was married to Mandy's mum, Ruby.'

Mandy nearly exploded. Why did the stupid woman have to bring that up now? She did not want Hugo to be reminded of that aspect of their relationship. Not now.

Carefully she controlled herself.

'But my father was Auntie Joyce's half-brother,' she said with a determined smile for Joyce. 'Bobby Cormack. So I'm a Cormack.' She paused to let that sink in, then added, 'Not a Sinclair, like Gina.'

Through her heavily mascaraed eyelashes she watched Hugo absorb the information. Well satisfied, she linked her arm again with Hugo's.

'Were we going to have some ice cream?' she cooed sweetly.

CHAPTER 42

'So how was your evening?' Hannah asked when Joyce returned from her evening with Middle Alec at the concert.

Joyce blushed.

'Well?' her mother probed gently.

'He proposed. On the way home,' Joyce told her.

The family were gathered in the sitting room enjoying a quiet evening together.

'So what did you say?' Gina asked.

'What could I say?' Joyce said sadly. 'I told him I liked him a lot, that I enjoyed his company, but I had my family to think of.'

She sat down heavily in one of the armchairs.

'Oh, Mum!' Gina protested. 'I think you like him more than that, don't you?'

Joyce shook her head again. 'It makes no difference what I feel...'

'Yes, it does,' Hannah said firmly. 'Alec Gunn is a good man and would be good to you. You know that. And he is good *for* you. As you say, you like him a lot and enjoy his company.'

Joyce nodded.

'So if you love him…' Hannah's steady grey eyes were fixed on her daughter. 'If you love him, tell him and let *him* work out what to do with your nuisance family!'

'You're not a nuisance!' Joyce protested. She looked round at her mother, her daughter and her son. 'Not one of you!'

'But…' Hannah prodded. 'Something about us is getting in the way and that won't do.'

'But, Mum,' Joyce protested, 'I have to think about you.'

'Well, I think I'm well able to look after myself,' Hannah told her robustly. 'I'd assume you'd live with Alec out at the farm if you married him?'

Joyce nodded slowly.

'Well, Gina and I will simply continue living here. We'll manage fine, the pair of us, won't we?' Hannah twinkled at her granddaughter. 'We might even enjoy just being the two of us!'

'That's true!' Gina agreed with a grin.

Joyce's eyes flicked over to Robbie. 'But…'

'Ah,' Hannah said, 'I wondered when you were going to mention Robbie. So you think there might be a problem?'

'Not a problem with Alec,' Joyce said slowly. 'He gets on fine with Robbie and Robbie with him. Alec's been very good about everything and you know he has good ideas to make Robbie's life more appropriate for a young man of his age. But…'

'But?' her mother prompted. 'What is the problem?'

'It's Young Alec,' Joyce said. 'For some reason he simply can't cope with Robbie.' She threw a swift worried glance at her son. 'It's not your fault, darling. It's something with Young Alec. And of course, the farm is his home, and one day it will be his…' She sighed. 'I can't see any solution there. So that's one big problem. And the other? Well, to suggest he take us both on, it just seems a lot to ask.'

'And have you asked?' Hannah put in quietly. 'About either problem?'

Joyce shook her head.

'Maybe you need to talk to the man,' Hannah told her daughter. 'Find out what the problem is with Young Alec, and make sure *your* Alec knows what he'd be taking on.' Her grey eyes flashed. 'Better to sort it out now before you say or do anything you might regret later.'

Joyce nodded. 'I know you're right,' she said. 'It's just I'm enjoying being taken out, enjoying Alec's company. I don't want to spoil it.'

She rose from the armchair and moved towards the door.

'I think I'll go to bed now.'

At the door, she paused and hesitated.

'Oh, by the way,' she said, 'Mandy was at the concert.'

She darted a quick look at Gina.

'With Hugo.'

CHAPTER 43

Shock surged through Gina. So Mandy was going out with Hugo? How had she managed that? The pain in her heart was so sharp Gina thought she would faint. And that was enough to make her pull herself together. She would not faint a second time because of that man!

'Oh, that's nice,' she managed to say, then produced what she hoped was a convincing yawn. 'Oh dear, I am tired. I'm off to bed too. Good night, all.'

She hurried up the stairs to the refuge of her bedroom. Without switching on the light, she moved the armchair to face the window. Then she settled herself into it, chin on her knees and stared out at the sea, trying to make sense of her thoughts.

Yes, Hugo would be an attractive prospect for Mandy. He was rich, successful, and good-looking too. She must have gone to work on him almost as soon as Gina had told her he was back.

But if Hugo was livid at being fooled by her pretending to be Mandy, why wasn't he as cross at Mandy? It had been Mandy's idea…

But she knew the answer: it was because she was George St Clair's daughter. And Mandy wasn't. And that's why it was possible for Hugo and Mandy… But not for her.

Gina swallowed hard. Could she even admit it to herself? She had fallen in love with Hugo in Aberdeen. But it had not been a new *coup de foudre* type of love. It was as if her childhood adoration of Hugo had lain dormant like a seed in her heart all these years, and when he appeared again – even though she had no idea who he was – her heart had known, and that seed had burst into instant flowering.

Gina let her mind wander back to the terrible morning at the office when he had discovered who she really was, and all the moments since when their paths had crossed and he had treated her with disdain and hostility.

But, she thought, she still loved him. It wasn't the innocent idolisation of the child she had been, but a steady, grown-up, determined thing deep inside her heart. She knew who Hugo was now – short-tempered, prone to lashing out, brilliant at his work. And maybe, Gina thought, remembering that kiss, and now the news about Hugo and Mandy, maybe like his father, with a weakness for women.

So he was going out with Mandy. Gina's heart ached within her at the thought. Because Hugo would get hurt. Mandy took what she wanted, then flitted off to the next victim, leaving hurt and damage in her wake. Gina had seen it so many times… and heard Mandy's derisive comments: 'Suckers!' 'No-hopers!' Each one dismissed with mocking laughter.

And that's when the tears came. Could she bear to watch Hugo become Mandy's next victim? Could she stand by, till Mandy had had her fun – and be there to pick up the pieces?

And then the devastating thought came: Hugo probably wouldn't even want her to. He still saw her only as George St Clair's daughter, tainted irrevocably by her father's bad blood.

A quiet knock on her door roused her from her thoughts. She scrubbed at her eyes and looked round as her grandmother stepped into the room and switched on the light.

'I thought I'd look in on you before I went to bed,' she said.

Gina managed a watery smile of welcome as her grandmother settled on Gina's bed. She twisted the chair round to face her.

'I asked your mum tonight if she loved Alec Gunn,' Hannah began.

'And now you're going to ask me if I love Hugo Mackay?' Gina gave a bitter laugh. 'Is it so obvious?'

'I thought I might tell you a story,' Hannah said. 'A story about love, and men, and the kind of things we women do when the men we love don't seem to love us.'

Gina looked into her grandmother's loving grey eyes.

'Go on then,' she said. 'Tell me your story.'

'It is mine,' Hannah acknowledged. 'I loved your grandfather. It always seemed to me that I'd loved him from the moment I first knew him. I'd always loved him. It was as simple as that. And when we were young, it was simple.'

Gina nodded. Like her childish love for Hugo.

'But then Belle... It nearly broke my heart when my sister, thinking she was pregnant by another man, seduced my Rab and got him to marry her.' She sighed. 'Those were terrible days for me.'

They sat in silence.

'But you and Granddad did get married,' Gina prompted her.

'Yes. Though it was a near thing.' The familiar twinkle appeared in her grandmother's eyes. She smiled at Gina. 'When Belle died giving birth to Bobby, I thought surely Rab would notice me... And when he didn't, I thought maybe I'd have a try at showing him someone else was interested. Maybe make him a wee bit jealous...'

The smile became a cheeky grin. 'So that's where Alec Gunn comes into the story. Ould Alec, though he was a fine-looking young man back then. We were walking out for six months and he was perfectly good company. And then he proposed.'

'Oh,' Gina said. She had not known this part of the story.

'I didn't love him,' Hannah said simply. 'How could I love him? Rab had my heart and always would.' She smiled mistily.

'So you said no?' Gina asked.

'Well, it was a little bit more complicated than that. Your Uncle Bobby took a hand in proceedings. I'd been cooking and cleaning for them, doing their washing, seeing they were comfortable. I think Bobby realised what a loss I'd be to their lives if all that went to Alec Gunn!' The twinkle was back in force.

'No!' Gina exclaimed.

'Not far off maybe,' Hannah said.

'But you married Granddad!' Gina said.

'I knew Rab did not love me when he proposed to me,' Hannah said. 'But I believed I had enough love for the both of us. And I trusted in the Lord to see us through. So I married him. I had waited for him long enough and I wasn't getting any younger!' Again that cheeky grin.

'Granny!'

'Aye well, some decisions are maybe more pragmatic than romantic. But I knew I loved him.' She paused. 'The thing is Alec Gunn kept on waiting. When Rab went off to the war and was injured, missing in action, and everyone thought for sure he was dead and would not be coming back, Alec approached me again. Maybe a woman in my position – I had Bobby and Danny to look after – I might look more favourably on him.'

She looked over at her granddaughter and Gina could see the steel in those grey eyes.

'Maybe I'd got used to waiting.' Hannah shrugged. 'Maybe I'd become stubborn and couldn't give in!' Her smile invited Gina to share her amusement. She went on, 'But I told Alec I'd wait for my husband – and wait I did till he came back. And he was worth waiting for.'

Gina, listening carefully, wondered how this could help her. She could not see how it applied to her. She loved Hugo but he hated her, and now Mandy had stolen him...

'Let me finish my story,' Hannah said, seeing Gina's reaction. 'Alec took me at my word that second time and married Margaret Campbell. She was a good Christian woman and I think maybe she had been waiting for him.'

The grey eyes were filled with affection and understanding.

'My dear, sometimes we can't see how our dreams will ever come true. How we'll ever have the happy-ever-after we long for.'

Gina's eyes filled with tears. Her love for Hugo was so hopeless she couldn't even dream of a happy-ever-after. Not now.

'Sometimes we have to wait. Just trust God and wait – as I did for Rab, more than once.'

Hannah paused, her gaze focused on her granddaughter's hurt face. She continued thoughtfully.

'And sometimes we have to stop waiting for the wrong thing – the thing that will never happen – and move on to the right thing that is God's plan for us. Like Alec with Margaret. That turned out well for them. I believe they had a long and happy marriage.'

Gina was floundering. What was her grandmother telling her? Should she wait patiently for Hugo, like her grandmother had done for her grandfather? Gina sighed. She was not like her grandmother. She did not have that solid backbone of faith and trust in the Lord. Her faith was pretty wobbly and all too on-and-off to sustain her.

Maybe instead, she should simply give up and move on, like Ould Alec did finally – no matter how much it hurt. She would be better off going for that job in Dundee and taking herself away from the sight of Hugo and Mandy. No doubt Mandy would be round soon enough to crow over her triumph.

Gina realised with a start that her grandmother had come over to her chair and was dropping a kiss on her head.

'I'm going to bed now,' Hannah said. 'Take it to the Lord, my dear. He'll help you with what you need to do.'

CHAPTER 44

It was a fine Saturday afternoon. Down at the bottom of their garden, Joyce was opening the gate out into the lane. She had often taken Robbie out for walks when he was little, but as he grew and became stronger and more self-willed, it had become more difficult. Under Alec's encouragement, she was now initiating more outings and today she would have Gina with her for support.

'Shall we go and take a look at the Monument, Robbie?' Joyce asked. 'It's a nice walk.'

Robbie clapped his hands in approval and the three of them set off along the cliff-top path that led to the North Baths swimming pool and beyond to the tower that commemorated the battles Caithness men had fought in before the twentieth century.

It was a fine day and down in the open-air swimming pool, refreshed by water from the sea, children were splashing and having fun. Robbie stopped, his eyes fixed on the cheerful sight. He beamed with pleasure and clapped his hands.

Joyce and Gina exchanged glances. Silhouetted against the sky on the cliff-top path, it would only be moments before a child spotted them. Someone would recognise him and very quickly Robbie might become the target of hostile eyes – or worse.

'Oh look!' Gina exclaimed loudly, pointing ahead on the path. 'Was that a rabbit?'

'Rabbit?' Robbie was instantly distracted. He loved animals so Gina's tactic was sure of success.

'I thought I saw a rabbit,' she laughed. 'Shall we go and see?'

As she hoped, Robbie was happy to continue along the path with her till they reached the slender tower on the headland that was their destination.

They walked slowly round it as Gina recited the names of the battles engraved on the panels: Camperdown, Trafalgar, The Nile, Waterloo, Salamanca, Lucknow, Alma, Inkerman, Sevastopol, Kandahar…

Robbie listened with delight.

'Shall I do it again?' Gina asked.

'Again!' Robbie shouted. 'Again!'

So Gina took his hand and together they circled the tower as she read out the names again.

'What now?' she asked. 'Mum, is it time to go home? Or shall we go a little further?'

Robbie looked around, and it was clear that his attention was still attracted by the bright colours and gleeful shouts of the children in the swimming pool.

'Oh, I wish we could go to the pool,' Joyce said, tears coming suddenly to her eyes. 'I used to love swimming when I was a child.'

Sadly she tried to turn Robbie away from the view of the pool and back towards the headland.

'Mum,' he protested, and turning back, pointed to where the families were gathered.

Joyce shook her head. 'I'm sorry, love. I don't think so.'

But Robbie was not happy to be thwarted and his happy smile was turning thunderous.

Joyce bit her lip. 'Gina…' she began.

'Robbie, darling, we haven't brought our bathing suits with us, or even any towels.'

He scowled and Gina laughed. 'Think how silly we'd look if we went swimming going into the water as we are, in all our clothes!' She waved her hands at her summer frock. 'And we'd be horribly uncomfortable walking home dripping wet afterwards, wouldn't we? We might even catch our death of cold. Achoo! Achoo!' She pretended loud sneezes that made Robbie laugh.

Joyce smiled gratefully at her daughter. Gina was so good with Robbie and knew how to distract him. Relieved that the momentary crisis was over, she said, 'I know what! Let's go home and have some tea. I think there are some scones…'

'Scones!' Robbie declared. 'I like scones.'

'So you do, so we'd better get home before your granny eats them all up!'

'Home!' Robbie agreed happily now and Joyce and Gina led him back to the house at a cheerful pace.

But Joyce's thoughts were far from cheerful. It was so unfair, she considered, that Robbie wasn't able to enjoy all the things other young men of his age were able to do. When he was younger, she had been too afraid of people's reactions to take him out much and now, with Alec's encouragement, she was trying to do more, but it was still difficult. Robbie had missed out on so much.

To her surprise, when they got home, Joyce found Alec deep in conversation with her mother.

'Alec!' she said, self-consciously running a hand through her windswept hair. 'I didn't know you were coming...'

'I hope you don't mind? It was a spur-of-the-moment thing.'

'Not at all,' Joyce smiled. 'We'd gone for a walk to the Monument.' She proudly indicated Robbie and Gina. 'The three of us.'

'Oh, that's nice,' Alec said. 'A little outing. Well, I was wondering...' He paused. 'I was just talking to your mother about it. The thing is I saw a notice that said Strawberts Brothers Circus is coming to town today and will be bringing elephants...'

'Elephants!' Robbie repeated the word excitedly. 'Elephants! I love elephants! Where are the elephants?'

'That's right,' Alec told him. 'Elephants.' He looked quickly to Joyce. 'The circus is arriving by train this afternoon. Someone said they would have to walk the elephants through the town to where the big top will be erected at the Riverside.'

'Elephants!' Robbie was in raptures.

'I wondered, if Robbie would like...' Alec paused.

'Yes! Yes!' Robbie shouted.

'We could take him to see the elephants,' Alec continued, his eyes fixed on Joyce.

Joyce's eyes filled with tears. This would be an opportunity to give Robbie a very special experience.

'Oh Alec,' she said, 'what a wonderful idea. That is so kind. If you're sure?'

'I think so,' Alec said. 'I think we should try?'

Joyce nodded, her throat choked with emotion at the kindness of this man. If she had ever had any doubt of his acceptance of Robbie and kindness towards him, this surely removed every trace.

But, she remembered sadly, there was still the problem of Young Alec.

CHAPTER 45

Over tea and scones, the proposed trip was eagerly discussed. Alec had clearly thought about where to park the car so they would be well-placed to see the elephants making their progress from the station to the Riverside. Finally, he looked at his watch.

'I think we should be going.'

Robbie clapped his hands excitedly. 'Let's go!' he exclaimed. 'Elephants! Go see the elephants!'

Alec helped Joyce into the back seat of the Mini, then looked at Gina. 'Are you coming with us?' he asked.

She shook her head. 'Thank you, but no. I think I'll just wander down town under my own steam.'

'OK,' Alec said. 'We'll maybe see you there.'

Gina watched as he helped Robbie into the front seat; then she set off down the street towards the centre of town. She hoped with all her heart that it would be a successful outing but she feared that Robbie was becoming over-excited. Surely though, with Alec to help her mother, everything would turn out all right? And in any case, it was a good idea for Alec to understand what her mother faced with Robbie. If he sincerely cared about her… And she rather thought he did.

She sighed. Lucky Mum. It would be nice for her to have someone to care about her. And suddenly she realised that in Hugo, Mandy would have someone to care for her now. Poor Mandy – she'd never really had much luck. It seemed as though Mandy was never wanted. Her mother always had other things to do. And even when Ruby married Hugo's father, Mandy kept being sent off to her grandmother's house in Lybster. Her own failed marriage, all those hopeless relationships, the men she chased after – poor Mandy, always searching for love.

Gina swallowed hard. Maybe she was being selfish. Maybe Mandy needed Hugo – more than she did. She fought back the pain and concentrated on finding a good place to see the elephants.

At last they appeared. They were not the huge towering elephants of her imagination but quite small ones, processing in a line, each elephant holding in its trunk the tail of the one in front. Children exclaimed in excitement and waved, and the elephants plodded sedately down the street from the railway station towards the bridge in the centre of town.

It was a happy sight, full of noise and delight, but Gina became aware of a sharper, louder noise. She recognised it at once. It was her brother Robbie. His excitement had risen with the crowd's and he was shouting out loudly.

'Elephants! Elephants!'

Gina strained to see where he was standing in case her mother needed any help. As the people around Robbie pulled back in dismay, she could see him, clapping his hands and jumping up and down in excitement. Then suddenly as the elephants came past, he surged out of the crowd towards them.

'Elephants!' Robbie cried and reached out to touch the nearest elephant.

It was as if the world froze and everyone held their breath. Gina found she had shut her eyes in horror. People would say he wasn't being kept under control, that he wasn't fit to be allowed out, that he had to be locked up. Would someone get the police? Would he be taken away? It would be terrible. Her mother would be devastated.

She forced her eyes open and was surprised to see that everything was calm. There were now two other men standing in the middle of the road with the elephants, where a moment ago it had only been Robbie. One of the men was Alec Gunn and the other was clearly the keeper in charge of the elephants. They seemed to be talking together in a pleasant manner. The keeper didn't even seem to mind that Robbie was patting one of the elephants, who also seemed completely unconcerned.

Gina slid out of her place and moved quietly up the lines of watching people to where her mother was standing, hand clamped over her mouth, her eyes wide with anxiety.

Gina put her arm round her mother and leaned close.

'I'm here, Mum,' she said. 'Don't worry. Alec's got it covered.'

Together they strained to hear what was going on. They could see that the keeper was smiling. Robbie was beaming. Alec and the keeper shook hands. The keeper offered his hand to Robbie but Robbie simply engulfed him in a bear hug, from which the keeper emerged still smiling. Alec smiled and offered Robbie his hand, Robbie trustingly put his hand in Alec's, and the pair made their way back to where Joyce and Gina were waiting.

The keeper called after them, 'See you later, young man!'

Robbie waved delightedly.

'Elephants!' he said to his mother and pointed as the elephants continued their slow procession across the bridge.

Gina became aware of mutterings in the crowd around them, hostile mutterings, and pointed fingers, just as Alec noticed them too.

'Let's get back to the car,' he said. 'Gina, are you coming? I don't think there's anything else to see...'

He swiftly led them out of the crowd and back towards the railway station where he had parked the car.

Joyce was nearly in tears.

'Oh Alec, I'm so sorry!' she said. 'Robbie...'

Alec turned to face her. He reached out and took her shoulders in his hands so she had to look at him.

'There is absolutely nothing to be sorry about,' he told her. 'We've had a nice outing with a little more excitement than we expected but it's all turned out well.'

He turned to Robbie. 'Hasn't it?' Alec asked him. 'You've had a nice time. *And* you've got another treat in store!'

Joyce stared at Robbie, who was smiling broadly, and then at Alec.

'What do you mean?' she asked.

'Robbie wanted to touch the elephants, didn't you?'

Robbie nodded enthusiastically. 'Elephants! Nice elephants!'

'So that's what he did.' Alec fixed Joyce with reassuring eyes. 'It was not a problem, my dear. In fact, the keeper was delighted and has offered Robbie the chance to visit the elephants when they're settled at the Riverside... and to help with them if he'd like to. That is, if you'd allow it?'

'The keeper... what?' Joyce gasped.

Robbie bounced up and down, beaming widely.

'Help. With elephants!' he said. 'Me help! With elephants!'

'And I'll be happy to take him,' Alec continued. 'If you'd permit. What do you say?'

Joyce's eyes shone. She leaned forward and kissed Alec on the cheek.

'What I say is that you're a good man, Alec Gunn. Thank you,' she said. 'Oh thank you!'

CHAPTER 46

It had been an interesting day, Hugo thought. He was well aware that Mandy was determined to show off to everyone in town that they were going out together. He didn't really mind. She treated him to smiles and batted eyelashes and had obviously set out to be an entertaining companion. It was quite amusing really and it kept his mind off the troubles at work.

Now as they ambled back towards the bus station, Hugo was surprised to see that crowds of people had gathered.

'What's going on?' Hugo asked.

He gestured to where crowds were lining the streets. A faint cheer rose in the direction of the railway station. But instead of the sweet curiosity he expected in response, Mandy sneered.

'Oh no!' she said. 'Some royal body turning up and expecting the peasants to cheer and kowtow.'

His surprised silence got her attention.

'I suppose you Canadians are terribly patriotic?' she asked in a decidedly patronising tone.

'I suppose we are,' Hugo said, thinking of his grandmother's collection of royal picture books. 'I thought you British were too?'

He remembered that excellent double-page spread Gina had written about the royal visit just that week. He had heard lots of praise for it and it clearly revealed the interest in and enthusiasm for the Royal Family among their readership.

But Mandy was distracted by the sight of the first elephant leading the procession down the street.

'Good grief!' she exclaimed. 'It's an elephant! What on earth is an elephant doing in Wick?'

'Ah, I think I saw a notice about a circus coming to town,' Hugo said, remembering the galley proofs he had scanned the other day. 'Would you like to go to the circus? It could be fun. We could go one evening...'

'Me?' Mandy said, horror in her voice. 'You can't be serious. Circuses are for kids. And they're smelly and full of animals...'

Hugo was confused. Surely the little girl he remembered would be delighting in the sight of elephants and the chance to go to the circus? He sighed. It seemed the little girl had grown up, and sadly the grown-up version had grown out of the younger one's enthusiasms and delight in the world.

He made no comment but simply watched the little procession come closer. The small elephants linked trunk to tail were rather charming. He hoped there was someone with a sharp eye taking good photographs for the newspaper. It would make a good picture. Swiftly he scanned the crowd to check.

And at that moment Robbie stepped out of the crowd and surged towards the elephants, reaching out a hand to stroke the one nearest to him. Before Hugo could react, Mandy was exclaiming loudly.

'Ugh!' she said in disgust. 'What's *he* doing here? He's not fit to be let out. I've said it all along. They should have put him away at birth. That's what you do with people like that.' Her revulsion was tangible.

But Hugo was watching the surprising scene unfolding. The keeper was speaking pleasantly to Robbie, even encouraging him to stroke the elephant. Then the man he had met with Joyce at the concert came forward, not to drag Robbie away in embarrassment, but to support him.

There was some conversation that quite clearly ended to everyone's satisfaction. The keeper and Alec Gunn shook hands. Robbie engulfed the keeper in a bear hug. Hugo remembered being the recipient of just such an enthusiastic embrace a few days earlier. Then the keeper turned back to his task, Alec gave Robbie his hand and unhurriedly they returned to the crowd.

Hugo could see Robbie's mother, Joyce, waiting in the crowd, her face a picture of alarm and distress. But Gina was there, with her arm round Joyce. And she was neither alarmed not embarrassed. She was supporting her mother steadily. Hugo saw her give Alec a grateful smile before the four moved away from the crowd.

He realised Mandy was speaking impatiently.

'Let's get out of here,' she was saying.

'That was Robbie,' Hugo said. 'Wasn't it? You know him, don't you?'

But Mandy brushed his question off.

'Not to say know,' she said dismissively. 'You can't *know* somebody like that.'

CHAPTER 47

Mandy was furious. That dreadful Robbie had spoiled her day. Up till that point, she had thought her strategy was working rather well. She had wheedled lunch out of Hugo and then she had guided him on a nice public promenade around town. It was a busy Saturday afternoon so she could be sure everyone would see them.

She had just been thinking how to extend the afternoon into the evening when those dratted elephants turned up. And Robbie! He should never have been allowed out, let alone make a spectacle of himself like that. If she was not careful, the conversation might have turned to the Sinclair family, and Gina. And that was something she did not want. Out of sight and out of mind was where she wanted Gina as far as Hugo was concerned.

On reflection she thought she had averted the danger. A swift change of subject and she had set herself to be witty and entertaining for the rest of the afternoon.

But Hugo had noticed. Mandy's reactions to the elephants and then to Robbie had surprised and disappointed him.

Trying to be fair to the lovely child he remembered, he wondered if she was simply one of those people who could not cope with disability in others. And in contrast he found himself recalling the obvious love and support Gina had shown to her mother and her brother. It was confusing. It didn't feel right.

He didn't have the time or the energy for puzzles so he simply smiled at Mandy's determined attempts at repartee and then, ignoring her protests, steered her to the early bus back to her grandmother's in Lybster.

'But I thought we might go...' she started to protest, with her prettiest smile, batting the carefully mascaraed eyelashes.

'To the circus.' Hugo found himself finishing off her sentence, knowing full well it was not at all what she meant to say. He watched her face and saw her eyes narrow.

Suddenly he had had enough of Mandy's company for one day.

'But you didn't want to go to the circus,' he reminded her. 'Dirty, smelly, and full of animals,' he repeated her words. 'Obviously not your scene.' He schooled his face to innocent blandness. 'So I thought you'd want to get home.'

She pouted. There was no other word for it, and Hugo felt the tug of memory as he looked at her face. But which of the two little girls had pouted like that? He brushed away the question and determinedly helped Mandy on to the bus.

'I'm not sure what I'm doing over the next few days,' he told her. 'I'll be in touch and we'll go somewhere more your style.'

As he turned away, he realised he had no idea what that would be. And the memory of those two little girls, he had to admit, had become rather fuzzy.

All he could be sure of was that Gina was George St Clair's daughter. That surely was all he needed to know. He took a deep breath and strode away.

CHAPTER 48

'Is Robbie ready?'

Alec Gunn, true to his word, had returned to the house in Willowbank at six o'clock to take Robbie down to the circus campsite where he had been invited to help get the elephants ready for that evening's performance.

Robbie was bouncing up and down in excitement, muttering 'Elephants!' over and over.

'Are you sure you want to do this?' Joyce fretted. 'Alec…'

Alec smiled. 'I'm sure,' he told her. 'It's a God-given opportunity. Don't you worry, I'll bring him back safe and sound, and maybe another night, we might go as a group to one of the performances?'

Gina came downstairs looking embarrassed.

'Mum thought…' she began. 'Please don't be offended but Robbie's used to me, and Mum thought it might be a good idea if I came along too. Just in case. I'll keep out of the way if I'm not needed.'

Alec glanced swiftly at Joyce.

'Please,' Joyce said. 'I'd feel more comfortable knowing Gina's with you. She knows how to manage Robbie when things get difficult.'

'I hope that won't be necessary,' Alec said. 'I'd like to think Robbie will be fine with me, but if it will put your mind at ease, then of course Gina comes with us.'

Robbie clapped his hands and stepped towards Alec.

'Elephants?' he queried. 'Go see the elephants?'

'That's right, my lad,' Alec said, with a reassuring smile to Joyce. 'Off we go!'

Down at the Riverside, the big top was already in place: pennants fluttered from the tall poles, and the striped material of the huge tent was bright in the early evening sunshine. All around, circus people were moving purposefully about their chores.

Alec found a corner to park the Mini and helped first Robbie, then Gina out. There was noise and smells and bustle and Robbie looked round excitedly.

'Isn't this fun?' Gina said, taking his arm. 'Shall we go and find the elephants?'

'Elephants!' Robbie repeated. 'Yes.'

Alec attracted the attention of one of the circus hands.

'We're looking for the elephants,' he said. 'The keeper said we could...'

'Ah,' the young man responded with a smile for Robbie. 'You're going to help with them tonight, aren't you? Jim told us they were having a visitor. I'll show you the way.' And he led them through a maze of caravans, the grass criss-crossed by fat electric cables and tent-ropes, to an area where large metal cages were lined up in a long row. Roars and growls came from the cages.

'Lions and tigers,' the young man said cheerfully. 'They're perfectly safe if you know what you're doing – and that means not going visiting without one of us,' he told Robbie with mock sternness.

Robbie laughed delightedly.

The big cats were beautiful, their skins glossy, and their eyes gleamed as Alec, Robbie and Gina walked past. Suddenly a young boy appeared from round the corner of the cages with a strange animal on a rope. It was big and white and fluffy, with a longish neck and dainty long legs, picking its way delicately behind the lad.

'It's a llama,' said the young man who was guiding them. 'Have you seen one before?'

They all three shook their heads and watched with fascination as the boy got the llama to run, prancing proudly alongside him.

At last they reached the tent where the elephants were housed.

'Jim!' the young man called and the keeper appeared at once. His face cracked in a wide grin and he held out his hand to Robbie.

'Ah,' he said, 'my young helper.'

'Yes, yes!' Robbie said, ignoring the hand and giving the keeper a bear hug.

The keeper laughed as he extricated himself. 'And this is your dad?' He turned to Alec, again offering his hand. 'Good to see you again.'

Alec hesitated. 'Unfortunately, that's not my privilege. Shall we just say I'm a friend of the family.' He cast a quick glance at Gina. 'For now.'

Gina gave him an approving smile.

Alec shook the outstretched hand, then continued, 'And this is Robbie's sister, Gina.'

'Pleased to meet you, Miss,' the elephant keeper said. 'Are you interested in elephants too or would you like to have a wander round while I get your brother to do some work?'

Gina looked at the group in front of her. Robbie was beaming happily, Alec seemed content and in command, and the keeper seemed to know what he was doing. She hesitated.

The keeper stepped a little closer to Gina so he could speak quietly. 'My own brother was like yours, Miss,' he said. 'We used to work with the elephants together till he got ill and died. It's a treat to do something for this young man. He's safe with me.'

Gina saw the sincerity in his eyes, and his sadness.

'Thank you,' she said. 'I'm happy to leave Robbie with you.' She grinned at her brother. 'I'll be back and I'll want to know you've made yourself really useful!'

Robbie laughed, and turned away importantly into the elephant enclosure with the men.

Gina choked back the emotion that welled up in her. There was such kindness and goodness in the world. So many good people. Her grandmother was right. God was good and brought good things out of what seemed bad at the time. Her gaze strayed over the circus campsite. She had never expected to find herself in such a fascinating place – and it was all thanks to Robbie doing something that had horrified her at the time!

And then she froze. Surely that was Hugo over beside the big top. No, it couldn't be! What could he be doing here? She strained her eyes. It looked like Hugo and, to her dismay, it seemed he had seen her.

Why did he have to be here and spoil everything? What was she going to do? Where could she hide?

She heard the lions roar from the cage behind her. Where could she hide safely amongst all these wild animals?

CHAPTER 49

It was definitely Gina.

Hugo realised she had seen him and was looking around wildly – for a way to escape, he was sure of it. It seemed to be her automatic reaction to him. But she had not chosen a good place. Behind her, in a neat row, were the big metal cages of the fierce wild animals: lions, tigers…

What on earth was she doing here? If Mandy didn't see going to the circus as a treat, surely George St Clair's daughter wouldn't be interested in such simple entertainment either? He turned to walk away. He had come on a whim. Mandy's dismissal of the circus had stirred his own memories and he had decided he might enjoy going to a performance on his own. All he had to do was find the ticket office.

But he found himself slowing down and ducking under a couple of tent-ropes so he could circle round and see what Gina was up to. To his annoyance, there was no sign of her. She was an infernal nuisance! If she had come in search of a story for the newspaper and got herself hurt through her carelessness, then his insurance would have to pay out. He would soon put a stop to that! All he had to do was find her.

Where was she likely to have gone? Where could she get a story? And he remembered Robbie's delight in the elephants as they were walked through the town. And he knew. She must have brought Robbie to see the elephants again. He'd bet his bottom dollar that's where he'd find them. With the elephants.

Hugo made his way to the elephant enclosure, keeping an eye out for Gina. From inside he heard voices – an excited loud voice that belonged to Robbie, and two deeper, older, male voices.

He looked into the enclosure and saw Robbie helping to wash one of the elephants. He had a long-handled broom and a bucket of water and he and the elephant were enjoying the splashing mess they were making.

As Hugo watched, the elephant sucked up some water from the bucket and squirted it at Robbie. Robbie dropped the broom and clapped his hands in delight.

'I love you!' he cried and pushed his face into the wet side of the elephant.

The only other occupants of the enclosure were a man who was clearly the keeper and Alec Gunn, the man who had been with Joyce at the concert. Hugo remembered how earlier in the day, he had stepped in when Robbie rushed out of the crowd to pat the elephants as they were being led through town. So somehow he was part of the family. But where was Gina?

The keeper caught sight of Hugo and came over.

'Can I help you, sir?' he asked politely enough, but Hugo could see there was a clear warning in his attitude.

Hugo held his hands up. 'I was just having a little look around.' He gestured to Robbie. 'He seems to be enjoying himself.'

'Oh, he has a way with animals,' the keeper said.

Alec Gunn came to join them, positioning himself alongside the keeper, almost like a defensive barrier between him and Robbie.

What was this? He hadn't said anything out of order, but still these two were ranged against him, clearly protecting Robbie.

'OK,' Hugo said and turned to leave, cannoning straight into a soft body coming at speed from the opposite direction and bouncing off him with a yelp.

'Oh no!' Gina said, her distress clearly visible. 'Not you again!'

'I think,' Hugo said, 'this is where we came in.'

CHAPTER 50

'I rather think this is where you'll be leaving,' Alec Gunn said to Hugo, exchanging a glance with the elephant keeper.

'Boys!' The keeper barely raised his voice and a trio of burly lads with pitchforks appeared at his side.

'OK, OK,' Hugo said. 'I'm leaving.'

'Good,' Gina said under her breath, but not so soft that Hugo didn't hear it.

'Gina!' another voice said loudly.

The human barrier in front of Hugo parted to let Robbie through. He flung wet arms round Gina.

'Gina!' Robbie carolled. 'Come and play! Elephants!'

Then he caught sight of Hugo. 'Hu-go! My friend Hu-go!' He reached for Hugo's hand and tugged. 'Come! Elephants!'

'Robbie knows you?' the keeper asked. Keen eyes assessed him.

'Yes,' he said, choosing his words with precision. 'My family have known the St Clairs from way back.'

'We didn't get a chance to be properly introduced the other night,' Alec Gunn said. 'I'm a farmer from out of Wick and a friend of the family. My son is teaching Gina to drive. And where are you from?'

'Canada,' Hugo said, trying to take in Alec's information. So was the young man he had seen with Gina a driving instructor? Hugo forced himself to concentrate. 'I'm from Manitoba... Though my dad's folks came from here originally.'

'And you're in Wick on business or looking up old friends?'

Long ago, before the devastation that George St Clair had created, Hugo knew he would have counted Gina and her family, as well as Mandy, among his friends. But he knew too much now.

'Business,' Hugo answered decisively. 'I have few friends left in the town.'

Gina flinched, the colour rising in her cheeks.

'I believe you were just going, Mr Mackay,' Alec Gunn said quietly. He turned to Robbie. 'Robbie, take Gina to meet your elephants.'

'Gina?' Robbie said.

'Yes, darling,' she said, smiling at him. 'I'd love to meet your elephant friends.'

Hugo relinquished Robbie's hand to Gina, who barely glanced at him as she passed between the protective human barrier that re-formed behind her even more tightly than before. Hugo looked at the men standing there, watchful and clearly willing to take action if needed.

Alec Gunn said abruptly, 'If you would be so good...' and he gestured to the doorway.

Hugo took the hint and left.

CHAPTER 51

When he had put a safe distance between himself and the elephant enclosure, Hugo felt the need to look back. Quickly he checked that the human barricade had dispersed, then he allowed himself a moment to stand and observe.

It was completely obvious that both brother and sister were enjoying splashing about with the elephants. Gina's face was alive with delight and laughter as Robbie clowned around with beaming face. She seemed completely at ease with her brother, enjoying his company and the elephants, unfazed by the mess and the water. Her hair was soaked into rats' tails, yet still she laughed. It wasn't what he'd expected. He compared Mandy's reaction to the circus. It was all rather confusing.

Thinking back, he had to admit he did not remember Robbie at all. Hugo racked his brains as he set off walking again. Did he remember another child? His pace slowed as he thought back. Surely there had only been Gina – Georgie as she was then – and Amanda? The two little girls. He could picture them as he had known them, playing, squabbling, laughing – but only two of them.

And surely it had been Amanda who had laughed and played and Georgie who had squabbled and sulked? It had to have been.

But today it was Mandy whose reactions had been sulky. If he had not managed things so well, their day together would surely have ended in a squabble. And now here was Gina laughing with Robbie, heedless of the state she was in.

Admittedly the short period of his life that he had spent in Scotland was now only a confused mass of impressions. He had been 13, in a foreign country, and suddenly without anyone to care for him. Ruby, his brand-new stepmother – whom he had disliked from the start – had run off with Gina's father. Both of them had been killed in that accident on Berriedale Brae when their car went over the cliff.

And then there was the personal disaster of his own father dying. Hugo had always thought his father had died of a broken heart. Not simply for Ruby, but for everything in his life that had come to naught, all the sorrows and disasters piling on to him till he couldn't take it any longer.

Hugo closed his eyes and gripped the nearest support. A snarl made his eyes snap open and he realised he had got himself into the area with the animal cages. He was holding on to a bar of a lion's cage. Hurriedly he removed his hand.

'Very wise, Mr Mackay,' said a soft voice.

It was the elephant keeper who now came to stand beside him. The man pointed to the lion, who was pacing backwards and forwards in the cage, his gleaming eyes fixed on the two men.

'Circuses can be dangerous places,' the man said. 'We lost a keeper to that lion a few years back. He didn't really know his job, was too confident, got too close…' He shrugged.

Hugo considered the warning. 'What's it to you?' he asked curiously. 'Robbie, and Gina?'

The man continued gazing into the lion's cage.

'I had a brother like Robbie. My little brother,' he said, letting the words sink in. 'I wouldn't want any harm to come to Robbie… or his family.' He turned and fixed sharp black eyes on Hugo. 'You understand me?'

Harm, Hugo thought. People seemed to jump to this idea that he was likely to bring harm to the family. But all he had done was uncover Gina's dishonesty – at the conference, and at the newspaper where she had got herself a job she did not deserve. How could that possibly be considered causing harm? The girl might have kindness for her brother, but in everything else she was rotten through and through – like her father before her.

Hugo squared his shoulders. He had nothing to be ashamed of.

'Animals are a lot simpler than human beings,' he said. 'At least with animals' – he gestured to the lion – 'what you see is what you get.'

CHAPTER 52

'Sometimes I think mealtimes here are more like feeding time at the zoo!' Hannah chided gently.

'Or the circus,' Gina laughed.

'You'd think there was going to be a famine in the land!' Hannah teased Robbie.

He grinned and ignored her, continuing to stuff huge portions of food into his mouth.

'And is that all you're going to have?' Hannah asked her daughter pointedly.

Joyce simply smiled and sipped her tea, the toast and marmalade on her plate barely touched.

Hannah exchanged a glance with her granddaughter. Gina grinned. It was nice to see her mother happy, and possibly in love?

'So what is everyone doing today?' Hannah asked.

'Alec…' Joyce began.

'Elephants!' Robbie shouted.

'One at a time,' Hannah decreed with a smile.

'Elephants!' Robbie won.

'You had a lovely time with the elephants yesterday, didn't you?' Gina said to him. She smiled at her mother and grandmother. 'We both had a lovely time with the elephants.'

Until Hugo turned up. The memory of his implacable hostility hurt deeply. Swiftly she smothered the feeling. She would not think about that man!

'Are you going to see them again today?' Hannah asked.

'Yes! Yes!' Robbie said.

'Alec thought we might go to the matinee, if we can get some quiet seats,' Joyce said.

'Oh, that would be nice…' Hannah began.

'All of us,' Joyce said. 'He's inviting all of us.'

'I'm too old for the circus,' Hannah protested.

'And you'd have more fun without us,' Gina put in.

'But I'd like you all to come!' Joyce insisted.

'Circus!' Robbie announced excitedly. 'Go to the circus!'

'Well, that's clear. Robbie must go. And you too, Gina. You'd enjoy it.'

And so it was decided, with Hannah adamant that she was too old to clamber into the seats at the circus and would be much happier at home waiting to hear all about it.

When the family returned, with Alec Gunn in tow, they were in high spirits. It took Hannah some time to disentangle the tumbled stories.

'A kangaroo?' she queried at one point. 'There was a kangaroo?'

Robbie was demonstrating the bouncing kangaroo, jabbing mock punches.

'Yes, indeed,' Joyce said. 'A boxing kangaroo.' And they all dissolved into laughter.

178

The outing had been a huge success. They had seen lions and tigers and a high-wire act and pretty ponies, the big white fluffy llama, several clowns and, for Robbie the highlight of the show, his friends the elephants.

'I must be going,' Alec broke in. 'I've had a lovely time. Thank you all for your company.' He caught Joyce's eye.

'I'll come out to the car with you,' she said, and they left Robbie and Gina telling Hannah more details of their outing.

'I did enjoy it,' Alec assured Joyce as they stepped outside. 'Robbie is a good lad.' He faced Joyce. 'I don't have a problem with him. You know that.'

'I know. It was a great treat for us all.'

'Robbie loves animals, doesn't he? And he's good with them...'

'Yes,' Joyce said.

'What would you think to him coming out to the farm to see how he gets on there? We've got cattle and sheep, as well as a couple of old horses, chickens, dogs and cats...' Alec said.

'I think he'd enjoy that,' Joyce said. 'And he's comfortable with you...'

'I hope you are too?' Alec said with a smile.

Joyce blushed.

'Aye, well,' Alec said, pleased. 'I know you said you had to think of your family. Let's see how Robbie gets on at the farm. Maybe it will help your decision.' He squeezed Joyce's hand.

'But what about Young Alec?' Joyce asked anxiously. 'He's not comfortable with Robbie...'

Alec's face was sombre. 'Please don't misjudge him,' he said. 'It's not Robbie that's the problem. It's something that happened a long way back when he was young.'

He sighed heavily. 'We had a young cousin, the same as Robbie. He and Alec were inseparable. When he died – it was a chest thing

179

and very sudden – Alec was inconsolable. Coming upon Robbie so suddenly, unexpectedly, brought it all back.'

'Oh, I see,' Joyce said. 'Oh, poor lad!'

'He was afraid of seeing Robbie again, of the grief again... But I'm thinking he actually needs Robbie – to help him get over his grief.' Alec searched Joyce's face for understanding. 'I feel very deeply that the good Lord has brought us all together so we can help each other. What do you think?'

'What I think,' Joyce said slowly, 'is that you're a good man, and I think you could be right.'

'I'd like Robbie to come to the farm,' Alec said. 'I know my son. He's a good lad. I'd like to give him and Robbie a chance.'

Joyce took a deep breath. 'I'll trust you, Alec, and the Lord,' she said with a smile. 'And we'll take that chance.'

Alec let out a pent-up breath. He smiled.

'Then I'll come over the day after tomorrow if that would work for you both?'

'Yes. Thank you,' Joyce said. 'That would be fine.'

'Mid-morning?'

She nodded and Alec waved before driving off.

She stood for a moment on the pavement watching the little red car vanish down the street. There was sudden tremulous hope budding in her heart. If Alec was right about his son, was it possible that there might be a future for Robbie at the farm? He did love animals...

And if there was a future for Robbie there, then could there be a future for her?

But what about Gina? And her mother? They said they would be perfectly happy continuing to live together in the house in Willowbank – but what if Gina wasn't reinstated in her job? What if she got that job in Dundee? What then?

Joyce paused for a moment before she returned to the house. If God could sort things out between Young Alec and Robbie, and give them a future, then she was confident He could sort things out for Gina too.

She sent up a swift 'thank You, and thank You in advance' prayer and returned to the house smiling.

CHAPTER 53

Buenos Aires, Argentina

'What are we going to do with this?'

Catalena Hernandez Cormack's oldest brother Rodolfo waved a hand at the box they had unearthed in the bottom of their late mother's wardrobe.

'Why on earth would she hang on to this?' her sister Carolina asked. 'It's got nothing to do with us – or her.'

'Throw it out then,' said youngest brother Federico.

In the aftermath of their mother's death, the siblings had started clearing her home and sharing out keepsakes and possessions. But this box with its strange collection of apparently worthless items, some completely unrelated to the family, had baffled them.

Cat was glad that she had managed to get back to Argentina in time to sit with her mother in the last days of her life. Her brothers and sister had welcomed her and shared the funeral arrangements and now there was this last job to do before she could get back to Scotland and to her beloved Danny.

She looked around her mother's bedroom, remembering the times she had clambered up on the bed and been welcomed in a scented, loving embrace. Often her father had already gone out, but if she had woken in the middle of the night with a nightmare and clambered into their bed, he too had been loving and welcoming.

She sighed. She had been blessed with a happy childhood. The only shadow had been her half-brother, Jorge, or George as he was known in Wick. He had broken her mother's heart, Cat knew. But she herself had gone on loving the increasingly estranged black-sheep brother.

If he had not gone to Wick and caused such devastation there, ending in his own death, she herself would never have met Danny and found such happiness. Strange, that she had her brother to thank for that.

She rummaged in the box they had found. A zarzuela programme from 1900. Some bonbon wrappers. A betting ticket from the Jockey Club. There were a few other keepsakes – the kind that young girls treasure. And at the bottom a battered old black-covered missal. As Cat reached for it, she saw that no, it was not a missal. It was a Bible. In English.

The little book was very much the worse for wear, its pages discoloured from many a soaking. Written in careful faded pencil on the flyleaf were the words, 'Hugh Mackay, from his mother', and the date 1897.

Cat thought back to Danny's latest letter. He had invited the new owner of his newspaper to stay in their guest room. And that new owner was Hugo Mackay – grandson of the Hugh Mackay who had been given this Bible. It was a strange coincidence that it should surface now in the bottom of her mother's wardrobe in Buenos Aires.

'I know whose Bible this is,' Cat said. 'I'll take it back with me.' She looked up at her brothers and sister. 'If that's all right with you? You're right, it isn't ours. As far as I know, it doesn't have anything to do with our family.'

'Take it,' Rodolfo said with a shrug.

'Yes,' the others agreed.

'What about these?' Rodolfo had dug further into the box and brought out a sheaf of letters. He unfolded one and read briefly, turning to the last page and scanning quickly. 'These aren't anything to do with us, either,' he said, handing them over to Cat.

Cat looked at the first letter. The address it came from was 2 Wellington Street, Wick, and the letter had been written in English by a young unformed hand.

'*Dear Hughie,*' it began.

Like her brother, Cat turned to the last page and read the salutation: '*Missing you terribly, my darling Hughie. I can't wait for you to have struck gold so we can be together. Your loving fiancée, Belle.*'

Belle? Cat searched her memory. Wasn't Belle her mother-in-law Hannah's sister? Belle had died in childbirth. But she had been married to Rab, not a Hughie…

She folded the letter and put it with the others in the back of the Bible.

'I think I know who these should go to. The girl who wrote these letters died, but her sister is very much alive. She's my mother-in-law!' Cat smiled. 'She's a lovely lady and she'll know what to do with these things.'

CHAPTER 54

Hannah looked at her family sitting around the breakfast table. It seemed that only Robbie was his usual self as he cheerfully shovelled huge spoonfuls of soggy cornflakes into his mouth. It was interesting that Joyce wasn't noticing the mess he was making or fussing and mopping up as usual. In fact she was absent-mindedly nibbling toast topped with Hannah's homemade crowdie. It seemed that her anxiety about her relationship with Alec had disappeared and in its place was a new contentment.

Gina, however, was visibly unhappy. She was half-heartedly opening her letters, scanning their contents and then setting them aside in a pile, her face more downcast with each one. Hannah caught her eye, an enquiring lift to her eyebrow.

'Replies,' Gina said despondently. 'To my applications for jobs.'

As she pushed the pile away from her, it fell to the floor and Robbie, dropping his spoon with a resounding clatter and splash into his cornflakes bowl, nearly fell off his chair as he made a dive for the letters.

'Letters!' he said, triumphantly grabbing them.

'Give them to Gina,' his mother instructed automatically.

But Robbie clutched them to his milk-spattered jumper, his face a picture of defiance.

'Robbie!' Joyce said. 'Please!'

'It's all right, Mum,' Gina said. 'Robbie can have them. He'll get as much good out of them as me, probably more.' She managed a wan grin at her brother. 'You keep the letters, Robbie. You have them.'

Her brother's face cracked into a wide grin.

'Letters!' he repeated. 'Mine!'

'No good?' Joyce asked her daughter quietly.

'No,' Gina said. She shrugged helplessly. 'I even applied for that job as a garage clerkess! And I couldn't get that!' She swallowed hard. 'So that's the lot for now… except for…'

'Which one?' her mother prompted.

'The reporter job in Dundee,' Gina said, looking sadly at her family. 'I don't want to leave you, but it's the only job I'm trained for. Not that I'm likely to get it. They said in the ad they wanted someone who could drive.'

'Is that what's worrying you, love?' Joyce asked. 'That because you haven't got your licence yet, you won't get the job? What did you say in your reply?'

'I said I was learning…'

'Well,' Joyce said, 'you *have* started learning…'

'And it's sweet of Young Alec, especially after the last time!' Gina commented wryly.

They all laughed, remembering Gina's rural exploits.

'He's said he's happy to continue the lessons a couple of days a week.' She shot a warning glare at her mother and grandmother. 'And don't even think there's any possibility of romance there! He's a nice lad but he's too young for me. And I don't fancy him in the least.'

She switched the topic neatly. 'What about you, Mum? You're going to the farm today, with Robbie, aren't you?'

'That's right,' Joyce said.

'Robbie will love that,' Gina said reassuringly.

'Yes, but Young Alec will be there. He and Robbie need to meet properly. Alec thought it would be a good idea and I agree. We have to give it a try.'

Joyce set aside the unfinished piece of toast. 'I must admit I am a little anxious. The farm will be Young Alec's one day,' she said. 'It's where he belongs.' She stood up, squaring her shoulders. 'And Robbie belongs with me, whatever happens.'

She picked up her plate and took it to the sink. Gina read the courage in her mother's frame. She admired her mother's dogged care for Robbie, never blaming him or his condition for the way her life had turned out.

But now, now surely, she would not have to sacrifice her last chance at happiness? Gina caught her grandmother's eye and knew she was thinking the same thing. But her grandmother had a serenity she could not feel. No doubt her grandmother would simply pray and leave it to her Lord to sort everything out.

Gina wished she had that kind of faith. She could do with the Lord taking a hand to sort things out for her!

CHAPTER 55

By the time Gina had left for work and Joyce had got Robbie into his outdoor clothes, Alec had arrived to carry them off for their day at the farm.

'Off you go, and see you enjoy yourselves,' Hannah told them. 'I'll be perfectly happy here at home.'

And though Alec tried to persuade her to join them, she would not be deterred. At last Alec got Robbie and Joyce into the Mini and Hannah waved them off.

She turned thoughtfully back to the house. Joyce was self-sacrificing and determined enough that if Young Alec could not find it in his heart to accept Robbie, Joyce would walk away from Middle Alec and her chance of a future with him. Gina was simply unhappy. It was clear that she loved Hugo *and* loved her job, but she could not see any way through to a happy ending.

At the moment neither could Hannah. But she knew Someone who did. Grateful for the silent, empty house, she settled into her accustomed armchair and the welcoming silence. When she rose an hour later, her heart was at peace. She knew her Lord had heard her prayers and she trusted Him to sort everything out in the way that would be best for each of them.

She had just put the kettle on when Cat appeared at the kitchen door.

'I did knock, but when I didn't get an answer, I just came in,' she said, and kissed her mother-in-law's cheek.

'Well, you're a surprise!' Hannah said with a delighted smile. 'Danny told us you were on your way back, but we didn't know when you'd arrive.'

'I got back last night,' Cat said. 'I flew into Prestwick, then managed to get a late train. I thought I'd pop round and see you.'

'I'm delighted,' Hannah said. 'Excellent timing!' She put an extra cup and saucer on the tray.

They went through to the sitting room and made themselves comfortable.

'I was sorry to hear that your mother had died,' Hannah said as she poured the tea and handed a cup to Cat. 'Though obviously it wasn't unexpected.'

'No. She had been ill for a while. I'm glad I got there in time.' She looked up at Hannah, a misty sadness in her eyes. 'And that I could stay and help my family with sorting things out.'

She sipped her tea, then set her cup down in its saucer. Leaning down from her armchair, she reached into her handbag and brought out a bulky brown envelope.

'I brought some things to show you,' she said. 'I wasn't sure what to do with them, but they're nothing to do with our side of the family, so I thought…'

'Your mother kept some of Geordie's things?' Hannah asked with dismay.

'No,' Cat said. 'Well, sort of…' She shook her head in annoyance at herself. 'I'm not making sense. Let me explain.'

She slid the contents of the envelope into her lap.

'My mother kept these. In a box in the bottom of her wardrobe. I can only assume they had been in Geordie's possession. But they are not his. They belong to…' She paused. 'Well, that's what I'm not sure of. The rights and wrongs of it.'

'So tell me,' Hannah said.

Cat rose and carried the contents of the envelope over to Hannah and deposited them in her lap.

'These are what we found,' she said. 'See what you think.'

Hannah looked at the little pile in her lap. She picked up the battered little Bible and stroked the cover.

'This has seen a pretty rough time of it,' she said.

Gently, she opened it and gasped as her eyes saw the pencilled inscription on the flyleaf.

'Hugh! 1897.' She looked across at Cat. 'But that's Hughie Mackay…'

And at once she saw again the scene at Wick railway station as Hughie and Geordie were leaving to make their fortune in the Klondike gold rush.

Hughie's mother had been there to see him off. Geordie Sinclair had said something mocking and Mrs Mackay had reached up to the carriage window and thrust… it must have been this Bible, into Hughie's hands. She had said something… Hannah reached into her memory. She had said something about reading it every day. And the Lord would look after him.

Hannah gazed sadly at the old Bible with its discoloured pages. Had Hughie ever read it? She hoped so.

'You've got Hugo staying with you,' Hannah said. 'This Bible belonged to his grandfather…'

'Ah yes,' Cat said. 'Our temporary lodger. I met him briefly last night. Danny explained who he was but I didn't have a chance to speak properly with him.' She smiled at Hannah. 'And anyway, I wanted to show you first. To talk to you about it and make sure I do the right thing.'

She gestured to the pile of letters that sat on Hannah's lap.

'Those were with the Bible. They are from...' Cat hesitated as Hannah's grey eyes fixed sharply on her.

'I'm sorry,' Cat said. 'They're from your sister Belle.'

CHAPTER 56

Hannah's hands trembled. She picked up the first letter and read what was written on the envelope.

'Yes,' she said. 'This is Belle's handwriting.'

She quickly checked through the other letters.

'Yes. They're Belle's letters to Hughie.'

Slowly she opened the letters one by one and scanned the contents, the sorrow in her face deepening with each one. At last she came to the end. She reached for her teacup and drained it.

'I thought since she was your sister you should have them,' Cat said.

'Thank you,' Hannah said quietly. 'But the Bible belongs to Hugo's family so it should be returned to him.'

'I'll do that,' Cat said. 'But what I don't understand is why my mother had them. How did they ever get to Buenos Aires? I knew Geordie St Clair had been up in the Klondike with Hugo's grandfather. And I know Hughie died there.'

She paused thoughtfully. 'I suppose Geordie took the Bible as a keepsake of his friend?'

Hannah sighed. 'Ah, my dear, it's not quite as straightforward – or nice – as that.'

She gestured at the letters piled in her lap.

'These letters. My sister Belle was secretly engaged to Hughie when he set out for the Klondike.' She smiled ruefully. 'Poor Hughie. I'm sure she persuaded him to go, so she could marry a rich man when he came back laden with Klondike gold. But it didn't work out the way she wanted.'

Hannah reached for the bottom letter on the pile and read aloud:

'*I never want to see you or hear from you again. As far as I'm concerned, there has never been anything between us. You can stay in Canada for ever with your dance-hall girl and your baby. Marry her instead of me. I don't want you.*'

'Oh!' Cat said. 'But how did Belle find out? Surely Hughie wouldn't have told her?'

'No,' Hannah agreed. 'That was Geordie St Clair's doing. He wrote and told Belle.'

'But why would Geordie have done that?'

'Because Geordie wanted Belle too,' Hannah said simply. 'Belle had sent him away with a flea in his ear – then had got secretly engaged to Hughie Mackay. And that rankled.'

'Oh, I see,' Cat said. 'So it was revenge? What happened then? Do you know?'

Hannah nodded. 'Nancy told me the whole story,' she explained. 'Remember we met Nancy at Hugh's funeral? Hugh's mother from Canada.' She paused, then added, 'She was the dance-hall girl.'

She watched Cat's eyes widen.

'Nancy?' she echoed. 'She was the dance-hall girl? Well... You'd never guess...'

'No,' Hannah agreed. 'You wouldn't.'

'So?' Cat prompted.

'When Hughie discovered what Geordie had done, he went out to the mine workings to have it out with him. They fought. There was a snowstorm, a blizzard. Geordie downed Hughie with a shovel, then fled, leaving him to die in the snow.'

'No!' Catalena gasped.

'He grabbed Nancy and held her hostage so he could get out of Dawson City alive. Hughie had relatives with a ranch in Manitoba.' Hannah gestured to the Bible and the letters. 'Geordie took Nancy there and made her pretend he was Hughie... He must have taken these with him. Maybe he thought they would back up his story.'

Cat listened wide-eyed.

'But the Alexanders saw through him,' Hannah added. 'They soon saw him off.'

'And from there he went to San Francisco, met my Uncle Federico, who took him home to Buenos Aires where he married my mother,' Catalena said, slowly piecing the story together. 'I see. And that's why my mother had those things. She doesn't speak English so I don't suppose she had any idea what they were.'

She looked questioningly at Hannah. 'I will, of course, return the Bible to Hugo.'

Hannah nodded her agreement. Cat looked at her mother-in-law with sudden anxiety in her eyes.

'Does Hugo know the whole story?' she asked. 'About his grandfather and Geordie St Clair?'

'I don't know,' Hannah said. 'It was Nancy's story to tell.'

'I'll have to say where I got the Bible,' Cat said. 'Oh dear, I'm worried it will just make things worse for Gina, stirring up the past. If Hugo knew...'

'If Hugo knew what?'

A harsh male voice broke across Catalena's words.

She gasped, turning to stare at Hugo. He had come silently into the room with Danny.

'If Hugo knew what?' Hugo repeated.

CHAPTER 57

Hannah held out the battered old Bible.

'This was given to your grandfather when he left Wick to go to the Klondike with Geordie Sinclair. I was there,' she told him. 'At the railway station. I saw your great-grandmother give it to him. Cat brought it back. We think you should have it.'

Hugo came forward and took the battered old book from her hand.

'Your great-grandmother instructed your grandfather to read it,' Hannah said with a gleam in her grey eyes. 'Maybe you'd like to honour her memory by doing that?'

Hugo nodded ironic appreciation of the comment. Then he turned to Catalena.

'So how did you come by it?' he asked. 'Why isn't it with my grandmother in Canada where it belongs? And what are you so worried about me knowing?'

'First things first,' Hannah said quietly. 'Cat?'

'My mother had it,' Cat said. 'I found it among her things when we were clearing her house. Our thinking...' She glanced at Hannah for support and confirmation. 'Our thinking is that her first husband – Geordie St Clair – had it in his possession when he died. And for some reason my mother held on to it.'

'And these letters,' Hannah said, holding up the small pile of letters.

Hugo's eyes flashed suspiciously. 'Whose letters?'

'From my sister Belle to your grandfather. They were engaged when he went out to the Klondike. Secretly engaged. But she broke it off.' Hannah nodded towards Catalena. 'Cat has returned them to me as Belle's next-of-kin.'

There was a moment of stillness while Hugo assimilated the information.

'I see,' he said finally. 'Yes, I can see the letters should go back to you, and the Bible to me, as last in the line. What I don't see is what Geordie was doing with them.' His sharp eyes raked the people before him. 'I also cannot imagine why you think that knowledge could possibly make things worse for Gina.'

'That depends on how much you know about *your* family background,' Hannah said quietly. 'Especially your grandfather's death?'

Hugo shrugged. 'Not a lot. Just that he died in the Klondike. I should imagine quite a lot of people did in those days. Conditions were harsh...'

'Ah,' Hannah said. She looked over at her son. 'Danny, perhaps you could help Hugo. The death notice was in *The Sentinel*. It should be in the 1899 papers, first half of the year.'

Danny nodded. 'Yes, I can easily find the bound copies for 1899. The old papers are in regular use.'

'I think you need to read that,' Hannah told Hugo. 'And if you have any questions, perhaps you'd like to come back and ask me – or, better still, your grandmother. Nancy was there, remember. She's the one with all the answers.'

And it was plain from the steely grey eyes that he was dismissed.

'Thank you,' Hugo managed to say, and allowed Danny to lead him away and back to the *Sentinel* office.

CHAPTER 58

'I have no idea what my mother is up to,' Danny said. 'But usually it's a good idea to just do what she says.'

Hugo laughed, but deep-seated anxiety was beginning to gnaw at him. Clearly Granny Cormack thought there was something important that he did not know. He did not like that. Not knowing was a rocky foundation... and he was beginning to feel his foundations less stable than he had thought. There was the conundrum that was Gina and Mandy. Could he have made a mistake about those two? And now this.

There was a big table underneath the bookshelf where the back copies of the newspaper were housed, bound year by year in huge black hardback covers. Danny soon found the correct year's papers and set the huge book on the table.

'I'll leave you to it,' he said and made himself scarce.

Hugo hesitated. What was it that all these people knew but he did not? What was the mystery and why did they think it would make things worse for Gina? Whatever it was, it had to have something to do with the Sinclairs. But what could possibly make him think worse of the Sinclair family than he did already?

Resolutely he turned the broadsheet pages, stopping in shock at a blaring headline:

WICK MAN MURDERED IN KLONDIKE
Killer escapes

He checked that the news report was indeed about his grandfather, and when he had verified it, he dropped into the chair at the table, thinking hard. 'Murdered.' His grandfather had been murdered.

He forced himself to read the details. And soon all was clear. Geordie Sinclair had killed his grandfather. There were reports of interviews with miners who had witnessed the fight between Hughie Mackay and Geordie Sinclair and seen Hughie left for dead. There were more interviews with townsfolk who saw Geordie make his getaway, with a hostage – a girl, an unnamed pregnant girl.

Hugo was reeling. He knew nothing of this. He started again from the beginning of the article, trying to match it with what he already knew or could guess. What was certain was that Geordie Sinclair was responsible for his grandfather's murder.

He sat back in the chair. Yes. It made things worse. Right from the start, the Sinclairs had been the Mackays' nemesis.

He became aware of a gentle floral perfume as someone paused behind his chair.

'Oh.' The voice was Gina's.

Hugo looked up to see Gina leaning over his shoulder scanning the article, her eyes wide with horror.

'Oh, indeed,' Hugo said. 'Seems the Sinclairs have been doing bad things to the Mackays for a long while.'

He heard her suck in a breath.

'Yeah,' she said in a wobbly voice. 'Well, you knew that. We're a bad lot.'

And she was gone.

CHAPTER 59

'I have got to leave!' Gina told her grandmother. 'More than ever! I have to get that job in Dundee and get away!'

It was Saturday morning after breakfast and Joyce and Robbie had been fetched by Alec for another day at the farm. After the success of the first visit, farm days had become a regular occurrence and a source of great delight to both Robbie and Joyce.

After they'd left, Gina and her grandmother had sat down for another cup of tea and a chat, and it had all come bursting out.

'Don't you see?' Gina said. 'My Sinclair forebears were bad people, rotten through and through. And that's all *he* can see – the harm and the damage they've done to his family for how many generations!' She sighed despairingly. 'It was there in the newspaper, in black and white, starting way back. Then there was my father and what he did to *his* father. And now there's me.'

'And why do you think that matters?' Hannah probed.

'What do you mean?' Gina looked at her in surprise. 'It's obvious: I'm the next Sinclair and he's the next Mackay, and I deceived him when we met in Aberdeen because I was pretending to be Mandy – not that I wanted to – and now he'll never trust me and…'

201

'Gina, stop and think!' her grandmother commanded.

Gina ground to a halt and stared at her grandmother.

'Breathe!' Hannah said firmly, but the twinkle was in her eye as she looked at Gina's upset face.

Gina did as she was commanded.

'Now, think. Calmly,' her grandmother said. 'First, you are correct about how your father and grandfather Sinclair behaved. But that's history. Past. Yes, Hugo is still bitter about what your father did to his father. But that wasn't you and has nothing to do with you. You didn't do any of it.'

'Yes but...' Gina's voice was small, an echo of her childhood. 'When I saw Hugo, back then when his father had died and I was just trying to be nice to him, he shouted at me.'

And suddenly Gina was in tears.

'He said he hated George Sinclair. Hated the name...'

She looked up at her grandmother, the tears trickling down her cheeks.

'I adored him! I couldn't bear that he would hate me, hate my name! I was Georgie Sinclair! So I changed my name. So he wouldn't hate me!'

'I don't think he ever hated you,' her grandmother told her. 'He was only thirteen, he was alone in a foreign country and he had witnessed his father's death and outright betrayal. It was all a huge shock. He was hurting, understandably, and he lashed out at the first person who managed to reach him.'

Hannah looked sadly at her granddaughter.

'And that person was you.'

Gina nodded. 'Yes, I know. I realised that. Later.'

She grimaced, managing a watery smile.

'Quite a long time later. And I forgave him.' She gulped. 'Of course, I forgave him. I loved him.' She paused, the tears flowing unheeded down her cheeks. 'And I still do. But it's no good. Even if he didn't really hate me back then, he does now. I can see it in his eyes every time he looks at me.'

'Don't be too sure about that, love,' her grandmother said. 'He's been hurt in the past so he's extra-sensitive about betrayal and dishonesty.'

'I know, Granny. And it's all my fault. I should never have let myself get involved in one of Mandy's schemes. They always end in disaster!' Gina sighed. 'I suppose it's not surprising everything's gone wrong since then: do something wrong and you get punished.'

Her grandmother stared at her from startled eyes. 'Where did you get that idea?' she asked. 'You know you're loved – by us and by God. If you confess when you've gone wrong, God forgives. And we'd never punish you. You know that!'

But Gina was shaking her head. 'Bad girls must be punished,' she said.

'How long have you believed that?' her grandmother asked.

'Always. Doesn't everybody?'

'No. Definitely not.' Hannah reached across and took Gina's hand. 'This isn't what Christians believe. We believe Jesus died so all our sins can be forgiven. Gina, love, you believe in Jesus. *Nothing* you could do would ever be so awful he wouldn't forgive you! There is no condemnation, no punishment...'

'But I thought...'

'I wonder where this idea came from,' Hannah pondered. 'Did somebody say it to you when you'd been naughty?'

'No,' Gina denied hurriedly. 'It wasn't me, it was Mummy...' Her eyes flew in horror to her grandmother's. 'Oh!' she said. 'Oh, I remember!' She took a deep breath. 'I was on the floor of Mum's bedroom, playing. She was packing our things. We were going to come and stay with you.'

Her voice began to shake. 'Daddy came back and he was angry. He hurt Mummy. She tried to stop him.'

Gina was aghast. 'I was too young to understand then. Granny, do you think he raped her? Oh, how dreadful! And then he realised I was there and witnessed it all. And he said Mummy had been bad and bad girls had to be punished. That's what he'd been doing.'

She fell silent, mulling over the horrendous memory that had surfaced. She looked over at her grandmother. 'Mum wasn't bad. He was. And he was using those words that have haunted me all my life to justify the evil thing he had done!' Gina's eyes flashed. 'Mum wasn't bad. I'm not bad. But oh, Granny, Hugo thinks I am! Because... at the conference, I think we were attracted to one another. I had no idea who he was but he was nice. We spent some time together... and he kissed me. Not big wolfy passionate kisses, just two... lovely gentle kisses...'

'Ah,' Hannah said. 'I see.'

And she remembered Nancy's letter. Nancy had said Hugo had met someone at the Aberdeen conference. That someone had to have been Gina. And Hugo had let his guard down. So when he discovered Gina's innocently meant subterfuge and who she really was, he had overreacted.

Once again, Gina had got beneath his barriers, and paid the price.

'Oh my dear,' Hannah said. 'Poor Hugo.' She reached over and patted Gina's hand. 'What I think is: don't give up.'

A loud knocking at the door interrupted them.

'I'll go and see who it is,' Gina said, getting up from the table.

She returned a few moments later.

'Post,' she said, holding up a sheaf of letters. 'I had to sign for one of them.'

She set them on the table, sorting them into piles: for her mother, her grandmother, herself. Then she took a knife and began to open her letters.

Her eyes widened and she stilled as she read through the first letter. Hannah watched as she set the knife down and carefully reread the letter.

'Is it from Dundee?' Hannah enquired. 'Have you got the job?'

Gina handed over the letter to her grandmother.

'Well,' she said a moment later, 'you'd better let Danny know.'

CHAPTER 60

Gina was glad to find her uncle alone in his office on Monday morning. She handed over the letter and watched as Danny read it through.

'Well done!' he said gruffly. 'I knew you could do it. Now let's see what Hugo has to say to this!' He waved the letter triumphantly.

'What Hugo has to say to what?'

Gina and Danny jumped. They had not heard Hugo enter the Editor's room. Danny cast a quick warning glance at Gina, then simply handed the letter to Hugo.

He took it, glanced briefly at the letterhead, then slowed and began to read. His face set in hard lines.

'Gina,' her uncle said, 'maybe you need to get back to work. We'll talk later.'

Gina looked at Hugo's furious face and beat a hasty retreat.

'Well?' Danny asked quietly. 'Will you now believe that Gina got her job on merit?' He pointed to the letter. 'She's just been awarded the annual prize for the best young journalist in the country!'

'You fixed this!' Hugo challenged him angrily. 'So she'll be reinstated…'

'I persuaded her to enter the competition, yes,' Danny conceded. 'Because I knew she had a very good chance of winning it. And yes, I thought it was the one objective way I could prove to you that Gina got her job, and holds it down, on merit. The result of the competition was up to a panel of judges – and they include the most distinguished senior folk in the industry. Nothing to do with me! I have no influence there whatsoever.'

He watched the conflicting emotions crossing Hugo's face.

'Their verdict is that Gina is the best young journalist in Scotland.'

Hugo sat down with a thump.

'It means kudos for *The Sentinel*,' Danny pointed out. 'For one of *ours* to win such a prestigious award...'

Hugo glared at the letter. 'One of ours' and he had threatened to fire her. He had put her on three months' trial... Which clearly she had not deserved. As all the staff at *The Sentinel* had known. And now all of Scotland.

He tried to organise his thoughts. So she was a good journalist and had earned her position at *The Sentinel* on merit. But that didn't wipe out her heritage or what her father had done... or her grandfather. The taint of generations of wickedness...

'*Yeah, we're a bad lot.*' That's what she'd said. And he had agreed. But what he had seen in her face was despair.

He had been wrong about her getting her job by deceit and nepotism. Had he been unfair about the Sinclair bad blood in her veins too? Or was it possible to be good at your job and still be a bad lot?

He ran his hand over his head. He couldn't think straight. In her favour, there was her obvious love for her brother, her care and support for her mother and grandmother...

The phone rang and Danny reached for it.

'It's for you,' he said, handing it over to Hugo.

'Yes, Hugo Mackay here. Oh.' Hugo's face paled. 'Right. I'll get there as soon as I can. Thank you for letting me know.'

He put down the receiver and turned to Danny, all other thoughts banished.

'My grandmother is seriously ill,' he said. 'What's the fastest way I can get to Canada?'

CHAPTER 61

Danny and Cat had come round to the Willowbank house for supper with the family. After the meal they all moved into the sitting room, the window open and the nets billowing in a pleasant breeze scented by the roses that scrambled up the outside wall of the house.

'I had hoped Hugo would go to the award ceremony with you,' Danny told Gina. 'As owner of *The Sentinel*, it was his place to be there. But I'm afraid you'll have to put up with me now!'

Gina smiled at her uncle. 'I'm perfectly happy with you!' she told him truthfully. 'In fact, much happier! Will you come too?' she asked her aunt. 'We'd have a nice time.'

Cat shook her head. 'I don't think so. I think it should just be you two newspaper types!' She looked across at Hannah. 'It *is* a pity Hugo can't be there. It would be good for him to see Gina recognised and fêted!'

'Indeed,' Hannah said. 'Did he get away safely?'

'Yes. We managed to get him a charter flight to Prestwick and from there he caught a flight to Canada,' Danny said. 'He'll be there by now.'

'It's a long trip,' Joyce commented. 'Tiring.'

'It's good of Hugo to drop everything and go to his grandmother's side,' Hannah said. 'It was a heart attack, wasn't it?'

'That's right,' Danny replied. 'Seems she'd had a couple of little ones in the past but this was the worst. The folk at the home where she lives felt Hugo should know – and he took the decision to go.'

'Poor Nancy,' murmured Hannah. 'We're none of us getting any younger.'

'How old is Hugo's grandmother?' Gina asked curiously.

'I think she's three or four years older than me,' Hannah said. 'That would make her around 86. She's been in a nursing home for a number of years but I hadn't realised her health was so poor. She didn't mention it in any of her letters.'

Hugo made the same point when finally he arrived in Manitoba.

'How long have you been having these "little turns" as you call them?' he demanded as he settled himself into the chair beside his grandmother's bed.

Nancy was looking frailer than when he had last seen her, but she was smiling and seemed to have weathered the latest upset with her usual equanimity.

Hugo fixed her with his eyes. 'I do have a right to know,' he said.

'True,' Nancy admitted. 'About a year or so.'

'You should have said,' Hugo told her. 'I wouldn't have gone globetrotting if I'd known…'

'I didn't want to worry you,' Nancy replied. 'And anyway, you have your life to live. I know you're busy.'

Hugo flushed. 'Gran, you should know I'm never too busy to come to see you, and when you need me, I want to know about it.'

'You're a good boy,' she said and patted his hand.

'Boy!' he laughed. 'I'm 32!'

'You'll always be a boy to me!' Nancy smiled. 'I can remember when Katie put you in my arms the very first time, all red and wrinkled.'

Hugo snorted.

'I'd be happier if I felt there was someone to look after you, after I'm gone,' Nancy said. 'I did wonder when I got your letter that perhaps you had met someone…?'

'I don't want to hear you talking like this,' Hugo said, carefully avoiding the issue she had raised. 'After you're gone, indeed!'

'Hugo, we all have to go and I'm not afraid of dying,' Nancy told him. 'The good Lord has looked after me all these years and I don't think He's going to give up on me now!'

'Did He though?' Hugo queried suddenly.

Nancy looked surprised. 'For sure He did. I wouldn't be here now…'

'I meant back then… In the Klondike. When Geordie Sinclair took you hostage…' Hugo looked into her shocked face. 'That was you, wasn't it? I've been puzzling about it and I can't see how it could have been anyone else. Was God looking after you then?'

Nancy looked at her beloved grandson. Thirty-two he might be, but what she saw was a confused, hurting boy searching for answers.

She sent up a quick silent prayer: *Help me, Lord. Help me help him.*

'Is it time for me to tell you my story, Hugo?' she asked him.

He nodded. Hannah Cormack had said to ask his grandmother. She looked so frail but determined. Maybe now was the time – before it was too late.

But Nancy had one more question. Fixing him with bright fearless eyes, she asked, 'All of it?'

CHAPTER 62

'I feel I really know very little about your past,' Hugo said. 'Granny Cormack said I should ask you.'

'I see,' Nancy said. 'That was wise.' She looked closely at him. 'And what brought this on? Why now?'

He reached in his pocket and brought out the small battered Bible.

'Danny's wife, Catalena, brought this back from Buenos Aires. They'd been clearing her mother's house.'

'Ah yes,' Nancy said. 'I heard from the family that Sofia Maria had died.'

Hugo held up the Bible so she could see.

'This was with some letters to my grandfather Hughie…'

'Hughie.' The word was the merest whisper.

'I don't understand why Geordie Sinclair had it,' Hugo said. He looked up at the wall above his grandmother's bed as if searching for inspiration. 'I know Geordie was responsible for my grandfather's death. Granny Cormack told me to check it out. And there was an article about it in the paper – the newspaper I've bought!'

'Ah yes,' Nancy said with a wry smile. 'There would be...'

She reached out and took the Bible from him, laying it in her lap and stroking it gently with a blue-veined hand.

'So?' Hugo prompted.

'So,' Nancy said with the faintest smile. 'Let's see: Geordie and your grandfather went out to the Klondike together. They came to Dawson City and they found some gold. Your grandfather had a ring made and sent it to Hannah's sister, Belle, his girlfriend in Scotland. They were secretly engaged.'

Hugo nodded. He knew this part of the story.

Nancy continued. 'But Geordie was also in love with Belle and Belle had spurned him. He had nursed his desire for revenge and when he realised Belle was engaged to Hughie, he was determined to do them a mischief.'

Nancy sighed and closed her eyes.

'Are you all right?' Hugo asked nervously. 'Please don't tire yourself out. Shall I call for someone?'

Nancy shook her head and opened her eyes.

'I need to tell you,' she said. 'You have a right to know.'

She sighed again.

'And if it makes you think the worse of me, then it cannot be helped.'

She looked down at the Bible and seemed to gather strength from it.

'I was working in one of the dance-halls in Dawson City. It was a rough place and we girls were expected to do whatever was asked of us.' She looked up briefly. 'You understand what I'm saying?'

Hugo nodded slowly.

'I wasn't there by choice,' Nancy said. 'If it makes any difference, I was born there. My mother was one of the girls and when I was born

213

she went off with a man, leaving me to the other girls to bring up. So you could say I was born to it.'

She made herself continue.

'So when Geordie Sinclair came to me with a proposition, I was in no position to turn it down. What Geordie paid me to do was get friendly with your grandfather.'

Nancy paused, looking at Hugo's shuttered face. She remembered Hughie's friendly openness and prayed that her revelations would not destroy her relationship with her beloved grandson.

'Your grandfather was a nice boy. But then I got pregnant. To my surprise, instead of being furious with me, Geordie was pleased. And he wrote and told Belle.'

Again, Hugo simply nodded.

Nancy went on. 'Belle sent back the ring and broke off the engagement in such a way as to let Hughie know she not only knew about me but also my pregnancy. But I hadn't yet told Hughie. Geordie had told me not to.'

'So one of those letters...' Hugo said slowly.

'Would be that letter.' Nancy completed the sentence. 'Yes. So Hughie realised he had been betrayed. At first he thought it was me – but when he came after me, he discovered it had been Geordie.'

Nancy took a deep breath. 'And that is what they fought about, out there at the workings, in a blizzard.'

'And Geordie struck him and left him for dead,' Hugo said.

'Yes. And when the locals heard, they would have lynched him if they could. Instead they forced him out of town. He took me with him as a hostage.' She shivered, remembering the events of those terrible days. 'I remember he grabbed Hughie's saddlebag. I expect the Bible and the letters would have been in it.'

'It was all he took with him when he was run off the Alexander ranch,' she added. 'So I suppose it went with him to Argentina.'

'I see,' Hugo said. 'But what happened to the ring that Belle sent back? Shouldn't it have been with the Bible and the letters?'

CHAPTER 63

'The Mizpah ring?' Nancy asked. 'It was a pretty thing. Hughie had an ivy leaf shaped out of gold and fixed on the ring he had made for Belle.'

She gave a little mirthless chuckle.

'In the language of flowers, ivy stands for faithfulness,' she explained to her grandson. 'Not very appropriate as things proved. I've always thought of it as the Mizpah ring because it had the word "Mizpah" in raised letters across it.'

'And that means?' Hugo prompted.

'It's from the Bible,' Nancy said, carefully opening the old book on her lap and gently leafing through the stained and torn pages. 'Here we are. Genesis, chapter 31 and verse 49. "The LORD watch between me and thee, when we are absent one from another." That's what it means.'

'Oh,' Hugo said. 'And do you think He did? Between Belle and my grandfather? It doesn't seem to me like He did much of a job.'

'I'm not so sure about that,' Nancy told him with a smile. 'I found out later that Belle wasn't a nice person at all. She wouldn't have been good *to* him or *for* him. You see, she used people to get what she wanted. And I think now that she was using your grandfather – because she wanted to be rich – and he was easily led. Poor Hughie.'

'So the ring?' Hugo prompted.

'Geordie insisted that I wear it. He took me to the Alexanders – they were relatives of your grandfather – here in Manitoba. They owned the ranch you were born and brought up on. Geordie passed us off as Mr and Mrs Hughie Mackay, a married couple expecting their first baby. I needed to wear the ring to back up his story.' Nancy paused. 'You need to understand that Geordie was violent and dangerous. I was very afraid of him and did whatever he asked...'

'But you said he was run off the ranch?'

'Yes. Marie Alexander admired the ring one day and what I said made our story begin to unravel.'

'But they allowed you to stay. Why would they do that?' Hugo asked.

'They were good Christian people,' Nancy said, smiling fondly. 'I am so grateful to them. Marie led me to faith in the Lord. They loved me like a daughter, and through them I met my beloved Clem...'

Hugo shook his head, trying to sort out all the information.

'You were a...' He paused. 'Dance-hall girl.'

'That's polite,' Nancy said with a tired smile.

'Pregnant by a customer.'

'That's not so polite, but true.'

'Then suddenly you're married to a pastor.'

Hugo stared at his grandmother in sudden horror.

'Did Grandpa Clem know? Did he know what you were?' he asked.

Hugo closed his eyes to try to block out the awful realisation. All this time he had charged Gina with dishonesty. Condemned her for the Sinclair bad blood that showed itself in deceit. But now, here in his own family…

He forced himself to ask the question.

'Did he know? Or… did you deceive him?'

CHAPTER 64

The question stuck like a rock in Hugo's throat. The woman he had trusted all his life. The one woman he would have trusted with his life. Had his grandmother simply been one more deceiver?

As he drove to the nursing home next morning, he reviewed her words. He had indeed been shocked by her revelations. The dance-hall girl and all the rest of it. This was not the woman he had thought he knew. She had always been such a godly woman...

But maybe that was Grandpa Clem's influence? No, wait, didn't she say it was Mama Marie who had led her to the Lord? So that was some time before she met Clem Paston. And there it was again, that terrible thought. Maybe Clem had not known. Maybe she had deceived him.

Hugo's eyes were hard when he entered her room. She was propped up on pillows, a fluffy pink bed-jacket over her nightdress, her white hair neatly brushed. Her eyes brightened when she saw him. But only briefly.

Nancy swallowed hard at the look in his eyes.

'Come in, Hugo.'

She indicated the chair next to the bed and he took it.

'How are you this morning?' he asked.

Polite formality, Nancy thought sadly. So, as she feared, her story had disgusted and alienated him.

'I am doing well,' she replied evenly. 'The doctor has been in and he is pleased with me. It seems that I am recovering.'

'That's good...'

'Let's not waste time,' Nancy interrupted him. 'Yesterday you asked me a question. Today you get the answer.'

She waited for his nod of acquiescence, then began.

'When your father was a few months old and thriving, Mama Marie said it was time we got him christened.

"Would you like that, *chérie*?" Marie had asked.

"Yes," I told her. "But... *I've* never been christened. I'd really like to get *baptised* if that would be possible."

'I'd read in the Bible that when people came to faith in Jesus, they got baptised. So I wanted that. I said it would feel then that I'd made a proper new start...

"That's a lovely idea, *chérie*," Marie had said. "I hadn't thought. You should ask Pastor Clem about it when he comes over on Friday."

"What I want is a proper baptism. Would he do that? I've seen him do christenings of babies, when he sprinkles them with water. What I want is like the John the Baptist story and what Paul says about baptism – going down into the water and then coming up again new! That's what I want."

'Marie smiled at me then. "If you want that much water, you'll need a river that won't chill you to the bone and there won't be one of those till summer!"

"True," I agreed. "But do you think Pastor Clem would be willing to do a baptism in a river? I've only seen him do christenings in church and people's homes."

"I don't see why not," Marie said. "You can ask him yourself and see what he says."

'Clem was in the habit of coming over for Friday supper and holding a Bible study with us, so I waited till then and broached the subject. To my delight, he said yes. With the same caveat as Marie: "If you want a total immersion baptism, outdoors, we'll have to wait for the better weather! I wouldn't want either of us frozen to death!"

"I really think you should be considering becoming a member of the church too," Clem added. "You've been attending with Bill and Marie this past year, and from our conversations I'd say you have as good a grasp of the faith as anyone else there!"

"More than that," Marie put in loyally. "Nancy put her faith in the Lord Jesus a while back and she really believes, don't you?"

"Oh yes," I told them. "Knowing Him – and you! – has changed my life!"

'A loud cry came from the crib in the corner.

"So has baby Hugh!" Marie laughed as I rose to see to the child. I brought him back to the table and rocked him back to contented quiet.

"Hugh Mackay, you were just feeling left out!" Marie teased.

'And that's when it hit me... Marie noticed something was the matter and asked, "What is it, *chérie*? Are you feeling unwell?"

"No. It's just... I hadn't thought..."

'I looked at her in desperation. What was I going to do? I looked at Clem, dreading how he was going to react.

"You were going to baptise me and christen Hugh on the same day… but…"

'I looked over at Marie, hoping against hope she had realised what the problem was.

"Don't be afraid," Marie said. "Tell us what it is that troubles you, *ma chère.*"

'And it was just too terrible. I was so ashamed.

"Don't you see?" I said. "We can't do it! Because then everybody will know! They'd realise…"

'Clem stood up, his sweet face filled with concern.

"Mrs Mackay," he said in a strong reassuring voice, "I'm sure we can solve whatever problem you feel there is. The past is not your ruler now. Jesus is. There is no condemnation for those who belong to Him…"

"No condemnation!" That made me laugh. "Oh, but there will be… when you christen Hugh Mackay and then baptise his mother…"

"I don't see the problem," Clem began.

"I do," I told him bluntly. "When Papa Bill went into town to register Hugh's birth, he named him Hugh Mackay, after his father, as I asked him to. But I'm not Mrs Mackay and I never have been! And when people know, that will bring shame on all of you!"

'I remember looking round at them, the people, next to your father, that I loved most in the world.

"I can't do it!" I said. 'I won't let you be shamed like that! Let Hugh be christened, but leave me out of it!"

'I know I wasn't thinking clearly but I just couldn't bear it any longer. I felt that the past would never let me go. I'd never be free of my background and what had happened to me.'

Nancy looked into Hugo's eyes, pleading for understanding.

'And then I ran away,' she said. 'I left your father behind, with a note, and I ran out of the house, heedless of where I was going. I just didn't care any longer.'

CHAPTER 65

'They came after me,' said Nancy. 'They were such good people I suppose I should have expected it. And I was a hothouse plant.' She looked up at Hugo with a wry smile. 'A dance-hall girl.' It was spoken with a kind of defiance. 'I just had not thought that I was leaving the house in the evening, in the winter! I wouldn't have survived the night.'

She paused thoughtfully. 'Maybe that was what I wanted. I couldn't see any future for me any more.' She looked steadily at Hugo. 'There was no way I would go back to what I knew. I truly believed I was a new creation in the Lord Jesus. And I couldn't take my own life. So I had taken a horse – and ignorantly chose the one who went lame within a half-hour!'

She smiled, a sudden radiant smile. 'You asked did the Lord look after me? I am so sure He did that night. Because my horse went lame so soon, they were able to catch up with me quickly, before I came to any real harm.'

Nancy remembered the warmth of the welcome she had received from Marie and Bill. And from Clem.

'It was Clem who found me. He put me up in front of him on his horse, and all the way home he told me all the theological stuff about being a new creation in Christ, past put behind us, no condemnation… and how that was all mine. Even mine.'

She turned her wedding ring round on her finger. 'And when we got back and I'd got warm, he asked to have a private word with me. He told me he'd solved my problem for me. If I was willing.'

'On the ride back to the ranch, I had told him all about my past and who I was,' she said. 'That my mother was a dance-hall girl in Dawson City and I was the unwanted and unexpected offspring of… how was it you put it? One of her customers.'

Nancy watched as her words hit their target. Hugo closed his eyes briefly.

'And despite knowing all, Clem offered me his name in marriage. So I could be baptised.' She waited a moment, then added, 'But he offered me so much more. Reassurance that I could indeed make a fresh start, with someone who believed in me – as my own self, not what I was born into, nor what I had done before I knew better. Clem never judged. He simply loved. And I will be forever grateful.'

She looked at the young man sitting staring at the wall.

'So there's your answer,' she said simply. 'Yes, Clem knew. Of course he knew. I couldn't have married him otherwise. A marriage with lies at the heart is no marriage and will never prosper.'

She looked down at her left hand. 'This is the wedding ring Clem gave me,' Nancy said. 'I gave the Mizpah ring to your father. He gave it to your mother and she wore it happily, proudly.'

'I don't remember,' Hugo said.

'You were very young when she died,' Nancy reassured him. 'You can't expect to remember everything.'

'Did he give it to' – Hugo paused, then ground out – 'the next one?'

'I think he did, briefly,' Nancy said. 'But she didn't like it. She wanted something a bit more "normal" so he got her something sparkly to please her.'

'Didn't work,' Hugo growled, his head bent low, eyes on the ground. 'Nothing pleased her.'

'No, I'd agree with you there,' Nancy said.

'And... Ruby?' Hugo hesitated on the name.

'Yes, I believe he gave the Mizpah ring to her.'

'So where is it now?' Hugo asked. 'Was it lost when Ruby was killed?'

'I really don't know,' Nancy said. 'It certainly wasn't found with her body. If anyone knows, it will be her daughter. Amanda.'

'Mandy,' Hugo corrected absently.

'Mandy?' Nancy enquired. 'Does that mean you've met up with her again?'

Hugo nodded.

'And is she still the spoilt young madam she was?' Nancy laughed. 'When I think of the tantrums she used to throw...'

But Hugo was looking puzzled.

'Mandy? No,' he said, 'that was Gina – Georgie as she was then.'

'No,' Nancy said decidedly. 'I may be getting old but I remember those two little girls clearly. Mandy was a brat. Little Georgie was the one who used to follow you around like Mary's little lamb. She was a delightful child and quite stole my heart.'

Hugo stared.

'Are you sure?' he asked.

'Perfectly,' Nancy said. 'But of course you'll have met Gina by now. She's the star reporter on that newspaper you bought.' She smiled at her grandson's confusion. 'Hannah and I have kept in touch over the years. I've followed Gina's career with great interest.'

Hugo put his head in his hands. It was all too much. Focus. What had he been asking about? Ah yes, the Mizpah ring.

For the moment, there was only one way to find out what had happened to it, and that was to ask Mandy.

CHAPTER 66

Lybster, Caithness, Scotland

'Who's it from?'

Granny Flett sat on the other side of the kitchen table, her straggly grey hair in curlers and a cigarette dangling from her lip.

Mandy glowered. 'None of your business,' she said, reaching for a knife to open her letter.

'You're just like your mother,' Granny Flett said.

Mandy ignored the familiar refrain and slit open the envelope. It was from the firm in Edinburgh who had sent the stuck-up woman to Inverness to interview her. But to Mandy's surprise, the letter was not a rejection. Instead, it was an invitation to a second interview in Edinburgh with the boss himself.

Well, that was interesting – especially since they were offering to cover all her expenses. She would write and accept, and then plan a few days away, a nice hotel…

But as she picked up the envelope to replace the letter, another – a flimsy airmail letter – detached itself from where it had got caught.

Mandy grabbed it, her eyes alight with excitement. Yes! It was a letter from Hugo! She held it to her chest. Hugo had written to her from Canada! Here was proof that her strategy was working and soon she would have a ring on her finger!

She smoothed out the flimsy airmail paper and began to read.

'*Dear Mandy,*

As you know, my grandmother has been unwell and I came over to see how she was doing. It's been good to spend time with her. I've been hearing her stories of the past.'

Mandy snorted. How boring! She read on:

'*It's strange how things can get forgotten and even mislaid. But maybe we've got a good opportunity to sort things out. I need to ask you something when I get back. I hope I'll find you able and willing to give me the answer I need.*'

Mandy's reading ground to a halt. He was going to ask her a question! That could mean only one thing: he was going to propose to her! She closed her eyes in triumph. She had done it. She'd won! Her future was assured. For a few moments she let her imagination roam over the kind of life she was going to enjoy – the foreign trips and holidays, the lovely home, plenty of money, expensive clothes, jewellery...

The letter finished quite formally.

'*I'm glad to say my grandmother is much better and I'll be able to return to Scotland shortly.*

Yours, Hugo.'

But Mandy didn't mind. Clearly the cursory salutation hid a passionately beating heart. He would be coming back to Scotland to propose to her and then marry her! No doubt soon after that, they'd go to Canada and...

'And what are you so almighty pleased with yourself about?' her grandmother demanded crossly.

Mandy glared at her but her triumph won through. She waved the airmail letter at her grandmother.

'Hugo Mackay has written to me,' she said airily. 'We're going to get married.'

'Is that so?'

'Yes. He says so in this letter. When he comes back, there will be a ring on my finger!' Mandy gloated.

Her grandmother's eyes narrowed.

'Why wait till he's back?' she asked.

She hauled herself up from the table and shambled through to her bedroom where Mandy could hear her rummaging through drawers.

Reappearing with something concealed in her hand, she said, '*His* father gave it to *your* mother, so I reckon it's yours now.'

Granny Flett opened her hand to reveal the Mizpah ring.

'You can wear it till he gives you a big sparkly diamond!' she told Mandy.

CHAPTER 67

Mandy grabbed the ring from her grandmother's hand and sat down at the table to examine it.

'It's a bit dull,' she said, but she slipped it on to the third finger of her left hand and held her hand up to view. 'I prefer sparkly. You're right. I want a nice big diamond and I'm sure Hugo can afford one.'

She started to remove the ring but her grandmother's words stopped her.

'It's not how it looks that matters,' Granny Flett told her. 'It's what it means. What it stands for.'

'So what does it mean?' Mandy asked crossly. 'It's just a boring old ring.'

'What it means is gold and the Mackays,' Granny Flett said. 'Hugo's grandfather went out to the Klondike to make his fortune and this ring was made out of some of the gold he found there. It's been the family engagement ring from the start. That's what it was made for.'

She nodded wisely, roller-bound hair bobbing.

'Anyone who knows about the ring – or about his family – will know what it means if you're wearing it.'

'Anyone?'

Mandy stared at the ring, brow furrowed in thought. Then her face lit up with satisfaction.

'I see what you mean. Well done, Granny! In that case, I must get ready and go out! I've things to do!'

Granny Flett puffed on her cigarette and watched the excited girl dash from the room. She was so like her mother. All that energy, and impetuous with it.

Mandy rushed into her bedroom and stripped off her Saturday-at-home clothes. Carefully she chose one of her favourite outfits – smart miniskirt and a little jacket over a blouse. Twirling in front of the mirror, she practised showing off the ring – casually.

When she was ready, she ran through to the kitchen.

'I'm off now,' she told her grandmother as she reached for the door. 'Don't know when I'll be back…'

The roller-bound curls bobbed in acknowledgement.

'You never do,' her grandmother muttered as the door slammed behind her.

Mandy could scarcely control her excitement as she sat in the bus taking her into Wick. She could not wait to see Gina and push the ring under her nose! She would know what it meant, and if she didn't, her grandmother certainly would. Granny Cormack knew everything. And this time, Mandy vowed, she would turn that to her advantage.

When the bus arrived in Wick, Mandy alighted and hurried across town to Willowbank, wings on her feet.

'Well, you're a surprise!' Gina's mother, Joyce, opened the door to her. 'Come in, come in.'

In the hallway, she called upstairs, 'Gina! Mandy's here!' She turned to Mandy. 'Do you want to go on up?'

Mandy grinned. 'No, I'll stay downstairs,' she said.

This was not news to be shared privately. She wanted Gina's downfall – and her triumph – to be public and final.

'Well, come into the kitchen,' Joyce said, a puzzled frown on her face. 'Robbie's there…'

Everyone knew Mandy could not cope with Robbie and avoided him wherever possible.

But Mandy waved that away. 'That's not a problem,' she said. 'Granny Cormack?'

'Yes, of course,' Joyce replied, surprised. 'Mother's here.'

'Good,' Mandy said.

She walked into the kitchen and smiled at the two occupants. Deliberately, she walked round the table and set herself down beside Hannah, taking her time to place her handbag on the floor with her left hand. She waited with her hand on her knee underneath the table till Gina appeared.

'Hi, Mandy!'

'Gina,' acknowledged Mandy, bringing her left hand up and setting it casually on the table.

'Oh!'

Granny Cormack's sharply drawn breath drew Gina's eyes, but then she looked where her grandmother was looking. At Mandy's left hand. At the ring.

'Is that what I think it is, Mandy?' Granny Cormack asked softly. Her grey eyes were cold as steel.

Mandy lowered her eyelashes. This was working well. She moved her hand to where Granny Cormack could see and touch the ring. Hannah's hand came out slowly, as if unwilling, and a finger reached out and traced the word 'Mizpah' in raised letters across the ivy leaf that adorned the front of the ring.

Her eyes fixed on Mandy.

'It's the Mizpah ring,' she said.

'Yes,' Mandy agreed, and displayed it for the others at the table to see. She waited a moment. 'Hugo and I are engaged, so of course I'm wearing the Mizpah ring. It *is* the family engagement ring, isn't it?'

With great satisfaction, she saw Gina lose all colour and reach out to grab the table to steady herself. Granny Cormack's eyes narrowed. Joyce put a hand to her mouth. A hand on which a ring with a small diamond winked in the light from the window.

'Ah yes,' Hannah said quietly. She turned to her daughter. 'Now isn't that a coincidence?' She gestured to the ring on Joyce's finger. 'We have another engagement to celebrate.' She smiled. 'Joyce is going to marry Alec Gunn, and she and Robbie will be moving out to the farm.'

She looked at Gina. 'Put the kettle on, Gina.' Hannah's sharp eyes bored into Mandy. 'I'm sorry we haven't anything stronger to celebrate with you, but maybe a cup of tea will be welcome?'

CHAPTER 68

Mandy seethed. How dare the old woman take her news so calmly? Worse, how dare Joyce Cormack upstage her? This was *her* day, *her* moment, and no one was going to spoil it.

She looked across at Gina's back as she reached for the kettle to make tea. Gina was hunched, her shoulders slumped. Good. She had managed the direct hit that she wanted.

Mandy waited till Gina had served the tea.

'Thank you,' she said with the most polite smile she could manage. 'I do hope you don't mind?'

She waved the ring at Gina and watched the pain in her face.

'But of course you could never mean anything to Hugo except...' She paused, choosing her words carefully. How had Gina described Hugo's reaction to her when he had found out who she was? 'Disgust? Well, you can't blame him, can you – bearing in mind who you are.'

She could feel all eyes on her and they were hostile. She sipped her tea as if unconcerned.

As she put her cup down, she said, 'Oh well, bad blood is bad blood and there's nothing you can do about it. You'll always be tainted by your father.'

She reached down for her handbag and rose. Her work was nearly completed.

'I'm so glad I don't have any bad blood.' She looked over at Granny Cormack and triumphantly played her ace card. 'I'm a Cormack, like you.'

But Granny Cormack was staring at her, and there was anger in her face. And something else, something that looked strangely like sadness.

And then she was rising from her seat and facing Mandy, squarely.

'I wouldn't be too sure of that,' she told Mandy quietly. 'I suggest you need to be very careful…'

But Mandy tossed her head. 'I've nothing to worry about!' She flaunted the ring at them and laughed. 'I have none of that Sinclair bad blood in me! And now Hugo's going to marry me and we'll be off to Canada and a wonderful new life there!'

With that she headed for the door. But Hannah had the last word.

'Mandy,' she said. And Mandy turned back automatically.

'Ask your granny. Granny Flett. I think you'll find Granny Flett can tell you quite a lot that you don't know, that you maybe need to know. She was there, you see.'

Mandy snorted and left. Ask her grandmother indeed! What did she need to know? Hugo was a rich man. He was coming back to marry her and she would live happily ever after.

She looked at the ring – made from Klondike gold. The Mizpah ring. It was definitely a good sign!

CHAPTER 69

Hannah and Joyce exchanged glances.

'Granny, what was it you were trying to warn Mandy about? What was it you wanted Mandy to know?' Gina asked curiously. 'Maybe there are things *I* don't know?'

Hannah shook her head, sadness and concern clear on her face. 'I don't *know*,' she stressed the word. 'But I've always wondered...'

Joyce said gently, 'I think I always knew.' She looked at her daughter. 'Your father...'

'Who was a right bad lot,' Gina said.

'Yes,' Joyce said. 'That's fair. He was a right bad lot. And I believe that our marriage was a sham from the start.' She smiled ruefully at her mother. 'Over the years, I've given it plenty of thought, put two and two together...'

'And?' Gina asked curiously. 'What more is there to know?'

'I think his affair with Ruby started very soon after they first met. Before he started courting me,' Joyce said. Her face was calm and her eyes steady. 'I'm sure he only married me to get what he could from the family business. And all the while, Ruby was his mistress.'

'Have you never noticed how alike you and Mandy are?' Hannah asked Gina gently.

Gina shook her head. 'Well, why would I especially? Mandy is family! I just thought…'

She looked into the kindly, concerned faces of her mother and grandmother and ground to a halt.

'Wait a minute. Let me get this straight,' she said slowly. 'Are you saying that Dad and Ruby were an item long before Ruby met Hugo's dad? And before Dad married you, Mum?'

Joyce nodded.

'So what you're suggesting is that my dad was in fact Mandy's father, and not Uncle Bobby?'

'Yes,' her mother said simply.

'Granny?'

'I'm afraid so. It's what I've always thought.'

'But you don't know for certain?' Gina prodded.

'Mandy's granny will,' Joyce said. 'Ruby spent a lot of time in Lybster with her…'

'And she would know who came calling, Bobby or George,' Hannah said.

'My memories are of George having a lot of trips out to Lybster while Ruby was living there,' Joyce added quietly.

'Ah, I see,' Gina said, as she struggled to absorb what she was being told.

'So Ruby and my dad – George – are Mandy's real parents?'

Hannah nodded.

'It kind of explains why Mandy's not like us,' Gina said thoughtfully.

Then a look of horror came over her face.

'Wait a minute! Hugo damns me for having George Sinclair's bad blood – but Mandy's worse! It was her mother *and* father who took his dad to the cleaners and killed him!'

She stared at her mother and grandmother.

'What will Hugo do when he finds out the truth? And will he find out before the wedding, or after?'

CHAPTER 70

The view south from the road at Laidhay was, to Gina's mind, one of the most beautiful in the county. It never failed to lift her spirits and today, driving herself in a hire car down to Dundee for the all-important job interview, she was determined to be positive about the future.

She had passed her driving test first time and the family – including the Gunns – had celebrated. She was delighted that her mother was going to marry Alec Gunn and Robbie was going to live with them on the farm. Gina had seen how Young Alec had relaxed towards her brother and the two of them were now firm friends. Robbie had a valued role on the farm where both Alecs and the farm labourers made sure he had plenty to do and was safe. And Robbie loved it.

Gina was so grateful to Strawberts Circus and that kindly elephant keeper. Robbie's impulsive rush to stroke the elephants had played a significant part in the way things had turned out for good for him and for their mother.

If only things would turn out for good for her. Gina gave a wry smile. She knew she was quoting from one of her grandmother's favourite texts. Romans 8:28, 'all things work together for good to them that love God.'

Maybe if she loved Hugo less and God more… Maybe that's where she was going wrong.

As she rounded the next bend, she noticed a flash of deep metallic blue beside a tumbledown croft house on the nearby hillside. Standing beside the car and the croft building was Hugo.

Gina shivered. It was as if just thinking of him had made him materialise before her eyes. But what was he doing there? Had his car broken down again? Before she realised what she was doing, she had swung her car off the road onto the track and was parking it beside his.

He looked surprised. 'Gina!'

'I saw the car,' she explained. 'I'm on my way south… I wondered were you all right?' She gestured to his car. 'It hasn't broken down again, has it?'

'No, it's fine,' he said. 'I just thought I'd stop and take a look…'

'Why?' she asked curiously, before she could stop herself.

He waved at the broken-down but-and-ben, the old stone of the walls half overgrown with nettles and rosebay willowherb.

'My great-grandmother lived here,' he said. 'This is where my grandfather was born.'

'How is your grandmother?' Gina asked.

'She's doing well, thank you. Another heart attack but she's pulled through,' Hugo said. 'I reckon she'll last a while yet.'

'Oh, that's good.'

'I wanted to see the croft,' Hugo continued. 'See if anything could be done with it. My grandmother reckons it's probably mine if I want to claim it. The views are beautiful. It would be a nice place to live.'

Gina filled in the blank: It would be a nice place to live with Mandy, when they were married.

240

'Ah yes,' she found herself saying, her voice studiedly casual. 'Will your grandmother come over for the wedding? Or will you marry over there?'

She couldn't believe that she was asking him this. Was she determined to wound herself even more deeply than Mandy had done already?

But Hugo was looking at her strangely.

'What wedding?' he asked.

'Yours and Mandy's,' she said, the confusion at his question showing clearly on her face.

'Now, hold on there,' Hugo said, laughing. 'As far as I know, I'm not going to marry Mandy!'

'She said you were engaged,' Gina interrupted. 'She came to see us, wearing the engagement ring… Your family engagement ring.'

Hugo's eyes narrowed.

'What ring?' he asked softly. 'What did it look like?'

But Gina shook her head. 'Don't tease me, Hugo Mackay!' she flashed at him. 'You know perfectly well what it looks like! The Mizpah ring! You gave it to her! Don't pretend!'

She took a deep breath. 'Maybe I'm not the only one capable of doing a bit of pretending around here! But at least my pretence was innocent and honourable! All I was doing was helping out Mandy! Now I must go. I have an interview for a job down in Dundee.'

She walked steadily away from him, holding her emotions in check. She opened the car door, settled herself in the driver's seat and switched on the engine. As she turned the car back down the track, she took a last look at Hugo in her rear-view mirror.

He was standing watching her go, an arrested expression on his face.

CHAPTER 71

Hugo was back! Mandy paced up and down the kitchen floor of the little house in Lybster. She had heard he was back so why had he not rung or come to see her?

'What's the matter with you?' her grandmother complained. 'You're like something in a cage. Why don't you go and do something useful?'

Mandy rounded on her in fury.

'I can't, you stupid old woman! I've got to wait in for Hugo to ring me. He's been back three whole days and he's not been in touch...'

'Ah,' Granny Flett cackled. 'So that's what the problem is. You are so like your mother!'

'So what's wrong with that?' Mandy demanded. 'My mum got every man she wanted! She could twist them round her little finger. My dad...'

'Aye, she got him all right,' her grandmother said. 'Didn't do her any good!'

'Yes, it did,' Mandy glared at her. 'She did all right, marrying into the Cormacks...'

'So that's what you think,' the old lady crowed, eyeing her with malicious delight. 'I wondered if you knew…'

'Of course, I know,' Mandy said. 'And if you know different, you'd better tell me!'

'Ooh, the brave one,' Granny Flett mocked her. 'I wonder what it is you think you know? Maybe not so proud once you know the truth!'

'Truth!' Mandy jeered. 'Truth is what you want it to be.'

And she waved her left hand where the Mizpah ring glowed dull gold in the dim light of the smoky kitchen.

'You sit down and I'll tell you the truth,' her grandmother said.

That's what Granny Cormack had said, Mandy realised. Granny Flett had been there…

'Aye, now you're wondering,' Granny Flett said and took a drag of her ever-present cigarette. She stubbed it out in the already overflowing ashtray beside her on the table and peered at her granddaughter. 'Aye, you're like them both.'

'Nothing to be ashamed of there.' Mandy pouted. 'Ruby Flett and Bobby Cormack. No bad blood there.'

She smirked, remembering her successfully wounding words to Gina just a few days ago. *There* was the bad blood, and Goody Two-Shoes Gina was irrevocably tainted by it!

But her grandmother was shaking her head.

'Nah, nah, my dear. Bobby Cormack was never your father. It was the other one. The foreign one.'

She lit another cigarette, blowing smoke up to the ceiling. 'Never did her any good, that man. George St Clair.' She pronounced the name with heavy mockery. 'She was besotted with him. Would do anything for him.' Bleary eyes darted to Mandy's face. 'Including marrying Bobby Cormack when she knew she was expecting George's baby.'

243

'But…' Mandy began, horrified. 'But how do you know? For sure?'

'Oh, I know, my dearie,' Granny Flett said. 'She came to me first. Of course she did. I'm her mother!' She began to laugh and ended up coughing. 'Oh dear me! I sent her to him, to George, to see what he'd say to it. He was responsible after all.'

'And what did he say?' Mandy demanded.

'That she should marry Bobby Cormack. Like they'd always planned.'

Granny Flett sat back and watched her granddaughter process the information.

'Planned?'

'Oh aye. Your mother was a match for that Argentine lad. They had it all planned out between then. She would marry Bobby Cormack, he would marry Joyce Cormack, and that way they'd get their hands on the business and the money – and all the time they would continue as they always had.' Granny Flett leered through the cigarette smoke. 'You just came along a little earlier than expected. And with the wrong father.'

Mandy stared at her. A set-up, between her mother and – it took a bit of getting used to – George St Clair. Her father. They had planned it together. She let the pieces of the jigsaw puzzle fall into place – a new picture, admittedly, but suddenly, she felt a thrill of excitement as she recognised and welcomed her true identity. She was not the daughter of boring old Bobby Cormack. She had none of that goody-goody Cormack in her. She was the product of two smart, go-getting people – people just like her.

But knowing herself, there was one more question she had to ask her grandmother.

'You said Mum was besotted with him. That she was a match for him. What about him?' Mandy asked. 'Did he care about her – or was he just using her like he did everyone else?'

Granny Flett breathed smoke into rings that floated up to the ceiling. She watched them contentedly.

'I always thought so,' she said. 'He always came back. And at the end he took her with him.'

She paused.

'If George St Clair ever loved anyone but himself, it was your mother.'

CHAPTER 72

Loud banging on the front door woke the Willowbank household early next morning.

'Whatever is the matter?' Joyce muttered as she stumbled downstairs in her dressing-gown. She checked the clock on the mantelpiece as she went past the open kitchen door.

'Seven o'clock. It's a bit early…' she began. Then she took in the young man standing at the door, wide-eyed and uncomfortable with the solemnity of his task. 'It's Tommy, isn't it?'

'That's right, Auntie Joyce. Mum sent me… She said…'

'Come in, Tommy,' Joyce invited, but Tommy demurred.

'I can't, I'm sorry,' he said. 'I've a whole lot of other people to let know…'

'Tommy.' Hannah had come up behind Joyce. 'It's good of you to come so early. Tell us your message, then you can get round everyone else.' She fixed the young man with steady grey eyes. 'It's your granddad, I suppose, isn't it?'

The lad gulped and his face twisted as a wave of grief hit him.

Hannah reached out and patted his arm. 'Aye, it's sad news, I'm sure.'

The young man pulled himself together and managed to get the words out: 'Mum said to tell you that Granddad...' He hesitated a moment. 'Granddad died at five this morning. In the hospital.'

'Well done,' Hannah said. 'It will be easier each time you say it. Thank you for coming. It was kind of Nell to let us know so quickly. You tell your mother we say thank you and we'll be round to the house later.'

The young man bobbed his head awkwardly and hurried away.

'Mum?' Joyce turned back to her mother. 'Are you all right?'

'Yes, of course, my dear,' Hannah said. 'My brother Will's death was news we were expecting. After those strokes he's had, it was only a matter of time.'

She turned back into the house.

'Yes, I know but...' Joyce followed her mother into the kitchen and put the kettle on for a cup of tea.

'And anyway,' Hannah added quietly, 'death is simply one more part of life. It comes to us all.' She pulled her grey dressing-gown around her and sat down at the kitchen table. 'Well, with Will gone, I'm the last of us left. I don't suppose I'll be too long after him.'

'Mother!' Joyce protested. 'Don't say that!'

But Hannah laughed. 'Joyce, my love, do you know you only call me "Mother" when I've done or said something you don't approve of!'

'Oh, Mum.' Joyce laughed weakly and went and hugged her mother. 'I don't want to lose you. I don't know what I'd do without you.'

'Going some place?' Robbie stood in the doorway. 'Heard you,' he said. 'Don't go, Granny.'

Hannah rose and went to hold Robbie's hands. She placed a fond kiss on his cheek.

'My dear, we cannot know what the good Lord has planned for us but we can trust Him to look after us.' She looked into Robbie's eyes. 'You trust Jesus, don't you?'

'Jesus,' Robbie repeated, and nodded his head. The chink of the teapot distracted him. 'Tea!'

'Come and have a cup,' his mother said. 'You too!' she added as Gina appeared.

'What's going on?' Gina asked sleepily. 'I heard voices...'

They settled down with cups of tea round the table as Joyce explained that Nell's son Tommy had brought the news of Uncle Will's death.

'Oh,' Gina said.

She looked at her grandmother and she saw for the first time that she was getting old and frail. She would be, Gina calculated carefully in her head, 83 next birthday.

There were so many changes afoot. Her mother and Robbie would soon be moving to Alec's farm. She had not yet told them that after her interview yesterday, she had been offered the job in Dundee. She had asked for a little time to think it over, but in her heart she knew she would have to accept it.

She couldn't bear to see Mandy marry Hugo. Mandy would be sure to twist the knife in Gina's aching heart as much as she could. A horrifying thought struck her: would Mandy ask her to be bridesmaid? It would be better to get away so the question would not arise.

But there was another question. Would her grandmother be willing to move to Dundee with her?

CHAPTER 73

'I remember jellyfish here,' Mandy said, kicking at the sand at her feet. 'When we were children, coming on Sunday school picnics.'

Mandy and Hugo were walking on the glorious expanse of golden sand that was Dunnet beach. It seemed to go on for miles, not only to right and left, but straight ahead to where it met the long waves of a deep blue sea which then reached out to a sky of paler blue. And there on the right of the sea–sky horizon, Dunnet Head and the tiny shape of Dwarick House, the House of the Northern Gate, perched on the top like a cherry on a cake.

'I always wanted to live there.' Mandy pointed it out. 'Dwarick House. But some lady-in-waiting to the Queen Mum got there first. Pity.'

She turned to face Hugo with a bright smile. 'Otherwise you could have bought it for us, for when we're married. Unless of course we're going back to Canada? I really wouldn't mind either.'

Hugo looked into her bright, confident face. He knew he had to confront her over the ring and her misperception, so he had deliberately chosen this quiet place for that conversation.

'Married?' Hugo repeated quietly. 'Unless my memory quite fails me, I do not recall mentioning marriage.'

Mandy laughed confidently. She was in a strange mood, Hugo thought, almost fizzing with excitement.

'Don't be silly, Hugo! You haven't mentioned marriage in so many words, but you've come back to propose to me! You said so in your letter!'

She waved her left hand so he could see the Mizpah ring on her finger.

'I thought since we're as good as engaged, I'd just wear this... till you get me something better, something nice and sparkly.'

She smiled brightly, inviting him to agree with her.

Hugo's eyes narrowed. He recalled his letter. Yes, he had said he had something to ask her. But what he had been going to ask her was if she knew what had happened to the Mizpah ring. Unfortunately the silly girl had read into it what she wanted.

As he watched Mandy smile winningly, determined to get her own way, Hugo realised his grandmother had been right. His memory offered him a picture of two little girls sitting at Granny Cormack's kitchen table. One was wearing this confident, winning smile, sure she could get her own way but willing to throw terrible tantrums when she didn't.

That had been Mandy. If it was who she was now, it was just as well there was no one in sight or hearing for miles. Dealing with this situation – not giving her what she wanted – was likely to produce a tantrum of apocalyptic proportions.

Resolutely Hugo continued. 'I must beg your pardon then,' he said. 'My words misled you.'

Mandy froze, staring at him in disbelief.

'Yes, I had a question,' Hugo said. 'But I found out the answer quite by chance.'

And as he remembered Gina's words about the Mizpah ring, he saw in his memory her face, so hurt, yet dignified and courageous, even when he lashed out at her that first day at the newspaper.

An older memory jabbed at him. Yes, there had been another time when he had lashed out at Gina. When she was a little girl.

And he heard his grandmother's words about Grandpa Clem. Clem who never judged anyone. Clem who had loved and married Nancy, knowing all there was to know about her – and against her. But it made no difference to him. And he knew that Grandpa Clem would tell him to stop condemning Gina for what had nothing to do with her – the actions of her father and grandfather. Clem would tell him to let the past be past. Let George St Clair be as dead as Hugh Mackay was, and Geordie Sinclair and Hughie Mackay before them. What mattered was today, and who he, Gina, and Mandy had grown up to be.

Hugo dragged his thoughts together and chose his words carefully.

'So you see, I won't be asking any question now, and definitely not one that includes a proposal of marriage.'

'Wait a minute!' Mandy stormed, eyes blazing. 'You said... So I put the ring on...' She lifted her left hand and waved it at him.

'Yes, I noticed,' Hugo said. 'The Mizpah ring. I was going to ask you what became of it but I can see for myself.'

'I've told everyone we're engaged,' Mandy railed at him. 'You can't back out now!'

Hugo shook his head. 'I can't back out of something I was never in,' he said in a reasonable tone. 'Now, give me the ring.' He held out his hand.

Mandy glared at him. 'I've got it and I'm keeping it!'

'I think it belongs to me.'

'It was my mother's,' Mandy countered. 'So it belongs to me.'

'My father gave it to your mother in good faith,' Hugo said. 'If she had been faithful to him, then maybe you would have some right to it, but seeing how that story ended...'

He went to grab her hand but Mandy pulled the ring off and with a sweep of her arm flung it as far as she could into the sand dunes.

'There!' she said. 'Now no one gets the rotten ring! I never liked it anyway.' She faced him. 'And I never liked you that much either! I've got plenty more fish to fry. I don't need you! Now I want to go home.'

CHAPTER 74

Alec and Joyce's wedding day dawned warm and sunny. Gina managed to hold back her tears till her mother and Alec had left the church in the red Mini festooned with ribbons and clanking with tin cans. Handwritten 'Just Married' signs hung from the front and back of the car. She was sure they would make a quick stop once they were out of sight and remove the paraphernalia before they got on the road for their honeymoon trip.

'Mum looked lovely!' she whispered to her grandmother, and was not surprised to see answering tears of joy on her cheeks.

'OK, time to go home!'

She took Robbie's hand and the three of them set off for Willowbank. Robbie was staying with them for the duration of the honeymoon, before moving permanently to the farm.

'Letters!' Robbie declared, triumphantly scooping up the scattered envelopes from the doormat.

'Let's see,' Gina said, accepting the letters from her brother. 'Oh, this one's something official and it's addressed to you.'

She handed the envelope to her grandmother who examined it. She followed Gina and Robbie slowly into the kitchen and found a knife to slit open the envelope. Slowly she sat down at the table to unfold and smooth out the several thick sheets inside.

'Oh,' she said, and sat back, her hand coming up to rest on her heart. 'Oh dear.' She swallowed hard and closed her eyes.

Gina, who had been putting the kettle on for a cup of tea, turned round.

'What is it, Granny?'

Hannah opened her eyes. She looked sad. 'Well, I never really thought… More like, I suppose, I hoped… But… I think you'd better read it for yourself.'

She handed the topmost sheet to Gina who came over to take it from her grandmother. Gina read the document, barely able to believe her eyes. They were being given notice to vacate the house in Willowbank in one month's time. The other pages in front of Hannah comprised the legal eviction notice. All as Aunt Joanie had threatened.

'Oh, Granny!' Gina said, aghast. 'This is terrible! How could Aunt Joanie do this?'

Her grandmother gave her what Gina could only consider an old-fashioned look.

'I know,' Gina said. 'Aunt Joanie is…'

'Joanie.' Her grandmother finished the sentence for her.

Hannah took a deep breath, retrieved the pages of the letter from Gina and shuffled them together.

'My dear, you know this is not unexpected. Joanie has been threatening that the minute Will died, she would get us out of this house.' She humphed gently. 'She never liked Will letting us have it, so now she can do something about it.'

Hannah gestured to the sheaf of documents.

'But we must not get upset about this. God is good,' she said firmly. 'His timing is perfect.'

She fixed her granddaughter with steady grey eyes and smiled.

'Your mother has married Alec, and she and Robbie will be living at the farm. Gina, my love, you've been dithering about that job in Dundee.'

'Yes, Granny,' Gina agreed with a sigh.

'Well, now your way is open,' her grandmother told her. 'If it is truly what you want, write and tell them you'll take the job; then get down there and sort out accommodation.'

Gina nodded, but her eyes were unhappy.

'What about you?' she asked. 'Will you come with me?'

Hannah shook her head. 'I'm too old for city life!' she said. 'But it's sweet of you to think of it.' She gestured to the boiling kettle. 'Why don't you make the tea and then come and sit down? Those shoes are very pretty but I'm sure your feet are sore after standing so long on those high heels.'

CHAPTER 75

'You're right!' Gina said as she sat down at the table and kicked off the new shoes she had bought for the wedding: She thrust her aching feet into comfortable sandals. 'I don't know how Mandy manages to live in high heels! My feet are in agony!'

'We haven't seen Mandy for a while,' her grandmother commented.' I was surprised she wasn't at the wedding.'

Gina swallowed hard. 'She's probably too busy arranging her own wedding,' she said. 'I heard she'd gone to Edinburgh for a few days. Shopping for her trousseau, I expect.'

She tried to keep her voice light and unconcerned but her grandmother picked up on it.

'Do you really believe Hugo will marry her?' Hannah asked. 'I'd have thought he had more sense…'

'I don't know,' Gina said wretchedly. 'He seems incapable of telling one thing from another.'

Her grandmother raised an eyebrow.

'Well,' Gina said, 'I've always tried to do what's right. I know what my dad was and I'm determined it's not going to come out in me.

Yet Hugo damns me almost on sight and then takes up with Mandy! Mandy of all people!'

'Did I hear my name?' Mandy appeared at the kitchen door. 'I let myself in,' she said. 'I hope you don't mind.'

She took the nearest chair and settled herself at the table. She was wearing a smart new jacket and skirt in burnt orange, with matching gloves and shoes.

'So how did the wedding go?' she asked.

'It was lovely,' Gina told her. 'Mum looked beautiful and everyone could see that she and Alec are in love.'

'That's nice,' Mandy said absently.

'How was your trip?' Gina enquired.

'Very successful,' Mandy said with a sudden brilliant smile. 'I've come back with so many lovely clothes and shoes! And there will be plenty more where that comes from.' Mandy waved a hand and Gina noticed that the Mizpah ring was no longer in evidence.

Mandy saw the direction of her eyes.

'Oh, that old thing!' she said with a laugh. 'I chucked it, and him. He wouldn't do for me. You can have him if you want,' she told Gina airily. 'I've got the most amazing new job in Edinburgh – Personal Assistant to the Managing Director of a chain of department stores, and I get the pick of the clothes and shoes and anything I want. All part of the job.'

Gina stared at her. 'That's the job you had the interview in Inverness for – with the woman you didn't like?'

'Yes.' Mandy laughed. 'Poor woman – she's Adam's sister – she was trying so hard to be stern and serious, but she's a lot of fun really.' Mandy preened. 'It's going to be really good. Much better than a boring life as Hugo's wife.'

Gina was reeling. 'That's all happened very quickly. What did you say his name was? Adam?'

'Adam Finlayson,' Mandy said. 'You know? Finlayson's, that fabulous department store in Edinburgh? And there's one in Glasgow, one in Perth...'

Gina heard her grandmother's gasp. She glanced quickly at her and was surprised to see that she had her eyes closed and was not looking at all well.

'It's lovely to see you, Mandy,' Gina interrupted her, 'but I think maybe we need to get out of our glad rags...'

'Gina.' Her grandmother's voice was surprisingly weak. 'I think what I need is a doctor...'

Gina stared at her grandmother. Her face had contorted in pain and one hand was clenched against her chest.

'Granny!' Gina said. 'What's the matter?'

'Pain,' Hannah said. 'Bad pain. It's my heart. Now go next door to Mrs Henderson and phone...'

'I don't want to leave you...'

'Go!' Hannah's grey eyes commanded Gina's obedience. 'Mandy can stay with Robbie and me.'

But Mandy was standing up.

'I will not! I'm not staying a moment here with him. I've said it before. He should have been put away long ago.' She glared at Robbie. 'Nobody wants you. You're in the way! Why don't you just get lost?'

'Mandy!' Gina protested.

'I'm only telling the truth,' Mandy said and marched out.

'Gina, please...'

Gina's eyes turned back to her grandmother. She saw the pain etched in her face.

'I'm going,' she said. 'I'll be back in a moment.'

CHAPTER 76

The next few hours went past in a blur. Gina tried to make her grandmother comfortable while they waited for the doctor to arrive. He took one look at Hannah and shooed Gina out of the room while he examined her thoroughly. Then an ambulance arrived and Hannah was taken to the Bignold Hospital.

Frantically, Gina tried to remember where she had put the contact telephone number for the hotel in Stirling where her mother and Alec were going to be staying that night. She checked her watch. They wouldn't have got there yet. But she could phone the hotel and leave a message for them before she headed to the hospital to find out what was going on.

Again she hurried next door and used Mrs Henderson's phone. She asked the receptionist at the hotel to relay the message to her mother and Alec as soon as they arrived. She decided it would be best if they stayed where they were till she had further news for them. No point spoiling their honeymoon if this turned out to be a false alarm. She tried to find low-key reassuring words for the message.

Waylaid by her neighbour who was understandably concerned, Gina realised time was moving on and she needed to get to the hospital before the end of visiting hours. Swiftly she locked the house and hurried along Willowbank, taking the shortest route she could think of.

At the hospital Gina was shown into the ward where Hannah was being looked after.

She was horrified at the change in her grandmother. In her hospital gown in the big bed, she seemed to have shrunk. She opened her eyes and Gina reached to take her hand.

'Granny.'

'Gina, my love.' The voice was whispery but the old eyes shone with love.

Gina bent and kissed her grandmother's cheek.

'Oh Granny, I'm so sorry!'

'What for, love?'

'I should have taken better care of you! I should have seen you were getting tired…'

'Don't worry about that. It's just my old heart. They wear out, you know.' And her grandmother's grey eyes twinkled at her. 'Mandy's news was a little unexpected,' she added.

'Yes,' Gina said. She hadn't had time to take it in properly. What was it Mandy had said?

'I know the name from somewhere,' her grandmother was saying. 'Adam Finlayson…?'

'Well, Finlayson's is a well-known chain. Lovely shops,' Gina said. She smiled. 'Mandy loves shops and shopping. Maybe she's landed on her feet again.'

'We must hope so,' Hannah said.

She squeezed Gina's hand to get her attention.

'Give Hugo a chance,' she counselled. 'The chance he didn't give you.'

Gina hesitated.

'Gina?'

She sighed and nodded. To please her grandmother.

They sat, holding hands peacefully.

Then Hannah asked, 'So who did you leave to look after Robbie?'

CHAPTER 77

Gina sat bolt upright. Robbie!

In all the upset over her grandmother, she had forgotten about him. Where had she last seen him? She tried to remember. He had been with them in the kitchen when Mandy was being so nasty.

He had probably gone up to his room. He never liked Mandy at the best of times and tended to make himself scarce when she was around.

Gina gulped and confessed. 'I haven't. I forgot. Oh Granny, I'd better get home and make sure he's all right.'

'I'm sure he will be,' Hannah said. 'He's a good lad. I always think he understands a lot more than people think.'

Gina, reassured that her grandmother was in good hands and seemed to be recovering from the heart attack she had suffered, took her leave.

'I'll be back,' she said. 'Next visiting time.' She paused. 'I left a message at the hotel for Mum and Alec. I'll tell them you're doing fine, shall I?'

Hannah smiled softly and nodded. 'Yes, you do that.'

As Gina hurried home, she thought of her grandmother's words. Robbie was 19 going on 20 now. Gradually, thanks to Middle Alec's advice, he was becoming more independent. He loved working at the farm.

Gina smiled. The Gunns, son and grandson of her grandmother's old beau, had turned out to be really good news for their family.

She let herself into the house. First she popped her head into the sitting room, then the kitchen but, not surprisingly, there was no sign of Robbie.

She stood at the bottom of the stairs and called up, 'Robbie! I'm home! Do you want to come down for a cup of tea and a scone?'

That usually did the trick. But all was silence. And it was the silence of an empty house. Gina stood for a moment, listening hard; then she tore up the stairs, breathlessly flinging open every door on the way and calling Robbie's name.

But there was no sign of Robbie.

On the top landing, she halted. More slowly now, her breath catching in her throat with terrible apprehension, she began again, methodically checking each room as she worked her way back downstairs.

First Robbie's room. Then her room, next door to his. After that, the small boxroom. Steadily down the stairs to the next floor. Her mother's room. Granny's room.

The sight of the neatly made bed and the Bible on her grandmother's bedside table nearly undid her. Gina found herself picking it up and idly flicking through the pages. So many underlinings and markings. Maybe she should take the Bible in to her grandmother this evening?

And then the sheer devastating situation hit her. Her grandmother was in hospital, after a heart attack! They could have lost her! They were going to lose their home! And Gina had almost certainly lost Robbie!

She wanted to sit down and howl. It was all too much.

She knew what her grandmother would do. She would pray. This quiet room almost breathed with the quiet prayers and strong faith that underpinned her grandmother's life. It was what Gina needed now. But Granny wasn't here to do it.

In sudden desperation, Gina flung her prayers into the stillness: 'Please, Lord Jesus, please help us! Please make it all work out for good like Granny says You do. Please help us!'

She opened her eyes and forced herself to continue her search. Bathroom. The walk-in drying cupboard on the turn of the stairs that used to be one of Robbie's favourite hiding places when he was smaller. Even more slowly now, Gina's unwilling feet took her to the little cloakroom under the stairs on the ground floor. She looked behind every coat. Then she searched the kitchen and scullery. And finally the sitting room.

Holding dread only just at bay, Gina opened the inner door into the vestibule, and then the heavy front door. She looked down the long garden and called, desperation cracking her voice, 'Robbie!'

Calling and calling, she set herself to search all the likely hiding places down the length of the garden. She opened the door to the garden shed, willing Robbie to jump out with a loud 'Boo!' But there was no trace of Robbie.

Where could he have gone? He'd never been anywhere on his own before. Something dreadful could have happened to him and she was responsible!

'Bad girls must be punished!'

But she knew the Voice in her head held no power over her now. She banished it, though she knew she was indeed to blame. She shouldn't have let Robbie out of her sight.

Somehow she had to do this her grandmother's way, trusting the Lord Jesus.

But her heart was racing and tears were filling her eyes as, with another whispered prayer, she pushed open the gate to the rough path that skirted the ends of the gardens.

'Robbie!' she shouted as loudly as she could. She brushed the tears away and stared desperately as far as she could see.

'Robbie!' she called.

But Robbie had vanished.

CHAPTER 78

'Gina!'

The voice calling her name was Mrs Henderson's, her next-door neighbour, calling from up at the house. Sudden hope flared in Gina's heart and she ran up the central path towards her.

'Have you found him?' she asked eagerly.

The grave look on the woman's face stopped her in her tracks.

'The hospital's on the phone,' Mrs Henderson said. 'You'd better come in and talk to them.'

She led Gina into the house and waved her to the telephone, taking herself out of the room to give Gina privacy.

Gina picked up the receiver. 'Hello?'

'Is that Gina Sinclair?' a kindly voice asked.

'Yes,' Gina said, wondering what on earth this could be about.

'Gina, I am so sorry to have to tell you. Your grandmother had a massive heart attack after you left here.' There was a pause. 'I'm sorry. We weren't able to save her. She died without recovering consciousness.'

'Oh,' Gina said numbly. 'Oh. Thank you. I'll need to…'

'Yes,' the soothing voice said. 'Please accept our condolences.'

'Thank you,' Gina said.

She put the receiver down and slid into the chair by the telephone table. She stared at the phone.

'Oh,' she said as the words began to penetrate her brain.

Mrs Henderson popped her head round the door.

'Is it… bad news?'

Gina lifted her anguished face and nodded.

'It's Granny. She's…' She had to force the unbelievable words out. 'She's dead.'

'Oh, my dear, I am sorry,' her neighbour said. 'Now you just go right ahead and make as many phone calls as you need to, while I make you a nice cup of tea…'

And she disappeared through to the kitchen, from where Gina could hear the rattle of china, the normality of the noise strangely surreal.

She tried to pull herself together. Granny was dead. Who needed to know? Who should she call first? But her mother and Alec would still be on the road somewhere en route for their honeymoon hotel in Stirling. She racked her brains. Who else? Uncle Danny. Of course. He would know what to do.

Her mother and Alec's wedding had been in the late morning with a light luncheon for the family afterwards; then they had all gone their separate ways. Gina picked up the phone and began to dial. *Please be at home*, she prayed earnestly.

'Hello!' she said with relief as she heard the line connect.

'Hello.'

But it was not her Uncle Danny's voice. It was Hugo's.

'Oh. It's you,' Gina said flatly. 'I need to speak to my uncle.'

'I'm sorry,' Hugo said. 'He's not here. He and Cat have gone away for a few days...'

'No! They can't!' Gina's voice rose in a sharp crescendo. 'I need them! Oh, what am I going to do?'

CHAPTER 79

'Gina. Calm down,' Hugo said.

'Calm down?' Gina replied and began to laugh weakly, shakily.

'Gina!' Hugo's voice was strong and commanding. 'What's wrong?'

'What's wrong?' Gina repeated. 'How about everything? Absolutely everything!'

She took a deep breath and started to catalogue: 'Auntie Joanie's evicting us so I've nowhere to live, Granny's dead, and I've lost Robbie. He's vanished into thin air. Mum and Alec are somewhere on the road to Stirling and I can't reach them, and now you tell me Uncle Danny and Auntie Cat have gone away too.'

She made a hiccupping noise as hysterical laughter gave way to tears.

'I've got to find Robbie! It's all my fault...'

'Where are you?' Hugo's voice was quiet and calm.

Gina responded automatically. 'I'm next door, at Mrs Henderson's.'

'Listen to me,' Hugo told her. 'I know you'd rather have anyone else but me but it seems I'm the only one around. Stay where you are and I'll be with you very soon. We'll decide what to do then.'

Gina didn't answer.

'Gina, do you understand?' Hugo asked. 'Don't go anywhere!'

'I hear,' Gina said wearily. 'You don't have to shout or boss me about…'

Gina heard Hugo's sudden laughter.

'That's my girl,' he said and then there was a click as the phone disconnected.

She put the receiver down just as Mrs Henderson came in with a tray of tea and shortbread.

'I've put extra sugar in,' Mrs Henderson said. 'You'll need it.'

She put the cup and saucer into Gina's hand and sat opposite her. 'Drink up,' she said.

Gina swallowed hard. She wasn't sure she could. She felt completely numb. It was a very odd feeling.

'It's shock,' her neighbour said. 'It will pass. And the tea will help.' She gestured to the cup in Gina's limp hand.

Oh well. Gina forced herself to take a sip of the tea. It tasted hot and strong and sweet and strangely it did seem to help. Before she realised what she was doing she had gulped it down and was reaching for a piece of Mrs Henderson's home-made shortbread. Suddenly she was starving and she wanted to eat and eat…

There was a knock at the door.

'I'll get it,' Mrs Henderson said.

Gina surreptitiously snaffled another piece of shortbread and was attempting to devour it when Hugo appeared at the doorway.

'Maybe we should go back next door,' he said. He turned to Mrs Henderson. 'Thank you so much for looking after Gina. I'll look after everything now.'

'It was the least I could do,' Mrs Henderson said. She nodded towards the phone. 'And if you need to make any calls, do please just use ours. I'll be in for the rest of the day.'

'Thank you,' Hugo said. 'That's very kind of you.'

He ushered Gina out of the house and watched as she unlocked the big front door of her own home and led the way into the sitting room.

'Now,' he said quietly. 'Tell me what happened, from the beginning.'

CHAPTER 80

And Gina did. Succinctly and clearly, she told Hugo how her grandmother had had a heart attack and been whisked off to hospital. How in the hubbub she had forgotten Robbie.

'Mandy was here and was nasty to him. I thought he'd just gone up to his room. That's what he usually does when Mandy's around.' Her eyes filled with tears as she said pleadingly, 'I thought he'd be all right! He's not a child!'

'Right,' Hugo said reassuringly. 'What happened then?'

'When I got back from the hospital, I searched the house – every room – twice! But there was no sign of Robbie. I went outside, looked in the garden, the shed, went out of the gate and shouted... and that was when Mrs Henderson called me to the phone and I found out...'

She faltered.

Hugo nodded and waited till she had composed herself.

'I had left a message at the hotel earlier for Mum and Alec,' she said. 'Just that Granny had had a heart attack and was in hospital but doing all right. I didn't want to panic them into coming back. But now...'

'There's nothing they can do,' Hugo said. 'We'll phone in a little while to let them know. I've a contact number for Danny and Cat too. For now, though, we must concentrate on finding Robbie.'

Gina nodded, her eyes filling with tears again.

'Have you any idea where he might have gone?' Hugo asked. 'He doesn't go out on his own, does he?'

She shook her head.

'So when you take him out, where does he like to go? Where does he know?'

Gina struggled to think. She tried to remember some of the outings they'd had recently.

'He likes the Monument,' she said 'Last time we went, he was really fascinated by the North Baths...' Sudden panic flooded her face. 'He can't swim! But that's what he really wanted to do... He could have gone there. Oh, Hugo!'

'Right,' Hugo said. 'That's the first place we need to search.' He took in Gina's panicked face. 'Don't worry. If we follow the path from the bottom of the garden we might find him somewhere along the way. I don't think he'll have got far.'

'I don't know,' Gina said worriedly. 'He's had quite a bit of time...'

'Has Robbie ever done anything like this before?' Hugo asked quietly.

She shook her head. 'Never.'

'So have you any idea why Robbie would? What would make him take himself off like that?'

And suddenly Gina remembered. First her grandmother's words: 'I always think he understands a lot more than people think.' And then Mandy speaking to Robbie: 'Nobody wants you! You're in the way! Why don't you just get lost?'

'Gina?' Seeing her horrified face, Hugo prompted her. 'What is it?'

'Mandy,' Gina said. 'She was here. Granny was in pain. She wanted Mandy to stay with Robbie while I nipped next door to phone for the doctor, but Mandy... Mandy said to Robbie, "Nobody wants you! You're in the way! Why don't you get lost?"'

Gina looked into Hugo's appalled face.

'Granny said she always thought Robbie understood a lot more than people thought. I think he understood what Mandy was saying. I think that's why he's run away.'

CHAPTER 81

Hugo was on his feet, anger on his face.

'Right,' he said. 'Time to go. Gina, maybe you should stay here. You've had a terrible shock...'

'No way,' Gina said. 'I'm coming with you! Robbie's my brother... and it's my fault he's gone.'

'There's no point beating yourself up about it,' Hugo said. 'And anyway, I don't think you're to blame. If blame there is, it lies at Mandy's door.' His lips were compressed in anger.

Gina locked the door behind them, then led the way down the garden and through the gate, onto the path beside the allotments, and down to the cliff top with its flimsy wire barrier.

'This is the way we always go,' she explained as they hurried down the long steep steps to road level. 'So this is the way Robbie would know.'

Carefully looking all around for any glimpse of Robbie, they crossed the road at the corner of Scalesburn, where Gina chose the shore-level path to the North Baths. As they went, she called and called, but there was no answering shout from Robbie.

When they reached the North Baths, Gina was glad to see the swimming pool was busy with children splashing in the water, their mothers and grandmothers sitting out on blankets and enjoying the fine day. There was no sign of Robbie in the pool, but surely someone would have seen him if he had come this way – especially if he'd tried to get into the water?

'Excuse me?' Hugo stopped at a group of older women knitting and reading magazines in the sunshine.

'Hello, Gina,' one of them said, eyes curious. 'What are you doing on a day like this?'

'We're looking for my brother, Robbie.' She waited while the women assimilated the information. 'Have you seen him?'

But all she got were shaking heads, pursed lips and disapproving looks.

'No, no.'

'Why ever would you ask that? He should be at home with you.'

'Oh well, it was your mother's wedding this morning. Did he get away when you were all busy?'

Hugo smiled pleasantly at the women. 'Thank you for your help. We must be on our way.' He took Gina's arm and pulled her gently away.

'Those… people!' Gina said in a voice trembling with anger.

'Shhh! Let it go,' Hugo said.

'It's all right for you,' Gina rounded on him, 'but it's what we – what Robbie has had to put up with all his life!' She cast a glance back at the avidly gossiping women. 'And he's worth more than them! He'd never say anything unkind. He'd never do anything unkind.'

'Unlike his cousin Mandy,' Hugo said.

Gina came to an abrupt halt and stared at him.

'Wait a minute,' she said, remembering Mandy's news. 'About Mandy… and you. One minute Mandy's flashing the Mizpah ring, saying you're engaged and getting married; the next she's back from Edinburgh boasting about her new job and saying she's dumped you!'

'Oh, is that what Mandy said?' Hugo laughed. 'Not exactly how I remember it! Still, if she's got herself a new job, I suppose we should be glad for her. In Edinburgh?'

Gina nodded.

'Gets her out of our hair,' he said.

Gina stared at him. 'I do not understand you.' Hugo heard Gina's hissed comment as she set herself to climb the steep steps up to the cliff-top path.

They reached the top and paused to carefully scan the scene below. Gina took a deep breath and shouted, 'Robbie!'

Several heads lifted and people stared, but still there was no answering shout.

She sighed.

'Where now?' Hugo asked.

'The Monument,' Gina said. 'It's one of Robbie's favourite places.'

But as they continued along the path, Hugo could see Gina's worry growing. Below them were jagged rocks washed by the sea. Seaweed and limpets made walking dangerous for anyone unsteady on their feet who might try to venture across them.

As they walked, Gina's gaze was searching, searching.

The tower offered a place to rest – but again no sign of Robbie. Gina slumped onto the grass at the base of the Monument.

'What can we do now?' she asked hopelessly. 'Where can he have gone?'

CHAPTER 82

'Would he have tried to get to Alec's farm?' Hugo suggested, racking his brain for places Robbie might have gone.

Gina shook her head. 'I don't think so. He wouldn't have any idea how to get there. Alec always came for him in the car.'

They sat disconsolately, backs against the Monument, staring out at the sea.

'What was it Mandy said?' Hugo asked suddenly. 'Gina, tell me again. There might be a clue…'

Gina frowned. 'It was something like "Nobody wants you. You're in the way. Why don't you just get lost?" I think that was it.'

'Just get lost,' Hugo mused. 'I wonder…'

Then suddenly he was standing up, grabbing Gina's hands and drawing her to her feet.

'I think Granny Cormack was right and Robbie understood more than folk realised.'

There was a strange light in his eyes, almost laughter.

'When someone threatens to run away, where do they often say they'll go?' Hugo asked.

Gina stared at him uncomprehending. 'Hugo, I'm in no mood for games.'

'No, no,' he said. 'This is serious. Bear with me. If it was me – or you – and you threatened to run away, what would you say? Think, Gina! You'd say that you were going to run away to…'

And Gina suddenly came alight.

'The circus!' she shouted. 'Of course, you'd run away to the circus! Oh Hugo! You're brilliant! Of course!'

And she flung her arms around him and hugged him tightly. Eyes glowing, she stepped back.

'Yes,' she said decisively. 'I think that's really the only other place he might go.'

'The circus is leaving today,' Hugo said. 'We need to get there before they leave. I left my car at your house.'

Without further words, they hurried back to Willowbank and piled into Hugo's car.

Down by the Riverside, the scene at first sight was one of utter chaos. The big top was being dismantled amidst shouts and yells. Men hurried here, there and everywhere, carrying heavy and awkward loads. The lions, obviously disturbed by the ruckus, were roaring and the elephants were trumpeting.

'I think we're in time,' Hugo shouted to make himself heard above the uproar.

'Let's find the elephants!' Gina cried and she was out of the car in an instant and running into the melee.

'Wait!' Hugo shouted, but she paid him no heed. He slammed the car door shut and hurried after her.

'Watch out!' he shouted and she swerved to avoid a boy leading a group of ponies towards a wagon.

Frantically trying to keep Gina in sight, Hugo did not see the foot put out in front of him and he went flying face down onto the muddy grass.

CHAPTER 83

'Well, well.'

Hugo struggled to get up, but a foot on his back held him down. It was the elephant keeper. On either side of him was one of the burly circus-hands who had been so unwelcoming the last time Hugo had seen them.

'And to what do we owe this pleasure?' the keeper asked sardonically.

'We lost Robbie,' Hugo managed to get out. 'I thought maybe he'd come here. Gina's beside herself with worry.'

'And what's it to you?' the man asked.

'I brought Gina...' Hugo said. 'He's her brother.'

'We know that,' the man said. 'And you, who are you?'

The question struck Hugo hard. Who was he? Once upon a time he would have stood up, brushed off the dirt, held out his hand confidently and announced, 'I'm Hugo Mackay. I'm a businessman. I buy failing companies and turn them round. I'm from Canada, though my ancestors came from round here...'

And suddenly he saw in his mind's eye the little tumbledown family croft – and Gina stopping to make sure he was all right.

Despite how badly – how unjustly – he had treated her. Like her Uncle Danny offering him bed and board when all he had done was muscle into the quiet newspaper and turn everyone's lives upside down, and threaten their livelihood and their happiness.

They were good people, and he – he who had prided himself on his excellent judgement, his business nous, and his total right to the moral high ground?

Everything he had prided himself on was nothing compared to the shining integrity and self-sacrifice of the girl he had condemned so unjustly. His bitter, festering unforgiveness of what *her* father had done to *his* father – it had nothing to do with Gina. The little deceitfulness she had practised in Aberdeen – that wasn't her either. It had been Mandy's idea. Mandy was the scheming, deceitful one.

He had got it completely wrong. He had treated the honourable loving girl as if she were worthless, and the scheming deceitful one – well, she had thought he was going to marry her.

The foot on Hugo's back moved irritably. Hugo lifted both hands in surrender.

'Me?' he said. 'I'm nobody.' And the sooner he got out of these people's lives and left them in peace, the better.

The foot lifted from his back and a hand reached down to help him up.

'Welcome to the human race,' the elephant keeper said with a grin.

'Hugo!'

Hugo looked beyond the keeper to see Gina hurrying towards him, a huge smile on her face, and with her a delighted Robbie.

'Hugo, I found Robbie!' she said as Robbie launched himself at Hugo in a huge bear hug.

'Hu-go!' Robbie said delightedly. 'Hu-go!'

He released Hugo and turned with beaming face to the elephant keeper and his two helpers.

'Yes,' the keeper said. 'He came to us and he's been helping us strike camp, haven't you, Robbie?'

Robbie nodded.

'And if you hadn't come for him, I'd have been happy to take him with us,' the man added with a grin for Robbie. 'You're a good worker, aren't you?'

'Yes, yes!' Robbie clapped his hands.

'Thank you,' Gina said, but the tears were filling up her eyes. 'It was all my fault. I was upset about my grandmother. She was rushed into hospital and I rushed after her and I...' She reached for her brother's hand. 'Robbie, darling, I forgot about you! I thought after Mandy was so nasty to you, you'd gone upstairs to your room. I never thought you'd take what she said and...'

'Get lost,' Robbie said helpfully.

The tears overflowed. Hugo thrust a handkerchief into Gina's hand and she gave him a startled smile but accepted it and put it to good use.

'He was never lost, young lady,' the elephant keeper said. 'The good Lord has His hand on His special people and He knew where to bring him so he'd be safe.'

Gina nodded. 'Granny died,' she whispered. 'I need to get Robbie back home now.'

'Yes, of course.'

The elephant keeper and the other circus hands said their goodbyes and turned back to the work of making the circus ready for its journey to the next town.

'I've got the car,' Hugo told Robbie. 'Shall we go back in that?'

'Car? Yes please,' and the three of them made their way carefully out of the busy circus ground and back to Willowbank.

'I won't come in,' Hugo said. 'You've things to do. But you know where I am if you need me.'

'Yes,' Gina agreed. She hesitated. 'Thank you. Thank you for everything.' And taking Robbie's hand, she turned away and headed for the house.

Hugo sat in the car after she had gone, one thought drumming in his head. He had made the most terrible mess of this. He had hurt Gina, but she had behaved at all times with dignity and... yes, that old-fashioned word that he'd never have thought to describe George Sinclair's family: integrity.

She had integrity.

CHAPTER 84

Joyce and Gina sat with Robbie, Middle Alec and Young Alec Gunn in the sitting room at Willowbank, surrounded by friends and relatives as the minister conducted Hannah's funeral service. Afterwards, as was the custom, the men and the minister left for the cemetery, leaving the women behind.

Gina watched with pleasure as the Gunns, father and son, took Robbie along with them, Robbie smart and proud in a new suit. His beaming smile was perhaps a little out of place for a funeral, but no one seemed to mind.

When the outside door closed behind them, Gina whispered to her mother, 'I'll just go through to the kitchen. Make sure everything's ready for the tea.'

Joyce nodded her understanding. She knew everything was ready but Gina needed to keep busy. Her grief was still sharp and new. And she was never comfortable in a roomful of gossiping women.

When Gina could no longer put off her return to the sitting room, she pushed the door open gently. Everyone seemed busy chatting so she stepped in quietly, aiming to get through to her mother's side. But Aunt Joanie waylaid her.

'You'll not be needing this big house now,' Aunt Joanie hissed spitefully. 'Now there's only one of you to live in it.'

Gina sucked in her breath and carefully controlled her temper. As she stood, slender and pale in her blacks, she raised eyes that were red-rimmed from weeping to her great-aunt's spiteful face.

'Yes, you're right,' Gina said steadily. 'I won't be needing it any more. But I'll be staying another week or two.' She managed a small smile. 'Don't worry. I'll be out before the end of the eviction period.'

She managed to sidestep her great-aunt and sat down beside her mother, who raised an enquiring eyebrow. Gina just shook her head. As her grandmother had once said, 'Joanie was Joanie', so her unpleasantness was only to be expected.

As the afternoon progressed, the men returned from the cemetery and Gina kept herself busy making sure their guests were plied with food and drink. She was glad that she had plenty to do and had no opportunity to worry about the future.

But it loomed large. Joyce and Robbie were happily settled on the farm with the Gunns. The Dundee newspaper was waiting for her to say when she would be joining them, and she really should take a couple of days off work to go searching for accommodation in the city.

But her heart wasn't in it. It was probably simply that it was another change coming so soon after her mother's wedding and her grandmother's death. Yes, she told herself, that's what it was.

She scanned the room. Everyone was well provided for and engaged in conversation. She would not be missed.

She opened the door and slipped into the hallway, then through the vestibule and outside. She stood outside the big front door, breathing in the clean, fresh air – then thought, why not?

Swiftly she took herself down the garden path and out of the gate.

She leaned against the wall and drank in the view of the bay, the water sparkling in the late afternoon sunlight. She was wearing reasonably sensible shoes. She might have time for a walk...

CHAPTER 85

'Gina!'

Gina looked up, startled. She had been deep in her thoughts and had not noticed Hugo follow her down the path.

'Where are you going?' he asked when he caught up with her.

'Oh, just for a breath of fresh air,' she said.

It hit her almost as a pain how handsome he was, tall and tanned in his smart suit. He had been at the funeral but she had managed to avoid him.

'Can I come too?' he asked.

Gina's eyebrows rose. This wasn't the Hugo she knew. He sounded far too humble!

'It's a free country,' she said lightly, and kept walking.

He matched her, step for step.

'Last time we did this,' he said, 'we were searching for Robbie.'

'Yes.' She concentrated on the steep steps down the side of the cliff.

'You'd do anything for your brother, wouldn't you?' It was abrupt.

She looked at him but could not read his face.

'Yes,' she said again.

'In fact, that's what you've been doing all these years,' he continued. 'Looking after your mum and your brother and your grandmother.' He paused. 'I asked around. People think you've given up a lot for them.'

'I love them,' Gina told him fiercely. 'What else could I do? After my dad...'

She trailed to a stop, then took a deep breath and said, 'My dad messed us up. I was the only one who could get a job and support us, so that's what I've done. And it hasn't been a sacrifice or any kind of martyrdom. I love them... and they love me,' she added more softly.

'Your dad messed us all up,' Hugo said. 'Your mum and your brother and you. And me and my dad.'

'Yes,' Gina said and kept walking.

'And I've messed things up too,' Hugo said behind her.

Gina slowed.

'I'm sorry.' His voice came from directly behind her.

Gina kept steadily walking, across the Scalesburn junction and up the high path towards the North Baths and the Monument.

'Gina, I'm sorry,' Hugo said, keeping up with her. 'I was so wrong about you. I don't think you've got a drop of bad blood in you. You're a good person... And Mandy...'

Gina squeezed her eyes shut. She did not want to hear about Mandy.

'Gina, I never intended to marry Mandy,' he said. 'I think I was just using her to annoy you. To hurt you. I suppose I messed her around too. She had every right to be furious.'

Gina opened her eyes and stared at Hugo.

'You saw her wearing the Mizpah ring?' he asked.

Gina nodded.

'I didn't give it to her,' Hugo told her. 'Her grandmother had it. She took it from our bungalow in West Banks when she came to fetch Mandy after her mother died.'

That made sense. But why give it to Mandy to wear if she and Hugo were not engaged?

'At no time did I propose marriage to Mandy, or suggest we would have any kind of long-term relationship. I wanted to find out what had happened to the Mizpah ring – so I wrote and said I'd a question to ask her. But she thought…'

Ah yes, Mandy would.

'When I found out she had been wearing the ring and telling people we were engaged, I told her I was not going to marry her, not ever.'

Gina wondered what kind of a scene that had produced.

Hugo smiled. 'Oh yes, that did not go down well. She took the ring off and threw it away. On Dunnet beach!'

'Oh, Hugo!'

'I went back there yesterday and scoured the beach.' He pulled something from his pocket. 'I found it.'

Hugo went on. 'When I met you at the conference in Aberdeen, I thought you were the most delightful, captivating woman I had ever met. It was so disappointing that you were *Mrs* Mandy Strachan.' He gave a wry smile. 'I suppose I shouldn't have kissed you but you were irresistible, there in the snow!'

His dark eyes were serious.

'Gina, that morning – my first at *The Sentinel* – you said we'd had "a chance meeting at a conference". Was that all it was to you?'

The tell-tale blush crept up Gina's cheeks as she recalled how that man and those two lovely kisses had haunted her dreams for months afterwards.

She shook her head.

'Good,' he said. 'Me neither. And I do understand why you were there – another of Mandy's manipulations.'

'I did get a good article out of it,' Gina confessed. 'One of the three that won the Press award.'

Hugo smiled. Integrity. That was Gina, through and through. He held out the old ring made of Klondike gold with the word 'Mizpah' in raised letters across the ivy leaf that symbolised fidelity.

'There's only one person I want to have this ring,' he told her, his eyes bright with sincerity. 'And that's you. I've been a fool, Gina. Can you forgive me?'

They were past the North Baths by now, she had kept up such a pace, and now they stood overlooking the rough rocks and splashing sea.

She looked at him, this man she had loved since she was a child. This man that she still loved. How could she not forgive him?

She nodded.

'I want you to have it,' Hugo said, and tried to put it into her hand.

But Gina shook her head and closed her hands into tight fists.

'I don't want it,' she said quietly.

CHAPTER 86

Hugo's face clouded. 'Does that mean you don't want me either? Is that it?'

'No, silly,' Gina said, near to tears.

'Do I have to go down on bended knee and ask formally for your hand in marriage?' he demanded.

'That would be nice.' She managed a wry smile.

'Gina, I'll do whatever you want! I love you and I want to share my life with you...'

'I still don't want the ring,' she said.

'Please!'

But she shook her head, quietly adamant.

'I don't understand!' Hugo said. 'I've told you I love you, I've asked you to forgive me, and said I want to marry you. What more do I have to do?'

'Nothing,' Gina said. 'I just don't want the Mizpah ring.' She glared at him. 'Don't you understand? If we're going to be together, forever and forever...' She looked up at his face to see him nodding determinedly. 'Then we don't need the ring.'

She traced the letters on the front: MIZPAH: 'The LORD watch between me and thee, when we are absent one from another.'

'Don't you understand?' she asked him. 'If we're not going to be absent from one another, we don't need it.'

Hugo's sudden whoop of laughter ripped through the quiet afternoon. And with a great windmill of his arm, he sent the ring flying out into the blue splashing sea.

'Hugo!' Gina protested in shock. 'The ring, the Mizpah ring!'

'You're right,' he said. 'We don't need it. You can have whatever kind of ring you fancy.'

'But it's your family heirloom,' she whispered.

'What it is,' Hugo said, 'is part of all this rotten family history that nearly kept us apart.' He paused. 'I say let the ring go, and with it all the mess of unhappiness and deceit and hurt that was connected to it. We need a fresh start.'

He smiled at her.

'Speaking of fresh starts, what about that job in Dundee?' he asked. 'Have you accepted it?'

'Ah,' she said.

'So did you accept the job?' Hugo asked. 'Were you planning on moving to Dundee?'

'I should have,' she said. 'But I kept putting it off.' Gina blushed. 'I don't know why.'

'I'm sure there are newspapers in Canada that would be happy to have an award-winning reporter from Scotland.' He grinned at her. 'For a while?'

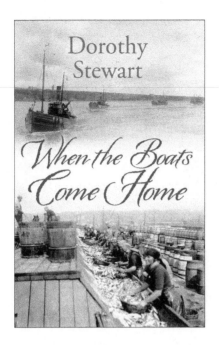

WHEN THE BOATS
COME HOME

DOROTHY STEWART

A Christian novel about family secrets, romance and revival in a
1921 fishing town.

October 1921 and the herring fishing fleets have converged on
Great Yarmouth for the autumn season. Wick fisherman Robbie
Ross has come to blows with his father and been thrown off
the family boat. His sister, war widow Lydia, reluctantly sets out
to bring him home, little knowing her world and her family are
about to be turned upside down.

Paperback 368pp, ISBN 9781909824676
Available on Kindle

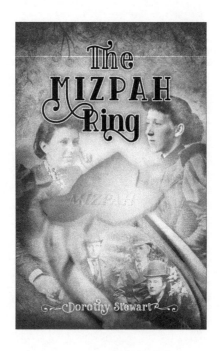

THE MIZPAH RING

DOROTHY STEWART

Book One of the Mizpah Ring Trilogy

'I wouldn't marry you if you were the last man on earth!'

And so Belle Reid sets in train three generations of heartbreak
and sorrow, death and disaster.

Geordie, her spurned suitor, sets out from Wick to make his
fortune in the Klondike gold rush of 1897 – but his ticket to that
fortune depends on the rival Belle has chosen over him. When
the lads find gold, and rival Hughie has the Mizpah ring made to
send to Belle, it's time for Geordie to make his move – and only
one of them can win.

Paperback 322pp, ISBN 9781909824997
Available on Kindle

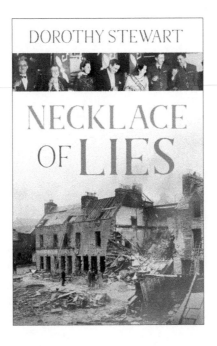

NECKLACE OF LIES

DOROTHY STEWART

Book Two of the Mizpah Ring Trilogy

Book 2 in the Mizpah Ring Trilogy introduces the second
generation of Cormacks, Mackays, and St Clairs as their lives
entwine and play out against the backdrop of Wick in wartime.
Must they follow in the footsteps of their parents, or can they
strike out afresh and make new lives,
new futures for themselves?

Paperback 272pp, ISBN 9781911211679
Available on Kindle